WHEN FOX IS A THOUSAND

LARISSA LAI

When Fox Is a Thousand

For Rosemary
With many fond
memories
Best always
Larissa Lai

PRESS GANG PUBLISHERS
VANCOUVER

First edition 1995

The Publisher gratefully acknowledges financial assistance from the
Canada Council, the Book Publishing Industry Development Program
of the Department of Canadian Heritage, and the Cultural Services
Branch, Province of British Columbia.

CANADIAN CATALOGUING IN PUBLICATION DATA

Lai, Larissa, 1967–
When fox is a thousand

ISBN 0-88974-041-0

I. Title.
PS8573.A52W54 1995   C813'.54   C95-910660-X
PR9199.3.L35W54 1995

Edited by Jennifer Glossop
Copy edited by Robin Van Heck
Cover photographs © 1995 Chick Rice,
"Tommy with Flowers," "Tommy Crying," and "Fox Shadowgramme."
Cover and text designed by Val Speidel
Type set in Cochin and Koch Antiqua display
Printed and bound in Canada by Best Book Manufacturers
Printed on acid-free paper ∞

Press Gang Publishers
#101 - 225 East 17th Avenue
Vancouver, B.C. Canada V5V 1A6
Tel: 604-876-7787 Fax: 604-876-7892

for my mother, my father, my sister

and for all the foxes

I know we won't meet again

in the season of blossoms,

And I won't sit quietly by

drunk in my chamber

— Yu Hsuan-Chi
9th century, Chang'an

Acknowledgements

IN THE SPRING OF 1993, three women began to meet regularly around a kitchen table. They showed each other stories and fragments of stories. They were Monika Kin Gagnon, Shani Mootoo, and myself. I am indebted to these two sisters for support, encouragement, and community which made all the difference in the world to this project. I am grateful to Monika Kin Gagnon and jamila ismail for generously given hours of honest and thorough assessment and critique. A big thank-you to Karlyn Koh, Karen Tee, Kathy-Ann March, and A. J. Verdelle for well-considered feedback on various drafts. I would like to thank Anne Jew and Jim Wong-Chu for encouraging me from the very beginning. Thanks to Jamelie Hassan, whose discussions about *The Thousand and One Nights* inspired the research for this book, and to the late Lloyd Wong for the idea of spaghetti noodles in hot dog soup.

In the spring of 1995, I was writer-in-residence at Cottages at Hedgebrook in Washington State. The staff and writers I met there supported and encouraged me in ways I had not known were possible, particularly Gabrielle Idlet, Chizu Omori, Adriana Batista, Claudia May, Brenda Miller, Karen Hwa, A. J. Verdelle, and Kathleen Saadat. Jennifer Rose and Laura Wollberg cooked the marvelous meals that fed our stomachs and our souls.

This work would not have been possible without the support, friendship, and committed politics of the writers, activists, and artists involved in the publications for which I worked while writing this book: *Kinesis: the Newspaper of the Vancouver Status of Women* and *Front Magazine*.

Thank-you to Jennifer Glossop for the index card trick and for a generous and thorough edit, and to Robin Van Heck for a sharp and patient eye.

Barbara Kuhne, Della McCreary, Val Speidel and Shamina Senaratne deserve a good swig at the Elixir of Immortality for their patience, kindness and hard work on the production of this novel.

A note on transliteration: I have left the names of historical figures in the form in which I found them. I did not feel the responsibility to standardize the names to one system. If anything, I felt a responsibility to leave them in the form in which I first came across them, reflecting the history of their passage into twentieth-century North America and my own relationship to that history. For indeed, the history of transliteration also marks the history through which writers such as myself have come to a place where we must access parts of our own history through various "specialists." This is not to say that there is any such thing as a "naturally acquired" knowledge of the past. Perhaps one can only say that the hodgepodge trail of these transliterations marks the disruptions in the (super)natural journey from past to present, from "there" to "here." On a more practical note, leaving the names as I found them will also make them easier to find should any of my diasporic, English-speaking sisters and brothers wish to look them up.

Thanks to the Explorations Program of the Canada Council, Multiculturalism and Citizenship Canada and the Astraea Foundation for funding this project in part.

This is a novel in three voices, denoted by:

for the Fox,

for the ninth-century poetess, Yu Hsuan-Chi, and

*for an unnamed narrator speaking of
contemporary twentieth-century life.*

PART 1

How the Fox Came to Live Alone

I COME FROM an honest family of foxes. They were none too pleased about my forays into acts of transformation. When they found out about the scholars I visited on dark nights, haunting them in the forms of various women, they were appalled. They love me too much to disown me for a trait that has run in the family for generations, although it is seldom openly discussed. They said, "Don't you know your actions reflect on us all? If you keep making these visitations, other fox families will talk about us. They will criticize us for not having raised you properly. It would be better if you chose a more respectable occupation, like fishing or stealing chickens."

They got even more upset when I started to counsel a house-wife. She was lovely. Her flesh glowed like translucent jade. Her husband owned vaults of silk and gold, as well as rice fields and horses. His eyes were quick, his beard thick and warlike. He dressed in elegant blues and browns, aristocratic, but not frivo-lous, and rode a muscular horse with a tendency to wildness. But he handled his wife the way he handled money, with cold, calcu-lating fingers. She responded warmly to his looks. But to his cold hands, she responded the way one does to winter, drawing the blankets tighter and waiting for it to end. He decided there was something wrong with her. Hadn't he, after all, treated her as though she were the most precious thing on earth?

He asked her to buy him a concubine, as men often asked their wives in those days. She agreed readily, pleased with the possibility that, if she chose right, she could endear him further to her and at the same time escape that wifely duty that had become increasingly disagreeable. She chose a plump and giddy girl who did not mind the cold. He was delighted and forgot about his wife altogether. She did not realize until too late that without his affection, she would lose her authority over the servants. The house fell into disrepair. Only then did she discover that she needed him more than she thought. She could do nothing but put gold and jade in her hair and wait. She might as well have packed her bags and moved into the vaults.

I moved in next door and began to give advice. So what if the body I occupied was not my own? One must take human form to engage in human affairs. It was difficult. I had not come fully into my powers, and could maintain the form for only a few hours at a time.

I instructed her not to bathe. I wrapped her perfect body in the flea-ridden hand-me-downs of a beggar. I set her to work on the soot-encrusted stove with a worn shoe brush. I smeared her face with fat and ashes and taught her to sing a heart-rending tune. The concubine took pity and offered to help, but the housewife chased her away. She scoured the floors. She scrubbed the chamber pots until they shone like the sun. The concubine came again to offer assistance, which my charge would have accepted had I not hissed at her from my hiding place outside the kitchen window. She grew thin and even the husband began to worry. He came and implored her to leave the work to the sturdier women of the house, but she chased him away crossly.

At the end of a month, I took her to my own room and dressed her in emerald silk. Long sleeves cut in the latest fashion. On her dainty feet I slipped a pair of shoes I had embroidered with my own hands. In the morning when the roses smelled sweet, I sent her into her garden, where the husband and concubine leaned over a chessboard. The husband was enraptured. He asked her to join them, but she refused, saying she was tired, and hurried off to her room.

The following day, I invited her over again. I draped her in a robe the colour of moving water. I gave her shoes made by my elder sister, who had a finer hand than I. At nightfall, when the scent of jasmine permeated the air, I guided her into the garden, where the husband and concubine sat drinking tea and composing couplets under the full moon. Again he approached her. She led him and the concubine to her chambers. In the hallway the concubine turned to her and raised a curious eyebrow. The housewife pushed them both into her room and locked the door behind them, whispering as she turned the key that she was tired and wished to be left alone. Then she went off to sleep in the concubine's room.

On the third day, she came to see me on her own. I wrapped her in a gown the colour of the sky before a storm. On her feet I placed shoes made by my younger sister, whose hand was so fine you could not discern the individual threads of her embroidery. I pushed her into the garden at midnight, when the scent of every rose and every orange blossom, every jasmine flower and every sandalwood tree infused the senses, so that those who lingered there were blinded and deafened by the aroma. As a farewell gift, I taught her how kisses come not from the mouth, but from a well deep below the earth. The husband was smitten.

Is it my fault if she ran off with the concubine?

Other foxes thought so, and chalked it up to the evil influence of the West, where personal whims come before family pride and reputation. Westerners had been coming and going from the capital for hundreds of years. Their ways of dressing had become fashionable among the students and courtesans. Their strange religions less so. Their horses—everyone wanted their horses, except, perhaps, us foxes.

Other foxes chastise me for my unorthodox methods. But I don't know why they should pretend to know so much about human affairs, since they don't engage in them. Their scorn, on the other hand, I understand well enough.

Human history books make no room for foxes. But talk to any gossip on the streets or any popcorn-munching movie-goer, and they will tell you that foxes of my disposition have been around since before the first dynasty.

I got worse when we emigrated to the west coast of Canada. The whole extended family came for the opportunities, not knowing that migration fundamentally and permanently changes value systems. My penchant for nightly roamings ceased to be a mere quirk of my character, but rather became a whole way of life. I like to fish, and I like to steal chickens. But I don't do either anymore, except on those rare occasions when courtesy demands it.

The foxes of my fox hole got used to what they called my unnatural behaviour in due time. They did not mind what I did or where I went, although they would never do such things themselves. "But," they said, "do you have to write about it?"

When I wrote about the thrill of new life that comes from animating the bodies of the dead, they swept their bushy tails in the dirt in disgust and said they didn't want anything more to do with me.

And that is how it happens that I live alone.

 IN THE YEAR 1071, ten thousand men wearing chain mail and wielding crosses sacked the fabled city of Byzantium. They stole gold and rubies and paintings of the people in their fields. They raped women. They burned houses. They took small children by the legs, whirled them around and smacked their heads into stone walls, shattering their tiny craniums like eggs. In a Greek Orthodox church, an English priest forced a local priest to show him where the religious relics were stored, threatening to torch the temple with its keepers inside it if he did not. Trembling, the Byzantine holy man led his captor into a dark hallway and undid the lock on a heavy oak door. Inside were many shelves, laden with all manner of strange and glittering things. There were pieces of the True Cross, upon which Christ had been crucified, a brass case decorated with a gold crown and studded with jewels that contained the skull of St. Philip the Apostle, and a silver case in the shape of an arm, engraved with the ecstatic faces of saints. Inside were the remains of the left arm of St. James. Greedily, the English priest stuffed the pockets of his frock, until they bulged as though he were pregnant. He thanked the other priest, gave him a good blow to the side of the head, and hurried into the streets, where his compatriots revelled, already drunk on holy wine.

None of this mattered to Mercy Lee, except that she had to remember it for the upcoming mid-term exam in Professor Frank's Western Civ class. The year was 1989 and she was sitting in a café at the Museum of History in Seattle, sipping a two-dollar cup of coffee and waiting for her friend Artemis Wong to come back from the gift shop. Well, perhaps it did matter but not to the extent of shaking the foundations of her faith. Absently, she opened the little designer purse that had cost her nearly half of what she earned in a month from her job at a department store cosmetics counter. From it she took out a pencil-slim vial of gardenia cologne and sprayed her wrists. Artemis was taking forever.

Artemis had been fascinated by the little jewelled cases that purportedly held pieces of the True Cross. She loved the box that was supposed to contain the skull of St. Philip the Apostle. She had exclaimed so loudly over the case containing the arm of St. James that Mercy had had to drag her away in embarrassment.

"Can you imagine people keeping that kind of stuff for generations and generations?" Artemis had asked.

"It's morbid. Besides, they could easily be fakes. Come on. There are some gorgeous paintings in the next room."

By early afternoon, Mercy's feet ached, not because of a feeble constitution but because those soft leather pumps that had been such a deal at Ingledew's last week were pinching. She excused herself from the visit to the gift shop, saying she really needed a cup of coffee. She could have just said that her feet hurt, but she hated people who complained of every minor ailment and didn't want to become one of them.

Left to her own devices, Artemis relaxed. The weight of companionship lifted from her shoulders. Mercy was all right, not very interesting, but nice enough. Mostly they were close because they took a lot of the same classes together. There weren't many Chinese in the Humanities as it was. There were even fewer studying Classical History. So they were close for now, and that was fine, although she suspected it wouldn't last any longer than it took to complete a degree.

She circled the outside of the building just for the lightness of the March air. In front of the double glass doors of the gift shop were twin maples whose leaves were just beginning to sprout. For a moment, she could have sworn someone was watching her from the branches of one of the trees, but, of course, that was impossible. She ignored the crawling sensation beneath her skin, chalking it up to the change in temperature from the stuffy building to the cool outside. She pushed open the double doors and breezed inside.

Whoever had produced this prodigious exhibit of Byzantine art had certainly spared no expense. She was greeted by two large stacks of glossy hardcover books with full-colour photographs of the most important pieces, a curator's essay, and two substantial pieces by well-known historians. She flipped through a copy briefly before stepping into the main body of the shop, where the other books on art and artifacts were interspersed with cases of jewellery and replicas of historical objects.

She gazed into the glass cases with a longing she could not have later described, let alone explained.

"Can I help you?" A young saleswoman approached her from behind.

"May I look at that silver box?" She pointed to a well-crafted little container less than three inches wide, encrusted with authentic-looking jewels of coloured glass.

"A replica of one of the boxes said to contain pieces of the True Cross," said the woman. "They're very well made. Painstakingly copied from the real thing by a professional craftsman. I think his name is on the card there."

Once the glass lid was up, Artemis was quite overcome with what could be described only as greed. She pointed to three or four other boxes and asked to see those as well. The young woman brought them up and laid them on the counter. At that moment an elderly man leaning on a cane tapped the saleswoman on the shoulder and asked her to point out the coffee-table books on pop art. She walked a little way towards the twentieth-century section with him. While her back was turned, Artemis' hand darted up onto the counter as if of its own accord, snatched up one of the elegantly crafted little boxes, and dropped it into her coat pocket.

"They're all gorgeous," she said to the saleswoman when she returned. "I'll think about it. Can I look at something in there?" she said, pointing to a case farther down the wall. The woman quickly put away the silver boxes, without counting them.

In the next case, on a rosewood platform stood the carved ivory figure of a woman, not six inches high. The hair had been exquisitely executed. It seemed to turn and billow in an imaginary breeze. The price was one hundred dollars U.S. It was a genuine antique. Still, it didn't make sense to spend so much money on something she didn't need, particularly after her little heist. On the other hand, she already felt guilty about what she had done, although it was too late to change her mind. The next five minutes found her laying the bills onto the oak counter and settling the carefully boxed figure into her bag.

Mercy was at the bottom of her second cup of coffee when Artemis got back to the coffee shop.

"Ready to head back to Vancouver?" she asked Mercy.

"Guess so. You buy anything?"

She pulled out the ivory woman, unwrapped it, and placed it in front of Mercy. The ivory woman gazed dreamily into Mercy's saucer. Artemis thought about the silver box. But there was no point worrying about it now.

The little red hatchback Mercy had borrowed from her mother hummed along the highway. Artemis was sleepy, but every time she closed her eyes, the car swerved dangerously, or so it seemed.

"Are you tired? Do you want me to take over?" she asked Mercy.

"I'm wide awake. I had two coffees in the museum, remember?"

There were fewer lights. The stars drifted even higher. The car slid out of the lane. A truck pared close and her eyes jerked open again. Mercy was still in control.

"Come on a youth group picnic with me next Saturday." Mercy's social life revolved largely around the church, one reason Artemis kept her distance.

"I told Eden I'd help him on a shoot."

"Didn't realize you two were so close. I thought he was just using you for your notes."

"Is it his fault if he has something better to do than suffer through Frank's boring lectures? And we are close. I've known him since high school."

"What's our story? Border's coming up."

"Why not just tell the truth?"

"What about the ivory thing you got?"

"Oh yeah. Don't say anything about that. Just tell them about the museum."

The border guard waved them through after the minimum number of questions. They cruised down the 99. Artemis strained to stay awake.

"I don't like doing that," said Mercy.

"What?"

"Lying."

"When did you ever lie?"

"Five minutes ago."

"Come on. That's just the border. It doesn't count."

 HER NAME IS Artemis Wong, and it suits her, since she belongs to no one. Her friends call her Art, or sometimes Artless, depending upon the degree of guile she is capable of in any particular situation. You say: A funny name for a Chinese girl. I will correct you. Chinese-Canadian. Make no mistake, because her name is a name that marks a generation of immigrant children whose parents loved the idea of the Enlightenment and thought they would find it blooming in the full heat of its rational fragrance right here in North America. So here she is, with a good mouthful of a first name to go with the short, crisp monosyllable last — Artemis, the virgin huntress. It's Greek. Think of her out on a moon yellow night, arrow pulled taut against bowstring and the taste of blood in her mouth. How seriously they considered the effect on destiny in the act of naming, I do not know. They had their pick of the pantheon. They could have called her Syrinx and had her running in terror from musically inclined men with hairy legs. It's true, she might have have been more docile, vegetative even. But she would have had a tune to hum to herself then, high and reedy, remembering river banks. If they had called her Persephone, they could have kept her, for half the year anyway, tending a fruitful garden. Though it is true that every fall her memory of them would drown in the icy River of Forgetfulness as she went into the underworld to live with her dreary husband, six bleeding pomegranate seeds glistening in his open palm. It might have been easier, for as it is, she remembers nothing of them at all, since they were forced to give her up for adoption when she was six months old. The name, which her adoptive parents decided to keep, thinking "Artemis Spinner" would never suit her, became her only keepsake. That and a trunk she looks into only reluctantly.

They could have picked the Roman equivalent, Diana. It would have been easier for teachers to get their tongues around, especially on those first nervous September days when they complained about not having much practice with foreign names.

In grade four, she thought of changing it. Diana Wong. Or

Diane, even; much simpler, and really, what difference would it have made to her family? It's not as if she would have been scorning the namesake of some ornery, forgotten grandmother way over in China with her funny high-collared suits and shuffly shoes.

But now she's kind of glad she didn't. It's an aesthetic, like fortune cookies, or spaghetti noodles in hot dog soup.

Ø
"Come with me. You can help with make-up."
"Can't. I told Mercy I'd meet her at the library."
"So stop by there first and tell her you
changed your mind."
"But I have work . . ."
"Work, schmerk. I'll help you with it later."
"And what am I going to say to her?"
☏

MERCY SAT by the fountain filing her nails as she waited. Her permed hair fell half over her face, the straight newly grown six inches contrasting sharply with the straggly grown-out ends. The ubiquitous student's canvas knapsack in faded forest green slouched beside her like an ill-fed companion beast.
"I've decided not to work tonight."
"Because you're hanging out with Eden. Fine."
"That's not the reason."
"Whatever. God will be your judge. Not me."
"Nothing is going on, you know."
"Then why bother."
"It's hard to explain. There's this . . . quiet . . ."

His stride was long and quick. Artemis found herself lagging behind him, following rather than walking beside. He made no attempt to slow down to accommodate her; in fact, he hardly noticed she was having trouble. He puzzled her. His treatment of her was inconsistent. Sometimes, like two nights ago when they had gone to the campus pub together after class, he was gracious and attentive, buying her drinks and regaling her with stories about his childhood years in Indonesia, where his grandfather had been a foreign diplomat. His large, crooked mouth spread into a mischievous, comically diabolical grin as he told a story about how he'd learned his first words, none of which were particularly polite, from an Englishwoman's mynah bird. And then there were times like this, when he requested her presence, but then seemed to forget she was there. An exasperated "Slow down, will you" perched on her lips, but she didn't know how to get it out without seeming whiny. She caught up with him at the top of the steel stairs, at the door to his studio. There she gave him a scowl that he didn't acknowledge. Instead, he turned his head to see who was coming up behind them.

Making a tremendous racket that echoed like a drum chorus in the empty stairwell, up clambered a young man, perhaps her own age, certainly younger than Eden. Little round silver glasses sat crookedly on a slightly hawkish nose. As he ran up the stairs, his chin-length hair flopped endearingly up and down like a puppy's ears.

"Sorry I'm late," he panted when he arrived at the top.

Eden smiled and looked him briefly up and down. "Get in there now. I'll show you how to set the lights."

The model was waiting in the studio when they went in. She lay stretched out long as a cat on the tattered green couch with most of the springs missing. She was a tremendous woman. Legs thick and muscled as a man's torso, arms that could hold up the world. Eyes set deep into the sockets, a strong nose, perfect lips. Her hair was a fine white-blonde, the same colour even in the thin wisps at her temples. Natural, not dyed. So pale it could almost be called colourless; there was a transparency about it, as though it might almost not be there at all, yet it was rich and luxuriant at the same time. Her breasts pushed against the fabric of an otherwise elegant scoop-necked floral dress.

"Found the key under the mat," she said. "Not a very original place."

"I guess not," said Eden in a soft voice Artemis had never heard before. His careless nonchalance fell away like a useless garment. She had never seen him purse his lips before, but pursed they were, tense with some unspoken terror or awe. It was strange to see that unusually large mouth lose its crooked, cocky grin, the ever-smirking corners turn down and lie still. He poured the woman a vodka tonic, sharp and colourless. He poured one for Artemis too, and then one for the floppy-haired boy, and one for himself. The woman got up and went behind a screen to change, taking her drink with her. Artemis moved to the couch. The impression of the woman's body remained, although any heat she might have left had already dissipated. Eden remained standing, drink in hand, absently, or was it nervously, eyeing the screen.

"How am I supposed to get into this?" the woman called out.

"It unfastens at the back." Eden took a large sip, put his drink on the table, and shuffled off to the corner where the light stands were stored in large black cases.

They could hear the dress open like a door on a squeaky hinge.

"You really want me to wear this?"

"It's more comfortable than it looks. It's lined." He unfolded a step ladder and began to set up a key light, relaxing noticeably now that his hands were occupied. He lifted a stand out of its hard black case and extended it to its full height. He clamped a light into place. The head of an alien on a long metal neck. He paid no attention to the floppy-haired boy fidgeting in the corner, waiting for direction.

She stepped out from behind the screen. The dress was made of polished steel. Sharp and dangerous.

"I can hardly fucking move."

Whatever she had been to any of them when they arrived, now, in the constricting dress, she became something terrible and frightening, something more alien than human, a giant insect inside a hard carapace. He flicked a switch. Hot white light poured over her. The dress glinted. A thin, high-pitched whine that must in actuality have come from the lights seemed to emanate from the dress's sharp angles. Only Eden seemed immune to the monster he had created. The wide mouth spread into a familiar grin. He pressed a button on the boombox and Brian Ferry's insistent, sinister music crashed out of it.

With the woman locked in her stiff dress and the music pounding as though a giant heart pumped beneath the floor, Eden too became someone else. No longer a mischievous imp nor a nervous boy, he moved with a kind of muscular fluidity, positioning the lights on their cool steel stands, adjusting their intensity and tone. He pointed the floppy-haired boy in various directions—connect these wires, flick that switch, move that case. And each time the boy jumped to it, although he struggled under the weight of a lighting kit almost as big as he was. Eden's mirthful hazel eyes had dissolved to a sharp unearthly green, there was something about the way they caught the light that was disconcerting. Every now and then, he would look up from his work to eye the model, safely contained within the steel dress. She tossed the last of her colourless drink down her throat and, lighting up a cigarette, turned to Artemis.

"Are you the one who's supposed to do my make-up?"

Artemis got up to fetch the case. Eden had explained to her what to do, assured her that with hands as steady as hers, she wouldn't have any difficulty. True, the make-up wouldn't be as good as if he could afford to hire someone, but it would be all right. The model wasn't a professional either. He had spotted her at the bus stop last week, and been so stricken by her height and figure and by the large, deep-set eyes that he had followed her onto the bus despite the fact that it didn't go anywhere close to where he lived. In nervous tones he told her how unusual-looking he found her. He asked if she would like to pose for him. He had been astonished at the effectiveness of his own charm.

She might seem intimidating, he had said, but she had never done this before so she wouldn't know what to expect. It had made sense when he asked Artemis to come along, but now this prodigious woman in that terrible dress did not exactly present an approachable figure. The woman couldn't sit, so Artemis beckoned her over to the ladder Eden had used to set the first light. She climbed until her face was level with the woman's face. She took a bottle of foundation that said *Fair Ivory* from the box and shook a little pool of pale, skin-coloured liquid into her left palm. It glistened against the lines and creases.

An intimate gesture, touching a stranger's face. Her skin was surprisingly soft and downy, covered with fine golden-white hairs that were invisible except up close. The loudness of the music heightened the unreality of their colour, glinting metallic as the dress at certain angles. Artemis smoothed the liquid on. Then she dusted green and silver shadow on the mothy lids of the enormous eyes and traced their edges with a black pencil. With a fine-haired brush she painted in lips.

"Powder," called Eden. "Lots, or she'll shine like a Christmas tree."

There was *Fair Ivory* powder too. Eden flicked the fill switch. When Artemis opened the box, a little funnel of powder rushed up the tube of light that caught them.

"Close your eyes," she said.

The heavy green lids lowered.

"Perfect," Eden whispered, suddenly close behind her.

She jumped.

"Didn't mean to startle you. She looks great. You should be a pro." His hands were empty and his eyes nervous again. "I'll just finish with the lights and go load up."

Artemis brushed pink across the woman's cheeks as Eden adjusted the lights one last time, casting an odd blue beam to make a pool in an unexpected place on the floor. He slipped film into the camera, wound and clicked it into place.

The woman strode into the lights. She moved, large and brilliant against the white backdrop. He raised the camera. She turned and rolled with surprising grace given the restrictions of her costume. He snapped steadily, confident now that there was a camera between him and his subject. He stopped every now and then to give directions to her—"Arm a little higher," "Tilt your head farther to the left"—or to the floppy-haired boy —"Fix her sandal strap," "Get rid of that wire behind her."

It was a relief when the woman was gone, the lights were down again, and the floppy-haired boy had vanished into the night. In the cool darkness, he kissed Artemis between the eyes like a small child and breathed in the smell of her hair. They walked out to the street together, into a light spring drizzle. He took her hand and swung it vigorously back and forth like a child being taken to the fair, and recited lewd limericks he had learned as a teenager in boarding school until she was in stitches and gasping for air.

"Tired?" he asked when they came to the street corner where his car was parked.

"Not really."

"Me neither. Come to my place. I'll make Irish coffees and we can watch the late movie on TV."

On his open king-sized futon, they sprawled on their bellies in front of a re-run of *Blade Runner* on one of the American channels.

The man who made eyes was Cantonese. Her heart hiccupped as she watched Roy and Leon descend on him, lifelike machines with human souls. They disconnected him from the suit in which he lived, climate controlled, making it possible for him to work in his icy cave, where the eyeballs cooked contentedly. Leon grabbed an unfinished eye from the tank and perched it on the eye-maker's shoulder, while Roy slugged out the questions. The eye-maker whimpered and grovelled. Artemis felt the urge to bury her head in Eden's shoulder later when Roy went to crush Tyrell's skull. Eden must have sensed her discomfort because he grabbed her hand.

"Say 'Kiss me.' " Deckard slammed Rachel into the wall.

"Kiss me," she stuttered. He kissed her.

"I want you. Say 'I want you,' " he snarled.

"I want you," she murmured.

The woman lying on the futon watched, clenched her free fist against the blood that flashed through her. The geisha on the video billboard put a breath freshener into her mouth. In the blue light emanating from the screen, Eden rolled away from Artemis. She looked down the length of him, a full six feet stretched out on the futon. He hooked a leg over hers, turned his head and smiled. His leg weighed into hers, water into water. He leaned over and brushed his lips against her neck. She closed her eyes just as Deckard shot down the snake woman. Eden moved back to his original position, but her eyes remained closed. In a few more minutes, she was asleep.

Late in the morning they awoke with the morning news muttering in their heads, still dressed in the previous day's clothes, which were wrinkled and stale smelling. They were barely in time for class.

 IT IS OTHER foxes who are strange, not me. They with their short lives and busy litters, caught in their petty rivalries and dreary surface-bound forays for ordinary meat. They go under the earth just to sleep, have only enough of an inkling of the vast possibilities that exist there to scare them. They do see themselves in me; that recognition is precisely what terrifies them, what causes them to hurry back to their mates and cubs, their animal carcasses and shallow dwellings as though to say, "See, here are the things that make us civilized, here are the things that make us *not like her.*"

When it amuses me, I laugh. When it hurts me, I laugh. And because laughing is not something foxes generally do, they twitch their noses in disgust and hurry away. I don't really care where they rush off to. They're silly to think they can hide from me in their pathetic little fox holes, clay dry and dug barely deep enough for dreams. They run away, but I don't run after them. I go to the hillside where all the graves face hopefully south. I go to look at beautiful corpses. Sometimes I choose the frail ones, with pale skin and snakes of black hair, small feet and long, intelligent hands. Other times, I choose them sturdier, those who in life would have been red and laughing.

See how gentle I am, warm muzzle against stone cheek, breath sweet as embalming wood. It is just a matter of breath, a matter of sighing into the proper hollows of the body. I am a glass blower, swelling this fragile form with the shape of life, lucid and eternal.

The word, I believe, is *animate,* although I much prefer *inhabit.* In this act I cease to be a mere animal. Nor am I a parasite. To inhabit a body is to create mass out of darkness, to give weight and motion to that which otherwise would be cold. And I, too, become warm inside an envelope of human flesh, less nervous and hungry.

But most wilt after a matter of hours, giving me barely enough warning to escape. There is no time for the gangly newness to wear away, no time for the grace that comes with knowing one's own limbs, possible symphonies in the muscles. I used to be able to inhabit the same body for longer than a night — a few weeks, a few months even, as I did to become the housewife's neighbour. But in time the body loses its shape. The synapses wear thin, refuse to accept any further commands.

I have inhabited a Poetess's body for more than nine hundred years, off and on. It is the only one I am able to return to each time without trouble, although only as long as I keep up my nightly scavenging. The need to find new bodies is pressing. Increasingly so these days, since I arrived in Canada. Perhaps it has something to do with the snow.

Those dreary excuses for foxes haven't any idea at all. They don't know about the places beneath the earth, the places where the roots of the broadest cedar go to find the rock-hard minerals that make it possible for them to shoot their branches into the sky. The trees house ancient souls, life coursing up and down their tawny lengths. Those foxes don't know how history gathers like a reservoir deep below the ground, clear water distilled from events of ages past, collecting sharp and biting in sunless pools. How stars dream like sleeping fish at the bottom, waiting to be washed into the bowl of the sky some time in the distant future when enough myths have collected to warrant new constellations.

I plan to see this come to pass.

Maybe it's not immortality the way those old scholars see it. There is no potion to drink that will make my breath sweet enough to breathe eternal life. No legendary moon rabbit pounding drugs beneath cassia trees on cinnamon-scented nights. No guilty Chang O hiding from her husband, belly gurgling with the forbidden elixir of life. Not for us foxes anyway, not even the most clever and resourceful. If I want to continue like this, new life must come from the reaches of the earth, from the sweet mouths of women who have passed on before their time. Each night is an experiment in survival.

I am not unhappy with my lot. I am working towards my thousandth birthday, the day I will have ripened past the possibility of decay, when my roamings through graves need not be so full of apprehension and the worry of not finding what I need. I look forward to a time when my dealings with humans need not be so uncertain, a time when I can tell at a glance whether there is a chance of trust and affection. (I need humans now, foxes are bad company.) It will be a relief. No more scholars with priestly leanings who may pronounce my existence unworthy, who will smoke me out by burning charms or setting out cups of poisoned liquor. By my thousandth birthday, only the widest-winged officials of Heaven will have any power over me, and then I can truly do as I please.

Until then, I cannot say I am discontent. The only complaint I have is that the more time I spend in human form, the more human I become. And the more human I become, the more I want a human past of my own—festivals, candy, costumed dancers, and simple magic that can be easily and delightfully disassembled like an acrobat's tricks. When I close my eyes and curl into a good morning's sleep, I can conjure only a fenced yard of chickens. And even then, I imagine it too close to the ground and a long distance off. It is not enough.

 IT WAS NOT vanity that made her want the camera turned on her. She couldn't explain the emotion. The word *shoot*. Like a gun going off or a star loosening from its fixed place in the heavens and burning down a long arc of sky.

As a child she had been fond of costumes. Not for the sake of beauty, but for disguise and outrage. To investigate the possibilities of what she could become. She chose odd things, badgers and tree spirits, fat ladies and ostriches. When she was small, her mother encouraged it, gave her the old velvet curtains, scraps of fake fur, buttons and glass beads from garage sales and discount fabric stores. Her father, somewhat confused by his odd child, nevertheless taught her to build. She learned to make castles and treehouses. At thirteen, when other girls had already discarded their first tubes of lip gloss and powder-blue eye shadow, she was still playing with grease paint. Her steady adolescent hands fashioned exquisite wings, lifelike ears, tiaras, and claws.

But this wanting wasn't quite like that. Not an exploration, but something more pressing. Something that weighed against her back and then washed through her. Something living. This wanting could push through her only when she let it. Wind pushing through a forest. It happened when she leaned over the bathtub after a long soak, trying to urge the fallen strands of her own hair down the drain. She felt the studio lights burn through her, heard the shutter click. It happened in Dr. Frank's office as he coached her on a paper about the Tartar invasions. She would really rather have written about the fall of Rome, but he said too many people had already chosen that topic. His breath was heavy with pipe tobacco and she could count his pores as he leaned close to show her a passage about horse breeding in an out-of-print text.

She didn't want to tell Eden about it. She was afraid it would break the quiet growing between them, the still, peaceful thing that drew them together. They were as comfortable as lovers in the quiet lull between moments of passion. Except that they were not lovers and the lull went on uninterrupted, gentle and continuous. Once, under a leaning oak, they made a little half-circle of candles at midnight and spread a picnic on the cool grass. But the hot lights flashed through her, breaking up the calm night.

To tell him about it might have stopped it. She couldn't say a word. Or wouldn't. Images came in the flashes. A pool of crushed silk. A bathtub filled with white roses. She waited for the invitation. She willed it, teeth gritted.

He told her a story about his father, who had lost his hand at the beginning of the Vietnam War, and his life near the end of it.

"It's very strange," he said, "but I mourn the loss of his hand more than the loss of his life."

"Why?"

"Because it feels as though it could have been prevented."

She thought about the severed hand, its pulsing absence. "You think we have control over everything in our lives except death?"

"It doesn't make sense, does it?"

"If he had lived, maybe eventually they could have given him an artificial hand."

"Or taught him to regenerate it, like how starfish regenerate lost limbs."

"I don't know. People are more complicated than starfish." In her mind's eye she sees the stump now, scarred over with a shiny layer of pink tissue, marine and alien.

"I've never done a shoot with you, have I?"

"No."

"Well, I just had this idea."

"Yeah?"

"You know that girl Mercy in our Western Civ class?"

"Of course."

"I was thinking of doing one with you and her."

She said yes, although it was not at all what she wanted.

Ø

"Did you give him my number?"
"I thought it would be okay."
"So I have to pose for these stupid pictures
just because you're trying to get some guy."

"That's not how it is. He's just a friend."
"He seems to think he's pretty special."
"I thought you would be flattered. If you're not
interested, you can just say no."
"I told him yes."
"Even though you don't want to."
"I'm trying to be your friend."

☎

"Mercy's not here yet. But you may as well change." The studio
was cool and dark. He pitched the garment playfully towards
her gut, so that she caught it like a football. Its weight and tex-
ture were a shock. Heavy silk. Antique. It fell against her limp
and heavy as a body. The stink of mothballs rose off it, strong
and poisonous. The odour threw her. The smell of mothballs
was the smell of China. The smell of the small wooden trunk her
biological mother had passed on to her adoptive mother the
week after the papers were signed. There was not much inside.
Two used padded jackets of no particular quality, one that she
grew into at the age of four, the other, she refused to wear at the
age of twelve. A Chinese-style quilt. They all reeked of mothballs and called to her from a distant past that she pushed away
with distaste. How thankful she had been for the whitewashed
walls and rose-pink carpets. The Suzuki-method violin lessons
and the wardrobe of pretty clothes.

The other place that smelled of mothballs was the Chinese dry
goods store her mother sometimes secreted her off to when her
dad was away on business. He didn't like her to go there. He
thought it would confuse her. There were packages of gray
wrinkled things that smelled like mothballs on the outside. She
didn't ask about what looked like insects or shrivelled fingers
and dried-out eyeballs. She knew somehow that all these creepy
things had something to do with her, and that she would have to
eat them later. Her mother took the child's quietness for reverence or the exercising of collective memory and decided not to
interfere.

Eden stopped fiddling with the light that would not clamp in
the direction he wanted. "It's real. But don't worry about it."

She shook it out. It was an old-style smock from the turn of
the century, sky blue with a wide band of purple trim, lined in

silvery white. She held it by the shoulders. In human shape it seemed all the more human. "Who did it belong to?"

"My father. He used to collect."

"I meant the woman. Who wore it."

"Oh. I don't know. People used to give stuff to my dad all the time. Come on, put it on."

At the home of her mother's best friend, her "Aunt" Sue, she had seen such a smock hanging on the wall above the fireplace, propped up through the arm holes by a long bamboo pole. It was pale pink with green borders that matched the sofa. It seemed sacrilegious to actually put on such a thing, but then, perhaps he was right. Why make such a sacred object of the past?

She started to undo the round button at the top left. Its fleshiness shocked her. Like a nipple, rolling between her thumb and index finger.

"I'm afraid I'll do something to it."

"It was made to be worn."

"I couldn't afford to replace it. All it would take to ruin it is a sweat stain. And these lights. They're hot."

"I'm sure my dad stashed half a dozen more somewhere. When you get that on, there's pants in my bag. And shoes, although of course you can't wear the shoes."

"They must be incredibly fragile."

"No. It's just that they're only about three inches long. I got you some slippers from Chinatown. They're a bit tacky, but we'll see. Otherwise you can just go barefoot."

He threw a switch and the room flooded with a blinding white light.

"Come on, hurry up. Then you can help Mercy when she gets here."

She stepped behind the brocade screen and pulled off her sweatshirt. Quickly she undid the round button and all the hooks down the side. She slid her arms into the wide sleeves. The garment fell against her back, cool and rich. She wished she'd worn a bra or an undershirt to have a barrier between herself and the smock's previous owner. As it engulfed her, it felt all the more alive.

"Does it fit?" he called from the top of a ladder in another part of the room.

"I think so."

"Pants are in the bag."

They had been tossed in carelessly, evidently at the last minute. She pulled them out and smoothed them over her lap. Underneath were the shoes. She picked one up and turned it over in her hand. The embroidery was exquisite. She had read about footbinding, knew that they had to break a girl's feet when she was young if she were going to fit the dainty shoes. Artemis was sure that she herself would not have the constitution to endure such torture, but then, she thought, we endure what is given to us to endure.

"Come stand in the light. Let's see."

She went to the centre of the studio and stood, spread her arms out and turned a slow, clumsy circle as she had as a child, parading newly bought clothes for her mother and father.

"Fits perfect," he said, climbing down the ladder. "Come here. I'll do your hair." He pulled a comb from his back pocket as he approached her. The way he touched her head was gentle, family-like. "My mother was a hairdresser for a short time. Before she met my father." He worked patiently through the snarls. "Is Mercy always late?"

"What time is it?"

"She should have been here an hour ago."

He wound the hair into a tidy bun and pinned it neatly into place. He found the Chinatown slippers, which were too small. Her heel hung over the edges. "Never mind. I'm not going to do any close-ups of your feet."

An hour later there was still no sign of Mercy. Artemis called her house but there was no answer.

"I say we have a beer and wait twenty minutes more," he said, opening the fridge in the back of the room and pulling out a large bottle of Kirin. On her toes, Artemis leaned towards the greasy mirror near the door. With a careful hand, she drew a blood red line around her mouth. She was brushing in an equally red shade of lipstick when he tapped her shoulder and proffered an ice-cold glass brimming with lager.

"It'll wreck my make-up."

"Never mind. There'll be time to do it again."

As she took her first gulp, there was a knock on the door. He put his drink down and shuffled towards it. "Perfect timing."

In the doorway stood a tall Chinese woman whom Artemis didn't recognize at all.

"Diane?" Eden whispered in the same awed breath he had used for the blonde amazon several weeks before.

"You said to drop by anytime, so here I am. I saw the lights on."

"Please, come in."

"Maybe she could do Mercy's bit," Artemis suggested, breaking the tension that hung between them.

"I'm Diane," said the woman.

"Oh, sorry! Diane Wong, meet Artemis Wong. Would you like a beer?"

We have the same name, Artemis thought. *Just different versions.* She ached to comment on it, but another glance at this carefully put-together woman made her think twice. Surely Diane would think Artemis stupid for raising the Greeks and the Romans. What came out instead was: "Why don't you ask her?"

"Ask me what?"

"We're just about to start a shoot."

"I'm interrupting."

"Not at all. We were waiting for someone." His hand shook a little as he passed her the glass. "But now that you're here . . ."

"I could take her place. That would be cool. I used to work for this photographer. What do I have to do?"

He handed her a bundle in brilliant red. Both Artemis and Eden let out a little gasp when, minutes later, she stepped from behind the screen, utterly regal.

Artemis had just begun to smooth foundation on Diane's perfect cheek when the phone rang.

"It's Mercy. She won't tell me a thing. She wants to talk to you."

Artemis took the phone.

"What's wrong?"

"I can't make it tonight."

"What happened?"

"I can't talk about it right now. I'll tell you later."

"We've been waiting for you for hours."

"I know. Look, I'm sorry."

"Eden had to find someone to take your place."

"I said I was sorry."

"Is that all you have to say?"

"Forget it."

"Can't you tell me what happened?"

"I said forget it. Forget it, okay?"

"Mercy . . ." But there was a click and the line went dead.

"Something's happened. We should go and make sure she's all right."

"Did she say what was wrong?"

"No."

"Then I'm sure she can take care of it. Come on, we're all set up here. We've been waiting for hours."

He positioned them sitting on the floor, knees pulled up to their chins, Diane leaning back into Artemis' chest so that Artemis could breathe in her hair. For another shot, he placed them face to face, staring into one another's eyes. "I know it's awkward. You won't have to hold it for long. In a photograph the gap always looks wider than it is." Artemis could see oceans bubbling behind Diane's brown irises. She wondered what Diane saw in hers.

Diane had to go as soon as Eden finished the roll. "I promised someone I'd meet them at midnight." She slipped behind the screen and was out of costume and back into the clothes she had arrived in—torn jeans, black T-shirt with a pendulous Eye of Horus around her neck.

Eden began taking down the lights, blinking them out one by one until the room hung in its usual gloom, lit only by a fluorescent tube low over the humming fridge.

 MY MOTHER'S BLOOD thundered in my ears and in my heart, which still beat in sympathy with hers. It skipped out of time the moment the promise was made, then fell back again into perfect synchronicity. My unfinished body did a somersault in the womb. The day I was born, the rhythm began to separate again, slowly finding its own pace and then rushing back to meet hers, reeling out and rushing back over and over, until the pressure from within became too great and the outside world wailed for me to enter it. Light flooded into my body so fast that my eyes stung and watered. For the first time, I felt small and fragile, confined within my own skin.

The colour of blood is the colour of luck, the colour of life. They say my father's heart was rich with all three the day he died. I am amazed how quickly the body can be turned to ashes, the blood turned to steam. We light incense to make the steam fragrant. The colour of death is no colour at all, only the traces of a concentrated essence going up and up. It finds its way past our lips, straight into the bloodstream.

The funeral was already over by the time the news reached me. I asked the house mother for a day off to go up to the Temple of Shifting Vapours to burn incense and paper money for his soul. It was raining that day, as it had been the day my mother died. My oiled-paper umbrella was still good, although three of the spokes were broken. I put on heavy shoes and a big coat and set off. In town I bought a large roll of joss sticks and many stacks of paper money, purple, turquoise, yellow, orange, and red. I bought a whole chicken and a few oranges, which, however, were slightly shrivelled, and no doubt sour. The rain had come quite suddenly and the ground was still warm. Steam rose from the earth like little wisps of lost souls, making the path hard to see. The air smelled of iron—freshly turned soil, or was it blood? If it weren't for that smell, one might indeed believe that the temple was in the clouds, suspended high above the mortal world.

I was greeted by a young novice. She seemed to be still unaccustomed to the robes. They weighed her down, keeping her close to the earth, to the cool stone floor which was in need of mopping. The muddy footprints of a recent visitor were still discernable. As we approached the main pavilion, I could hear the cooing of doves. A short slim snake darted past me on the right. Another shot right between my feet. I nearly cried out in shock. Suddenly a panic of white wings fled past my face. Doves. A thousand of them. And a thousand snakes. "A patron is doing a ritual for her mother-in-law," the novice explained. "A rich and beautiful patron," she added, with a shy half-smile. I looked at her and felt compelled to smile back.

The novice suggested that we should wait for her to finish. I agreed, so we stood behind a pillar and waited for the woman to finish kowtowing, three sticks of incense in her elegant hands.

Her white silk robe moved as she did, always just a moment behind, remembering each motion after it had already passed with a kind of sadness. Even under the high ceiling of the temple, she seemed tall. She wore an expression of deep concentration which intensified whenever she paused for a moment to take in the effects of the ritual. A few snakes still twisted around the base of the large ornate Buddha, whose head almost touched the ceiling. There among the rafters three doves fluttered, still desperately searching for a way out. "Sometimes," said the novice, "they die of exhaustion and fall out of mid-air onto the stone floor."

When she was finished, the woman strode out of the temple with a walk that suggested royalty. As she breezed past me, something cool flooded through my bloodstream like a thousand tiny birds. My breath darted into my mouth before I could stop it. The novice gave me that funny half-smile again, but I pretended not to notice.

I lit the incense for my father and placed it in the sandbox beside the woman's. Hers was still smouldering. I laid out the chicken and the oranges. I put the paper money into the burners and lit them, watching the bright colours dissolve in the orange light, and the smoke spiral up, past the three doves, still fluttering, up to where my father was waiting. For a moment I thought I detected a trace of the herb shop smells flowing under the fragrance of the joss sticks. Then it was gone. I knelt on the cold floor for a long time.

When I began my descent, the sky had already begun to darken, and it was raining steadily. Quietly, I cursed myself for not having been more careful about the time. My shoes, by this time, were damp both inside and out. I shivered a little from the cold. Two more spokes of my umbrella had broken. I scrambled down the hillside, not wanting to get caught by the pitch dark of a rainy night. A moderate wind came up from the north, blowing rain under the umbrella.

My coat was beginning to soak through when ahead of me on the path I noticed a lantern swaying with a step I thought I recognized. It was the woman who had made the dove and snake offering! I considered whether I should approach her, but thought better of it. The lamp stopped swaying. It glowed evenly from a fixed position on the path. She was waiting for me.

THE DINNER Mrs. Lee prepared was disturbingly simple. She was an old-fashioned Chinese cook with a dab of the New World thrown in, and usually there was never a meal in her house without at least six dishes, including two different kinds of meat and one Western-style dish like breaded shrimp, veal cutlets, or spaghetti. Tonight when Mercy sat down at the table what stared up at her from a lonely white plate was a gray pork chop, previously frozen french-cut beans, and an ice-cream scoop of rice.

"What kind of dinner is this?" demanded her fifteen-year-old brother, Tobin, already flexing his male authority.

Her mother didn't look at him, but at Mercy, as though she were somehow responsible for her brother's outburst. Mercy glanced briefly at his sullen face.

"Okay if I go out tonight, Ma? Just to the library to study with Art," said Mercy. Whatever was going on in this house, she didn't want to know about it. It gnawed at her; she felt vaguely guilty for not asking about it, but she knew she would feel better once she was out.

Her mother looked at her, scooped rice onto her own plate, sat down at the table, and began to eat. "Do what you want."

Mercy and Tobin exchanged raised-eyebrow looks.

"Where's Dad tonight, Ma?" Mercy asked.

"Gone to China."

"But he was just there."

"Well, he had to go again."

"A factory we own with Uncle Jim burned down," said Tobin, "with all these people inside. They couldn't get out because there were only six windows in the building and they were all up near the ceiling."

"Is that true, Ma?"

"Tell your brother it's not good to eavesdrop."

"Is that how you found out, Toby?"

"Yeah, and Dad said the government is going to fine them tons of money. So he's all mad because he's lost his factory and now he has to pay a fine too."

"Tell your brother he should know better than to speak that way about his father."

"All those people died and all Dad cares about is money."

"You're the one that's always spending it," said Mercy, lapsing a little.

Their mother ate silently.

"And he calls himself a Christian."

Afterwards, when Tobin had gone down the street to shoot some baskets with his friends, Mercy sat down beside her mother at the kitchen table. Her mother sat silently. Mercy settled in beside her, not saying a word. It was hard for her to imagine her father as a ruthless business tycoon. He was a quiet, gentle man, thirteen years older than her mother. Like his daughter, his face was on the fleshy side, and though it had once been as smooth as a woman's, it was now spattered with deep-brown age spots, which seemed all the darker because the frames of his thick glasses were exactly the same colour. He dressed in modest suits, preached hard work and a simple way of life, and kept the Sabbath day as meticulously as a prized invention. In his spare time, when he wasn't doing business with China or keeping up the Lord's work, he liked to tinker in his shop, mulling over inventions that were indeed his own, trying to come up with something that would make them instantly rich. Mostly, his inventions were things for the kitchen. He had come up with an electric pepper grinder, a tortuous-looking clamp for sectioning grapefruit halves, a pair of self-operating chopsticks.

He was an odd man, perhaps, but no more odd than anyone else. It was hard to imagine him as a vicious hard-hitting capitalist. But that was how they portrayed him on the news that night, which her mother insisted on watching on the black-and-white TV in the kitchen. Her face was still as a stone except for the corner of her lip, which quivered slightly when they showed smoke pouring from the wreckage of the factory followed by a clip of screaming, sobbing family members. Thank God Tobin was still out playing.

"It's not like people are going to cut us off, Ma. It's just business. Everyone understands that." But she knew as soon as the words were out of her mouth that she hadn't helped matters at all.

"Did you know your father used to write poetry? In all the classical forms. I wanted him to become a teacher. When we got married he said he would think about it."

"He would never have gotten a job."

"But he would have. He could have been so good at it."

"What's done is done."

The news ended. Mercy drew three coins from her pocket, the really old kind with the square hole in the middle. Her mother's eyes opened wide. "No . . ."

"Come on. You showed me how to do this yourself, when I was eight, remember?"

"Your father . . ."

"He isn't here." She pushed the coins into her mother's hands. Six times her mother tossed them, and six times Mercy recorded the results in a series of broken and unbroken lines on paper meant for telephone messages, with the telephone message pen. She consulted her own English-language copy of the *I Ching* and wrote the result beneath the hexagram.

> *Remain steady and allow*
> *the world to shape itself.*

"Don't go out tonight," said her mother.

They stayed up until almost midnight playing cards for the first time since Mercy was a small child, when her father had called it the Devil's game and burned her favourite pack with the grinning monkeys on the backs one by one in the fire.

 I HAVE BEEN thinking of my father a lot these last few months. I think of the herb shop, the little drawers of leaves, stems, roots, flowers, insects, bones, horns, claws, viscera . . . The smell of medicine always makes me nostalgic. They said my father was strange. That he would regret teaching me to read when I was five, that my water-clear soul would cloud over and fade away, and that I would never marry. He said I have my mother's face, the same forehead, the small, slightly pointed nose. I can't remember her at all. Can't remember her holding me. Can't remember her walking me out into the garden in spring to watch the cherry trees blooming. Can't remember how the fog came in like the tide and stayed for months one autumn, taking her life when it ebbed out.

What I do remember is the magic leaving my father's hands. When I was younger, it seemed there was nothing he couldn't cure, with just the right mixture of this root or that, the essences of flowers, plants, or animals. My mother started bleeding on the inside and he couldn't stem the flow. The house filled with steam from this or that infusion boiling away in the kettle. In fact, it reeked of steam and the rich fetid smells of life, the way you would expect it to smell deep beneath the earth, where the soil is rich and gently heated by the planet's bubbling insides. Strong and bitter as blood. I imagine my mother must have begun to smell that way too, stinking of life until the moment she died. I don't think that smell ever left the house, although it diminished after her death to the faintest odour, which would occasionally bloom with the pungency of memory when I shook out sheets that had been in storage for a long time. I don't remember her, but I remember that smell. It never entered the house with that intensity again.

After her death, he began to get the prescriptions wrong. His hands became clumsy in the measuring, his nose lost the ability to determine quality herbs from stale ones. His vision grew blurry. His eyes lost the ability to distinguish the various shapes and sizes of the raw materials he used to make his medicines. It was as though his senses were retreating deep inside his body, renouncing the world in favour of an ascetic's lifestyle.

He would come alive, sometimes, at night. He would collect the oddest assortment of objects — strange flowers in the deepest reds, plants with thick green leaves, mushrooms in brilliant oranges and russets, which must surely have been poisonous, branches that smelled sweet when burned, and sometimes even small animals or lizards, still wriggling. None of the traditional paper money or candles. Occasionally he would use incense I had bought at the market, if it was within easy reach as he stumbled through the kitchen into the backyard. He would set his offerings on fire, fully expecting the smoke to journey straight to heaven and bring her back to him. He would sit up late into the night waiting for her. It terrified the neighbours.

When a younger herbalist with a pretty and very much alive young wife set up business on the other side of town, business began to drift in his direction, as gently as the wind changes with the turn of the seasons. As my father's business dwindled and he had more time on his hands, his nocturnal rituals increased in frequency. It was unlikely that a marriage would be arranged for me at this rate, so I began to consider alternatives. There was a rumour of a village in the West inhabited entirely by women. Since I have always had trouble distinguishing what is a story from what is real, I packed a bag to take with me the moment I could find out how to get there. In the market, I asked numerous travellers, horse vendors, and fabric sellers if they knew the way, and everybody gave me an answer. The only problem was that the directions I received all contradicted one another, so I was no better off than had I received no response at all.

I arrived at a more practical solution late one night after a bout of tossing and turning. The wet smell of burning flowers and branches and mushrooms found its way into my head. Outside the window, my father sat beside a smoky fire, looking for all the world like a ghost. His hair needed trimming and he was as thin as a hungry dog. I almost wished my mother would appear to put him out of his misery.

In the morning, he was more or less himself, although his eyes were tired.

"Father," I said, "how is the shop doing?"

"You know it is not doing well."

"Yes, I know. I think that if you had a little money to invest, you might still make a go of it."

"Perhaps so."

"If you sold me to a teahouse, it might make a difference."

His hair suddenly became a white forest. "My only daughter," he said, "how could I?"

"If you don't, there will be nothing left for me here either. You won't be able to afford a dowry to marry me off. If you don't get another chance, the shop will fold, even assuming I could manage it on my own, after you have gone. If you sell me, I will at least be guaranteed a roof over my head, and you will have another chance with your business, or, at the very least, something to retire on."

He sighed. "I knew it was a bad omen."

"What?"

"Do you remember Chiu the oil seller?"

"Just a little."

"We were good friends before you were born. When your mother and his wife got pregnant at the same time, we promised that our children should marry. But then both women gave birth to girls. We should have known not to make promises under such uncertain conditions. I must be haunted by a fox!"

A month later, a well-known teahouse took me because I could write pretty lines. I sent my father the money. I was sixteen years old.

What is the value of human life? We are made up of so much water.

I have a nightmare about the ocean. Not a nightmare exactly. A dream, then:

I am walking along a sandy beach. It's warm and the sun is bright. Large rocks stick up from the sand like teeth, twice my height. I weave among them. They hide where I have come from, where I am going. Finally I come to a wide-open area that is all grey rock, stepping down in wide plateaus to the edge of a cliff, which drops impossibly down to where the sea is waiting. I lie on the cliff's edge and wait, for what, I'm not sure. I don't notice the water begin to rise.

It comes up behind me, making small animal noises. By the time I notice it, I have to hurry, but the plateaus aren't so wide after all. I'm climbing, trying to find footholds in an increasingly steep, smooth rockface. The sea is a thousand greedy hands, grabbing.

The woman I am about to tell you about was not afraid of the sea. She was afraid of the moon. The way it tugs at our blood. "It seems incredible that the moon does that," she said, watching the sea enter a narrow gorge it had cut for itself in the black rock. It swerved hard against the rock we sat on and sent salt water flying into our eyes. "The sea survives all droughts and floods, and still the moon can make it move. Have you ever thought about that?"

What about our blood? I wanted to ask. How can something clutch at us from such a great distance?

Now I want to ask her if that's how fate works, but she isn't here.

Ø

"I just wanted to see that you were okay."
"I'm fine."
"You want me to come and see you?"

"If you want."

"You going to tell me what happened?"

"Yeah. I guess. When you get here. Come at around two.
I have to take my mother to the doctor first."

☎

THE PEACOCK HEN was not the kind of place Artemis nor-
mally went into. It doubled as a café and bar and was fre-
quented mostly by fly young stockbrokers and film-industry
types. She passed it on her way to the bus stop where she was to
catch a bus to Mercy's house. She didn't even bother to look up
when someone rapped on the window from the inside. It was
only when a man on the street nudged her and said,"I think
someone's trying to get your attention," that she turned her head
and saw Diane grinning and beckoning her with a quick, playful
hand. The grin was warm, the kind you don't turn away from,
the kind that promises mischief or a juicy revelation. Artemis
went round to the wide, glass double doors and grasped a thick
brass handle cool from the air conditioning inside. The purple
carpeting was plush under her tattered hightops. The clothes
that had been hip and urban on the street became suddenly
straggly and cheap. She slid into the booth across from Diane.
The leather upholstery felt cool against her bare arms.

"Want to go shopping?"

"I don't have money."

"Me neither. I'll get us some." Her eyes glittered. "Stay here
and watch my stuff."

Only Diane could look so smashing in a lime-green spandex
dress as she shimmied up to the bar and drew her legs over a
high chrome stool, donning a forlorn look. Artemis waited. The
pause grew uncomfortably long. A waiter came to the booth.

"Waiting for someone?"

"Yeah."

"Would you like a drink while you're waiting?" Out of the cor-
ner of her eye, Artemis saw a stately looking man go up to Diane.
She ordered an iced tea quickly to get the waiter out of the way.
The man was jacketless. He wore a well-ironed white shirt and a
tie in tastefully aggressive colours, turquoise blue and yellow.
Artemis slid to the outside edge of the booth so she could hear.

"No, no. I just finance them," the man was saying.

"I would have pegged you for an actor," said Diane. "You don't have those kinds of aspirations?"

"No, I'd like to write and direct, if anything."

"And why don't you, then? You must have ideas, a story you want to tell?"

"Oh, of course. I've got this idea for a Western, about a homesteader who falls in love with an Indian woman. But he has killed her brother and she doesn't know." He laughed. "But I don't know if I would fund it myself." The bartender slid martinis across the counter. "Run a tab, will you, Allan?"

"Come on, now. You've got to have more faith in yourself, in your own creative process."

He shrugged. "I have my own little creative outlets. I'm a photographer."

"Oh?"

"It's a little sideline I've had since I was in college. I do boudoir photography. Would you believe women pay me to take pictures of them? They're dressed, of course. It's sexier that way, don't you think, when you can imagine what's underneath instead of having it all laid out in the open?"

"Absolutely."

"Sometimes I do it for friends, just for the hell of it. Now that money isn't really an issue anymore."

"I just finished doing some work for a photographer."

"I'm sure you looked lovely. Are you a model, then?"

She grinned that mischievous grin. "I do it sometimes when I'm invited. But I'm studying to be a singer."

"What kind of music?"

"Opera."

"Opera?!"

"My mother was an opera singer as a young woman in Tokyo."

"She must have made a charming Madame Butterfly."

"Not at all. In Tokyo they like Tristan. My mother would sing Iseult."

The image of a small Asian woman battling the octaves through two and a half hours as a tragic Germanic blonde must have been too much for the man. A confused grin bloomed across his face. "You'll excuse me. I have to go to the john."

"I should be going anyway." She opened her purse.

"Oh, please, no. I'm getting this. Here." He snapped open his wallet and placed a credit card on the bar. He leaned close to her and whispered, "I'll be right back." Then he disappeared around the corner.

"Good-bye, Allan!" Diane called sweetly to the bartender. She slid off the high chrome stool, sweeping the countertop with her hand and deftly palming the credit card. "Marshall is going to pick up the tab when he gets back from the can." The bartender, busy with other customers, turned his head, nodded, and smiled.

"Come on, let's go!" Diane quickly gathered her things from the booth and hurried Artemis out the door.

"Shit, Diane!"

"Shit nothing. Come on."

They caught a cab at the corner.

"How did I do?"

"That man's going to be a woman-hater for life."

"Nah. He was drunk. I don't think he'll even notice for another hour or two. And how much can he mind, really? A man like that must know by now that pretty girls come only at a price. That opera line was risky though. Those are the only two operas I know."

"This isn't right."

"Just creatively balancing one of society's more glaring in-equalities."

The driver put them down in the centre of a fashionable area of town. Diane paid him with the card.

"This is crazy. He'll have put a stop on it by now. We'll get caught."

"I figure we have a good two hours. You need a new dress."

"I don't wear dresses much."

"We'll find something. Come on."

Diane pulled her into a shop that sold suits for men and women. She rifled through the racks, choosing items quickly but judiciously.

"Try these."

"Diane . . ."

"Go on."

Artemis stepped into the dressing room with the two jackets, three silk shirts, and two pairs of pants. She tried them one by one. "I look like a gangster girl."

"Planning your career. That's good."

She stepped out.

"Perfect," said Diane, placing the card on the counter. "This too," she said to the saleswoman, taking a gray fedora off the rack and squaring it on Artemis' head at a roguish angle.

In the next shop, Diane pulled a dress off the rack, outrageous in red satin and vinyl. "So expensive for so little fabric, but a girl deserves a treat every now and then, don't you think?"

Out on the street, she looked at her watch. "Half an hour before the bomb drops. Do you like cologne?" They went to a nearby department store known for its fabulous perfume counter. Diane requested the largest bottle of Opium available, while Artemis sniffed at a number of exquisitely shaped bottles, with curves that suggested but did not mimic the lines of the body.

"You've go to spray it on, or you can't tell," said Diane.

"Will this be all?" asked the clerk, a heavyish but elegantly made-up woman in her fifties. She had succeeded in tricking the eye to diminish the size of her nose, drawing attention instead to her lovely green eyes with their large, carefully sculpted lids.

"No. It's my friend's birthday, and I need to get a scent for her. But she doesn't know what she wants."

The woman gazed thoughtfully at Artemis' unmade-up, slightly terrified face. "Something clean and simple," she pronounced, and produced several uncomplicated-looking bottles. She sprayed one on each of Artemis' wrists and a third on one of Diane's. Artemis lifted each of her wrists to her nose. All that she noticed was that her pulse was racing. She lifted Diane's wrist to her nose to sample the third scent, accidently hooking her lip against Diane's smooth palm as she did so. The smell was a little too chemical to be pleasant, but there was something green and smoky about it that appealed to her.

"This is it," she said to the saleswoman.

"The largest bottle you have," said Diane.

She put the card down.

The woman looked at it, and ran it through the authorizing machine. "Anderson's an unusual name for an Asian woman."

"I'm married."

"So young!"

"I think twenty-four is old enough."

"Young," said the woman. "But then I suppose you'll look the same at fifty. You Orientals never age." She smiled and pushed the slip and a pen towards Diane.

Diane picked up the pen and paused over the slip for a moment. Then, with a quick and determined hand she signed and pushed it back. The clerk glanced back and forth between the signature on the card and that on the slip. Artemis looked at the floor. The woman tore the top copy off and gave it to Diane. "Have a nice day."

"Can I have the carbons?" said Diane.

They fled to the lobby of a hotel attached to the mall. There was no reason to flee, really, except that it filled a need for the sensation of escape. Diane checked her watch and declared them out of time. In the elegant empty waiting room of the women's washroom, they opened their bags to gloat over their loot. Diane produced a small pair of folding scissors from her purse, cut the credit card in half, took it into one of the toilet stalls and flushed.

Artemis glanced at her watch. "Oh shit."

"What?"

"I got caught up. I totally forgot I was on my way to see someone."

"Not much you can do about it now."

"I can call at least. You got a quarter?"

Diane opened her purse and routed around among the things inside.

Outside at the pay phone, Artemis punched in Mercy's number. The phone rang. After eight rings she replaced the receiver.

"I wonder if I should just go there."

"How late are you?"

"About three hours."

"No point then. Why don't you come to my place and drink with me?"

It was beginning to rain. Artemis and Diane stood under the narrow roof of a bus shelter, clutching their bags and breathing in the cigarette and wet wool smells of the other evening commuters who crowded under the roof with them.

"Should have tried for a cash advance," muttered Diane, careful to keep her voice low just in case. "You can get them at bank machines now, you know."

"Never mind."

"But wouldn't you like to be sitting in a nice warm cab right now, telling some silly man where to drive you?"

"Oh well."

Diane hugged herself, pulling her thin leather jacket, which she fastidiously left unzipped, tightly around her. "Are you local born?"

"I don't know."

"How can you not know?"

"I'm adopted."

"And they won't even tell you where you were born?"

"I think they're insecure or something. Afraid I would leave them for my birth mother. Too many secrets in my family. Still, they let me keep the name she gave me."

"What do they do?"

"My father's an Asian Studies professor. My mother's a curator at the Museum of Ancient Cultures."

"Are they white?"

"Yeah."

"Asian-philes."

"What?"

"Orientalists."

"I don't know what you're talking about."

"Do they collect artifacts? You know, Chinese pottery, silk hangings, scrolls of calligraphy, stuff like that."

"There are a few items around the house. I have a trunk of things that used to belong to my biological mother. My mother wants to make sure I'm aware of my history."

"Or maybe you're just part of the collection."

"Of course not. I'm their daughter."

"Do you ever catch them looking at you funny?"

"I don't know what you're trying to get at, Diane. My parents are good people."

"Of course they are. I didn't mean to suggest . . ."

"I think I should go home. Look, here comes the Number 14. It goes straight to my corner."

"Change your mind. Come on, I'm sorry. Didn't you have a

fun afternoon? Come with me. I'll tell you about the skeletons in *my* closet."

The line-up filed on. "I'm tired. I'm upset about having stood my friend up. I should go."

"Look, here's my bus. Come on. I've got your cologne in my bag."

From where the bus let them out they walked eight blocks to the old peak-roofed house where Diane lived. To get to her apartment they had to climb three floors of rickety wooden steps on the outside of the building. The paint had once been peacock green, but was now faded and peeling. The steps were slippery because of the rain. Artemis clutched the wobbly railing nervously.

"I don't actually live here. I'm house-sitting for a friend for a month."

"And then where will you go?"

"I don't know. I move around a lot. But I like this place. I call it my aerie," said Diane, turning the key in the lock. "I like to come home to this place after a good day's worth of sophisticated delinquency."

"Princess by day, owl by night."

"Don't call me that."

"What?"

"Princess. I hate being called princess. Princess, goddess, star. I don't know what's wrong with people."

"You do have a certain air about you."

"Any confidence I might have I've earned, okay. I put a lot of work into learning how to take care of myself."

"I'm sorry."

"It's okay. Me too. I guess I'm tired." The apartment was small and dark. The ceiling sloped sharply down on either side. The walls were covered with political posters, one for a march against poverty, one for a rally against violence against women, one for a women's music festival in the park. The bed in the corner was neatly made, the short kitchen counter clean. Diane offered Artemis a chair at a somewhat cluttered table and handed her a cold beer from the fridge.

"You steal credit cards often?"

"No. Just sometimes. When I need to remind myself who takes care of who."

"Don't you have family that looks out for you?"

"I have a family that looks after itself. It looks after me only insofar as I'm part of it. You know what I mean?"

"Not exactly."

"As long as I am what they expect me to be, they take care of me. Step outside of that and forget it. It's not that they refuse me anything. It's just that they don't understand the other half of my world."

"What do you mean, 'other half'?"

"I had this brother, okay. Who left us. It was supposed to be this big secret, but I told my friend Kitty."

———

Smoking long skinny cigarettes after school with Kitty Lum against the cool brick wall behind the school, Diane gave Kitty the story in detail. Kitty told her mother, Sadie Lum, and Sadie told Junette Mah, whose mother was Japanese, which makes her half, although she tried not to let anyone know. Junette told her mah-jong friends all about Sally Wong's shameful son and so Sally slowly found out that everybody knew. Diane caught hell.

She walked into the store after school one day to find her mother in the back room, sticking price tags on tins of Campbell's soup. The back door was open to let air in, but it made the room cold.

"You are never to talk to anyone about your brother again."

"What's wrong, Ma? Haven't you always said there's no point in keeping so many secrets?"

"I never do anything to restrict your freedom. That is what we came here for, so you could be free. But I won't have you bringing such shame down on my head."

"Have people been gossipping?"

Sally Wong hung her head. "The more you run away from the old world, the more it catches up with you."

"You're going to have to be more specific, Ma."

"Just this once in your life I'm going to ask you to do something, and not ask questions about it." Sally looked her daughter straight in the eye. "Don't speak about Andie again. Not in this house. Not outside." Abruptly, she turned her head to catch the winter sky pouring through the open back door, and went back to tagging prices on chicken noodle soup.

It was near the end of eleventh grade. Diane sat on the low brick wall that separated the school from the parking lot, chewing spearmint gum, thinking it would mask the smell of nicotine on her breath. She and Kitty had just started smoking, but it didn't make the popular girls think them any cooler than they did before. They had headphones plugged into Diane's walkman and were listening to Simon LeBon.

They didn't hear the wheels screech to a halt because the volume on the walkman was too high, but they were startled by how close to their feet the tires of the little green MG bit.

"Hey Diane, want a ride?" It was her older brother, Andie, with his hair slicked back like John Lone. He had dropped out of school the previous year. Otherwise, this year he and Diane would have been in the same grade. Andie was a good soccer player, and good at taking apart things like radios, telephones, and cars, and putting them back together again. Anything else, he didn't care about. *Smart, but lazy,* his teachers wrote on his last report card. Diane, on the other hand, was good at school. She would never be caught dead in the library, though, or sitting out in the hallways leaning against lockers with the Chinese girls with glasses, quizzing each other at the last minute before tests. But she studied at home, late into the night, under the covers with a flashlight, like a rebellious small child defying her parents' orders to sleep. She didn't have to do this. When Shauna woke once to see the glowing mountain of her sister with a flashlight under the quilt, she said, "Go ahead and use the desk and reading light if you want. I can still sleep." Embarrassed, Diane turned the flashlight off and the mountain flattened. "I was going to sleep anyway." She made sure Shauna didn't catch her at it again.

Diane hadn't heard Andie. She pulled the headphones off her ears. They tangled in her knotted hair.

"Did you rent this to impress some girl?"

"No, I bought it. And I'm offering a ride to my favourite sister."

"This belongs to you?" Diane asked him, as she pushed the headphones generously into Kitty's hands. "Here, you keep this for tonight." She got into the car. In the distance, she could see Jane Croft and Marianne Scott eyeing her through the glass doors that led into the front foyer of the school.

They tore out of the parking lot with an impressively well-controlled swerve and the wind whipped their hair about as they picked up speed on the main road.

"Are you sure you didn't buy this to grab some chick's attention?" Diane worried about her brother, who dressed and swaggered like Hugh Hefner himself. She found it slightly embarrassing.

"The only girl's attention I want is my sister's," he said. "My favourite sister, who I'm gonna take to her favourite ice-cream place for a hot fudge sundae with peanuts." He meant Dairy Queen, which hadn't been Diane's favourite ice-cream place since she was eleven. She was about to say so, but his eyes had this desperate look that dropped into her belly like lead.

As they slowed to turn into the entrance of the strip where the Dairy Queen had sat ever since she could remember, she caught a whiff of the car's upholstery. An aroma which, due to excitement and then the wind, had evaded her until now. It smelled new, like a giant stuffed teddy bear you might win at the fair. She thought to herself that when she got a boyfriend, he wouldn't drive a car like this, but something more sophisticated, like an old Rambler.

The hot fudge was too sweet. It dug in at the back of her throat and made her ears ring. Andie wolfed his in big spoonfuls. Did he taste it at all? He looked at her with his big, round eyes, and she ate the sundae to occupy herself so she wouldn't have to look back. The fudge sauce gobbed in the white dribbly stuff that had been ice-cream until it melted. She poked at it with her plastic spoon.

"Tell me why you bought this car."

"I've been saving for a long time."

"I meant, what made you want to buy this car? If it's not for some girl's sake . . ." She looked at him finally, grinning at what she hoped he would take as an affectionate joke. His last girlfriend, Marie, had stopped calling over a year ago. He had been so proud of her blonde hair, even though she really wasn't what you could call pretty.

"No, Diane, not to impress any girl. I'm moving out."

"Andie, that's great! Have you told Mom and Dad yet?"

"No."

"Why not? You don't think they'll be upset, do you?"

"I do, actually."

"Why?"

"Because. I'm moving in a with a guy."

"What are you trying to tell me?"

"I think you know."

Diane was quiet for a moment and then she said, "Well, Andie, so what? It's cool with me. I don't think of you as any worse. I mean as any different. There's no need to make such a big deal of it."

He looked at her dumbly. "Mom and Dad are gonna freak."

"No. Andie, they won't. They may not be delighted, but they're not going to disown you. They're not like that."

"You don't understand anything. It's not what they say. It's how they'll look at me. Like I'm the biggest disappointment of their lives. I am the only son, you know."

"Come on. We're in Canada now. This isn't China anymore."

"Say what you want, Diane. I know how it is."

Everything was loaded into the rented van except the couch and a few smaller boxes. The couch was fake red velvet. Its thick arms had been worn bald. So had the cushion covers. In a few places the stitching was coming apart, and the threads stuck up like stray hairs in unexpected places. This couch was the first one bought by Sterling and Sally Wong after they got married. It had occupied a key position in the living room for the first fifteen years, and a comfortable place in the rec room for eight more.

"Are you sure you want this thing?" Sterling Wong hid everything behind his wide-rimmed glasses. "I'd be happy to give you money for a new one."

"I don't want money, Dad," said Andie. "I'll be fine. If you would just help me get it into the van." Father and son crouched on either side of the unwieldy piece of furniture, and with bent knees and held breath, raised it above the ground and heaved it into the van.

"Are you sure you don't need my help to unload it?" asked his father.

"It's fine. Stephen will help me."

"I don't know why he feels he has to hurry away from us like this," said Sally after he was gone. She watched the clouds of dust puffing up behind the van as it pulled away down the alley.

Sterling shook his head. "It's hard enough being Chinese.

Why does he want to make it worse? Especially in something he has a choice over."

"But he didn't have to leave us like this. Do you think he'll come back, Diane?"

"How should I know?" she snapped.

For a week the house and the store were deadly quiet. Andie's ghost filled every crevice of every room, but nobody knew what to say.

On Sunday, Diane and Shauna sat at the kitchen table peeling potatoes for the roast chicken their mother was making. The doorbell rang unexpectedly, and Diane's knife slipped, nicking her finger. She got up. It was Andie, and a tall young man with brown hair and hazel eyes.

"Andie! Hey, Dad, Andie's here!" she called into her father's office. The old man shuffled out from his hideaway beaming. Diane sucked her bleeding finger.

"Who's this?"

"Mr. Wong, I'm Stephen," said the young man gravely. He produced a bottle of chilled white wine from the depths of his well-cut brown wool overcoat, and handed it to Andie's father.

"This is my daughter Diane. This is Shauna."

"Hi!" they said, one after the other.

"Come in, come in, sit down." The elder Wong ushered them nervously into the never-used living room. Andie and Stephen moved ahead, coralled by the elder Wong. Shauna and Diane returned to the potatoes.

In the kitchen, Sally Wong broke a package of smoked almonds into a little bevelled glass dish with scalloped edges, and hurried them onto the glass-topped coffee table. Stephen miraculously produced a bunch of pink carnations floating like the heads of angels amidst an abundance of baby's-breath, and placed it graciously in her surprised hands.

Sally blushed. "Thank-you! No need to be so polite, no need, no need at all." She backed out of the room to get a vase.

"I hope you don't mind us coming unannounced," said Stephen. "Andie insisted it wasn't necessary."

"Of course it's not necessary," said Sterling, looking reproachfully at a cowering Andie. "My son is always welcome in my house, whether he calls or not."

"Stephen is a librarian," said Andie, trying to turn his father's gaze away from himself.

"A librarian?" said Sterling. "That is a good profession. So you like books, eh?"

Sally Wong came back into the room with a vase full of carnations in one hand, and a black lacquer tray with wine glasses and a corkscrew in the other.

As she turned to go back to the kitchen, Stephen said, "Won't you sit with us, Mrs. Wong, and have a glass of wine?"

"Have to finish making dinner."

This was a very practical response, which Stephen accepted. "After dinner, then. Andie and I will clean up and we can all sit together afterwards."

She smiled. "We'll talk about it later." She scuttled away before this young man could embarrass her again with his strange and overwhelming politeness.

"So what kind of books do you like, Mr. Wong?"

"Oh, all kinds. All kinds of books."

"Do you read in English or Chinese?"

"Oh, a little of this, a little of that."

"Ever read Pu Song-Ling's *Strange Tales of Liaozhai*?"

The elder Wong gave a little chuckle of pleasure. "So you know these kinds of books, eh? I bet my Andie doesn't know of such books."

Andie scowled. "Strange tales of what?"

"Liaozhai . . . Is that the right pronunciation, Mr. Wong?"

"Yes, yes I think so," said the old man.

"My father doesn't know. It's not his dialect," Diane yelled from behind a mound of potato peels in the kitchen.

"Well, that's right," said Mr. Wong. "But I can speak a little Mandarin. My ignorant children, of course, are not aware of this."

"Which tale do you like the best?" asked Stephen.

"Many of the tales are very fine. But I like the one about the Taoist priest on the mountain of Laoshan."

"That's the one about the man who tries to learn Taoist magic."

"Yes. But he's been too spoiled as a child, and does not have the necessary stamina to learn the Taoist art. He comes home and tries to show off the one trick he has learned, which is how to walk through walls. But when he tries it for his wife, he just gets a big bump on his head."

Stephen was the only one who laughed.

"My children should read these stories, especially my son."

"You never taught us to read Chinese, Dad."

"But the book is available in English translation," said Stephen.

Broke up with Stephen and moved to Toronto, said the postcard that Shauna separated from the phone bill, a flyer for a pizza place, a flyer for dry cleaning, and a large envelope of coupons that advertised "Over $500 worth of savings inside!" She checked the postmark, and it had indeed been stamped in Toronto.

"That Stephen was a good man," said Sally.

"He was an idiot," said Diane.

"I didn't think he was that bad," said Shauna. "I mean, since Andie likes guys now. That's what I don't get."

"So what if he does?" said Diane.

"At least he could have learned a few things from Stephen," said Sterling. "A clever boy, that Stephen. He could even speak a little Chinese."

"Why did Andie have to write on a postcard for all the world to see?" asked Sally.

"Don't look at me, Ma!" said Diane. "Anyway, he didn't even sign it, so who's to know it's from a son and not a daughter?"

This was the only correspondence the Wong family received from their son. Two months later, however, Diane got an envelope with her name and address neatly typed. There was no return address. Inside was an index card with typing on one side and a felt pen drawing of a thick coiled snake with shimmering scales on the other.

> *Dear Diane,*
>
> *Please don't show or mention this letter to anybody. You know I trust you not to. I am writing because I don't want you to worry about me. I sold the MG. I am living in a house with three roommates, one other man and two women. We have a big back-yard with two old apple trees and a swing. I'm working part-time at a garage that belongs to this Japanese guy. Get this: He's a nuclear engineer. Of course he couldn't find any work in this lousy country, so he opened his own shop.*

I was seeing this Chinese man for a week, but he looked too much like Uncle Sheldon.
Love, Andie

Diane stifled a giggle at the last, and hid the card in a blue tin that used to hold assorted cream-filled cookies. A month later, there was another one.

Dear Diane,
My roommate was dealing heroin. He went travelling for a few months, and so I took over the business. But I got sick of all the junkies wanting to hang out all the time. Anyway, we live in a basically good country, and I do have an honest job. Why rock the boat?
Stephen's been calling. I think he's a creep.
Love, Andie

The drawing on the other side was a space-age hot rod, with a helmeted driver. Spikes and guns of all sorts stuck out from every angle of the car and the driver's armour. For some reason, the picture made her weep.

———

"Did any other letters come?" asked Artemis.

"I waited for them. But not with the certainty that I had before. I never knew when the letters were going to come, you know. I couldn't predict the time."

"And so?"

"And so the expectation of their arrival just faded away bit by bit. I began to dream up worst-case scenarios."

The evening is thick and hot. The sun flushes the sky a scandalous pink. The entrance to Stanley Park swarms with people like bees on the lip of a honeycomb. Families walk slowly after a full supper. Young couples in golf shirts stroll by holding hands. Rollerbladers, both men and women, in tight neon suits, with brown, muscled legs fly past, hi-tech angels hurrying towards heaven before the gates close.

A full moon is rising and the sea lolls against the seawall with its full lazy weight, aching to spill over and swallow the asphalt path. Where the sea first curves into the land, a Vietnamese family has staked out territory beside the seawall. Their throaty dialect, which he can almost understand, is soothing to him. The mother and father stand in the ocean, thigh high in their rubber boots, each holding one side of a fine green net as though to catch the sea itself. They hold it taut, waiting for the waves to push smelt, those ounces of silver life, into the narrow mesh. On the edge of the seawall the grandmother presides over white pork-rind buckets, full of fish. When the parents drag the net in, the children gather around. Their small hands tug eagerly at the wriggling inches of life fighting vainly for water.

The sky is dark now, and the first stars are poking through velvet. He walks jauntily, in long strides, searching the eyes of men walking in the opposite direction. There aren't many. He meets progressively fewer people coming the other way as he walks. No more couples, families, or rollerbladers. He passes the last fishing family, casting a hopeful net for a final try. Men's eyes come out of the darkness and vanish again. He passes the rock shaped like a woman waiting for her lost lover, and it is there that a thick arm encircles his throat. "Faggot!" His groin screams. "Chink!" His eyes, please, not his eyes! He falls down, and there are steel-toed boots slamming into his mouth, his spine, the crack of his bum. Blood pours hot and sticky over his face. There are pinpricks of light in the darkness, and then there is nothing.

"Did you ever find out what happened to him?" Artemis took a gulp of her third beer.

"It was the way I imagined it. He was killed. Except in High Park in Toronto, not Vancouver. I have the newspaper clippings somewhere. Want to see them?"

"No! I mean, you don't have to show me, unless you want to."

"I wouldn't offer unless I wanted to."

Only one clipping, from a gay and lesbian rag, had photographs. A picture of the dead man, his face barely the breadth of two fingers on the page. A photograph of the site where the body was found, the foot of a tree with thick, snarling roots. All gray against a gray background. Diane had not turned on any lights and the sky was almost dark. The two women leaned over the image on paper already starting to yellow.

"My father got an eye infection the week this came out. His

vision's been a little off ever since. I didn't mean what I said before about family. We take care of one another the best we can, you know. I'm trying to get up enough money for my mother to go back to Hong Kong to see my grandfather before he passes on. She hasn't been there in twenty years."

"You miss your brother."

"Yeah. For sure I do."

"I'm sorry." Artemis moved her hand across the table to take Diane's. The slender fingers were ice cold. Their eyes locked in the last of the evening light that came in through the small window on the far wall. They leaned closer towards one another and their lips caught like a sudden match flaring in the dark.

Diane pulled away. "That was weird."

"It doesn't have to mean anything."

"Then let's just say it doesn't."

PART 2

The Familiar Shape

THE WOMAN with the lantern smelled subtly of
roses. She asked my name. When I told her she
seemed pleased. "My husband reads your poetry,"
she said. "He quotes your lines to me sometimes."
Although her umbrella was glossy and whole, the rain had
drenched her clothing also. In the light of the lantern, I could
make out the shape of her body beneath her damp dress.

Later that week, in the front room of the teahouse where I
worked, I was introduced to a travelling scholar. He said he
came from a family of hunters. He was tall and his skin was
luminous as the surface of a lake. He looked at me with a light in
his eyes that made me think perhaps he was remembering someone else. His gaze weighed on me. I wasn't sure whether to be
worried or pleased.

We played chess until late in the night. Some men, when they
discovered that I play chess, found it distasteful, since it is not
a very ladylike game. But this scholar seemed to enjoy it. I
watched his hands as he lined up his men, his horses, and his
cannons. His palms were narrow, the fingers long, and nails
clipped so that they were round and pink with neat white borders. They moved with a decisive swiftness that made me think
of carp, darting about to capture bits of bread tossed into their
shallow pool. He beat me once, I beat him twice. He complained
of faulty horses, and suggested we play a game of rhymes
instead.

He asked if he could stay the night, but I said no. As a rule, I
didn't sleep with the clients. Since I earned my keep with my
poetry and other amusements, the house mother didn't pressure
me.

He came again the next night, saying that the roads were too
muddy to travel. He brought me a gift—a packet of rose-scented

incense. I lit some. The smoke and sweet odour filled the room like fresh air from a place far away. I found myself remembering a rainy dusk on the hill leading down from the temple, and a figure standing on the path. I pushed the memory away, recalling that I was working and ought to put my energy into that. It would not, I thought, be at all unpleasant to have this man as a patron. He asked me if I could sing. I told him I had been studying with one of my sisters, who had been an opera singer. Spiders scuttled from my elbows to my wrists. I don't often get nervous. I wasn't sure whether it was because singing was a relatively new thing, or because I was so anxious to please my guest. I stood up, conscious of the weight of my embroidered sleeves, and then the weight of the whole garment, the way it flowed blue to the floor, cascading birds and flowers. The silk lining began to feel rough and slightly sticky against my skin, and I noticed my hands were not as steady as usual. When I opened my mouth, the voice began to come. It was frail at first, conscious of itself alone in a quiet room. Then it grew to fill the space, streaming from my lungs with the force of a tidal wave. It enveloped me firmly, guiding me through myself like a long path to the ocean.

The next day there was a typhoon. It started slowly on a mountain far away. Then the rain came smashing onto the street. It moved over our heads and was gone like a great beast, passing through the sky. The air was filled with steam. Next the wind came, bringing shards of rain, cutting wildly into the air, making gashes in trees and houses, pushing people to the ground like an angry tiger in a great hurry to lay the blame on someone. I stayed in my room and lit some of my new friend's incense to calm my nerves. Outside, earth and water and leaves and branches slammed into the side of the building. I thought I would go to bed early to try to hide from the storm, and had just begun to undo my hair when I heard the house mother calling me. Quickly, I rearranged my hair and went out into the foyer. The scholar was there. He was drenched to the bone, and his clothes were streaked with mud. No sedan would take him, he explained, so he had walked.

I suggested he might like a warm bath. He suddenly grew shy. His clothes were dripping, leaving murky puddles on the floor. I felt something like generosity well up inside me, and offered to bathe him myself. He agreed, but made me promise that whatever I saw, I would not hate him. I laughed, somewhat surprised at what I assumed to be a vulgar reference. I promised. When the water was hot, he went into the alcove alone and drew the screen. I watched his shadow undress. A long back emerged, a little crook where the waist went in and a hip flared out. There was something familiar about the shape. Then, he stepped into the tub and called to me. I went behind the screen. Slightly distorted by the water in which it was immersed was the body of the woman with the lantern.

"Remember your promise," she said, unable to read my face.

"I don't hate you," I said.

The revelation overwhelmed me, in spite of all those brief flashes of thinking I had seen a hand move that way before, or known someone with a similar step. I didn't know what to say. Outside the wind whirled like a mad dancer and the rain clattered, clamouring to get in. It seemed so far away. I picked up the bar of soap and rubbed it between my palms. I like the way a half-used bar of soap feels, all smooth and irregular from contact with hands and water. The smell of sandalwood and steam rushed into my lungs as I smoothed it over her shoulders, her chest, into the soft space between her breasts. Her skin was smooth and stretched taut over her flesh, fine over the lip of her collarbones. Even with the temperature of the bath, there was a heat which came distinctly from her body. It seeped through the skin of my palms, up my wrists to my elbows, and flooded straight into my heart. Then the room was quiet, only the sound of bathwater lapping and my blood roaring in my ears.

I bent over the tub and kissed her. She pulled me into the water.

 THE CHURCH was impenetrable. Gray stucco with heavy oak doors. There was an electronic device on the outside of one, perhaps an intercom or an alarm. The windows were dark. The lower ones were an intricate lattice of clear bevelled glass. Above them were long stained-glass arches depicting biblical scenes. From the outside there was no way of determining what lay within. Artemis lifted the iron door handle, expecting it to be locked.

The door swung smoothly open. It took her eyes a few moments to adjust from the bright sunshine outside to the cool darkness within.

The windows were the first thing her eyes adapted to. God creating the world in blues and greens, a large compass in one hand. Eve tempted by the Serpent. Jonah vomited out by the whale. A startlingly gory image of soldiers hammering the hands and feet of Christ to the cross. Through these strange images light poured, casting shards of coloured light across the pews and spilling over onto the floor. She stepped into the body of the church, conscious of how small she was, and how made of flesh and bone. The size and emptiness of the place conspired to this. Light and spirit where she was blood and muscle, now sprinkled with jewels of coloured light. Her mind flitted involuntarily to a memory of Diane's mouth, the heat of it.

A small figure knelt in one of the pews. It was absolutely still.

"Mercy?"

The small head reared up. "Last place on earth I thought I'd see you."

"I've been calling and calling. Your mother told me I'd find you here."

"You didn't come when you said you would."

"Nor did you, if you recall."

"That was different. I had a family crisis. Where were you?"

"I, well, I ran into this—"

"Never mind. It doesn't matter. I mean, it's your business, isn't it? I hate my brother because he's so nosy, but I'm more like him than I thought."

"You don't really hate your brother."

"No, I suppose not. He's just a boy, like any other boy. I don't know. What would you do if you discovered you didn't like any of the members of your family? Not just that you didn't like them, but didn't respect them."

"Move out, I suppose, if I hadn't already."

"Yeah, so okay, then what? Does that make you any less related to them?"

"No, but at least you wouldn't have to see them all the time."

"Would it stop them from doing what they're doing? It wouldn't. I'm helpless and guilty at the same time."

"It can't be that bad."

"I don't know. I don't know if it's that bad or not. My father owns this factory in China with my uncle. It burned down with the workers still inside. There was only one door and they couldn't all get out in time. The human rights people are having a field day."

"The older generation is ruining the world for us."

"He's my father, Art. My family. A part of me."

"You can't think like that."

"Why not?"

"Because then it makes you responsible for what he does."

"But I am, don't you see?"

"You've got to change the way you think about it."

"I told you, we're family. We care for each other the way people who are not family don't."

"Your friends care for you."

"Yeah, like who?"

"Well . . . like me."

"Then where were you when you were supposed to come see me?"

 SHE DIDN'T come back again for a long time. Days swallowed one another like a line of fish, each one bigger than the previous until they were monstrously huge with wide eyes and distended bellies. Each day was an unbearable wait until nightfall, when perhaps she would walk out of the blue darkness and through the front door. Guests breezed dizzily in and out of the house. Not my usual self, I avoided them as much as possible, which, however, still meant a considerable number of engagements. The bright light and the heat weighed on me, and I longed to burst through it for a single breath of cool air.

A party was arranged at the local temple to celebrate the autumn moon. I dressed slowly in my room, cloistered by the compressed light coming through the paper screen doors. The gauzy sleeves of my robe slumped heavily as wool blankets. I tied my sash carefully in front of the mirror and gazed at my reflection for a long time. I combed my dull hair and arranged it, somewhat mechanically, so that while the form was impeccable, it weighed like stone.

When the other girls stepped out of the house onto the bright street, I followed them, but soon I was lagging behind, absently examining the lush leaves of plants that flourished in this kind of weather. Ahead of me, the laughter and chattering diminished to the sounds of a faraway ocean, continuous and indeterminate. I got lost in the echoes of my own footsteps and the smell of a village full of garbage rotting in the heat. Rows of brick houses flowed by monotonously. Outside town, something broke the evenness of my footsteps—a scrambling of claws into earth, irregular, a four-legged creature with a lame leg. I listened to it for a long time before I could bring myself to turn and look, even though the possibility of danger flashed briefly through my gut.

It was an old woman with a walking stick, gray and gnarled as though it were an extension of her own fingers. She must have had good ears, or known this path exceptionally well to be able to walk it unaided, for her eyes were turned up to heaven, staring blackly at her own blindness. Her face was as bleak and dry as the Gobi Desert and crisscrossed with deep ridges like those the wind builds in sand. She scrambled after me, one two three hiccup, one two three hiccup, and when I got used to the rhythm it struck me as having an odd kind of grace. I looked at her again and thought to myself that she must have been beautiful once. I slowed to a stop and she approached me, taking my hand with the ease of someone who can see. I couldn't help but wonder with what faculties she sensed me and knew where my hand was. She turned her face towards me. Her mouth opened and her voice was as rich as heavy silk or sweet fruit just on the verge of turning bad.

"You will get what you want," she said, "but you will be sorry you wanted it."

"What are you talking about?"

She smiled, revealing a single brown tooth, turned away, and began hobbling back down the path.

"Wait!" I turned and took a step towards her, but a wall of thick summer heat hit me in the face and gushed into my lungs, burning my heart and making my eyes tear. When I looked again, she had disappeared around a bend in the road, or perhaps vanished altogether.

A fat sweet moon was pushing up from the ground like a

mushroom when I reached the temple. It had stolen a few drops of the sun's gold and left a pink mess of blood and flesh on the other horizon. The sky sank into a bottomless ocean which drank the blue out of it, so that it wilted, indigo to sapphire to midnight to black. The temple was festooned with clever lanterns, some in the shapes of animals and fish and flowers, some in more conventional styles, with riddles penned elegantly onto the translucent rice paper. Women in dresses that might have been spun from spiders' threads strolled in light, silver and viscous as mercury, hot flowers adorning their hair. Slender, refined-looking young men mixed with full-bearded soldiers, their stout bodies carrying the weight of skirmishes and wars that were becoming increasingly frequent in the hills to the north. Three young dancers in different-coloured robes of matching design teetered on three-inch feet enclosed in dainty slippers embroidered with birds, leaves, and flowers. A few men looked on admiringly, and a few women snuck curious glances of envy or contempt. I had heard from a dancer who lived in our compound that more and more dancers were binding their daughters' feet. She said it was very painful, but that it all but guaranteed a good career. In a quiet corner a few bearded men were drinking a newly fashionable drink, tea, and marvelling at its fragrant bitterness.

Two young men caught my eye. What I noticed first was how much alike they looked. The same height, the same lean boyish frame and slender face. Twins gazing into the mirror of one another's eyes. They had the same way of tilting the head to ask a question. One of them was her. The other must have been a man, since there was a fine sparse growth of hair trailing from his chin. He leaned into a thick arc of light cast by an orange carp, his hands gesturing earnestly. I moved closer, pretending to ponder the wiry riddle posed on a round white lantern. They were arguing about whether the empress Wu-tse Tien, one hundred and fifty years dead, had been a good ruler.

"After her coup succeeded, she put so many of the people who supported her into office that the bureaucracy almost sank under its own weight," said the bearded man.

"But she accepted criticism for that, and punished the man who tried to slander the critic."

"She believed too much in fate. It made her easy to flatter. I remember a story about how she promoted a man who told her he dreamt she would live for eight hundred years."

"And I remember a story about how she invited flattery with a pear tree branch blossoming out of season, but rewarded the man who criticized the flatterers."

"I seem to remember that story differently," he said. "Let's ask this little sister what she remembers." And he turned to me, for indeed, I was there at his elbow before I realized it. "Do you know the story about the empress and the pear tree branch?"

"Well," I said, startled at this directness, "I've heard it only once."

"Everybody knows that story," said the bearded man. "Come on, tell us what you know."

He gazed too intently at me as I opened my mouth to speak. I felt self-conscious about the sidelong glances I could not prevent myself from taking at her. She caught my eye for the briefest moment and knew that I recognized her. "The story goes that the empress produced a branch on an autumn afternoon as she sat in council with her ministers. Since pear trees bloom only in the spring, the ministers all murmured how auspicious it was that spring should come in autumn. But the prime minister said it was because yin and yang were not in harmony, and as the harmony of yin and yang was his responsibility, he should be punished. The empress praised him for his honesty."

"So," said the young man, his eyes sparkling in a way that suggested he thought I might have guessed at the gender of his companion, "the minister was not punished for treason, but for failing in his responsibility for the actions of nature. An unfortunate situation either way."

"No one really knows whether he was punished or not, only that he was praised for his honesty," said the disguised woman.

"And how do you explain her killing her own son in order to accuse her rivals of the deed?"

"Yet emperors kill their sons and fathers and brothers all the time. We call it politics and take scant notice."

That night back in my own quarters, I sat up late. After the first taper I lit burned down to a stump, I took the luxury of lighting a second. I wanted to write my own poem for the autumn moon that hung outside my window, begging for an inscription. Holding the ink-soaked brush at a perfect angle, I thought, for next year, perhaps I will have the right words. The night was very still, a night for secrets. Even the faintest gust of wind rustled the leaves violently and forced confessions from the roots of shrubs and trees. When the sound of foot falls echoed under my window, I could not mistake them for anything else. I leaned out. She stood in a pool of moonlight. The light was so precise that when she smiled I could count her teeth. She pulled a man's hat from her head and tossed it up at my window. As my fingers snatched it out of mid-air, her hair sprung loose, a glossy black cascade engulfing her. She winked at me through the bright strands. Then I heard her silver laugh as she hurried away under the cover of trees.

The next day the offer came to buy me out.

THE SKY had been clear for three days in a row. The air smelled green with an undercurrent promise of balminess to come. Diane was supposed to come by Artemis' place at noon. They were going to the beach. At one o'clock she still wasn't there. Artemis called the house where she was staying.

"I'm still in bed," she said. Her voice was rough and smoky.

"What's wrong? Are you sick?"

"Not exactly. Why don't you just come over? I'll give you the address."

Artemis got on the bus and sat by an open window, feeling the breeze on her face as the city wound away beneath her, as though she were ascending straight up instead of meandering eastwards.

She walked several blocks through a quiet neighbourhood. The sun was hot. She felt the back of her T-shirt beginning to soak through.

The house lay in the leafy shadows of an old chestnut tree. She knocked on the door, and heard Diane yell from the upper floor, "It's open." She pushed the door gently and the doorway accepted her like a mouth accepting communion. The ceilings were high. All the windows in the house were open so that the cool shadows blew in. The floors were strewn with large and small rugs, Chinese and Persian. A kimono hung, displayed on a wall in the front hall, and looking into the living room, she could see a Chinese opera costume under glass above the fireplace. Futon furniture. Cushions covered in Central American fabrics.

"I'm upstairs."

The stairs creaked pleasantly as Artemis climbed them.

"In here."

Artemis walked into the room. Diane lay in bed with bare shoulders that suggested utter nakedness. Beside her, with his eyes closed and long lashes brushing his rosy cheeks, lay a man who might have been carved from marble except for the vivid brown curls splayed against the white pillow. His cheek and collarbones were so clearly articulated she could imagine a sharp blade and the hand of a master chiselling. A master with a practiced understanding of how muscle lies over bone. He opened his eyes and smiled warmly at Diane's guest.

"You like this house?" Diane asked. "It belongs to white girls."

The god laughed, self-consciously.

"Yeah, I could live here," Artemis said.

"That would have been great, but they want to kick me out. The woman whose room this is, she's coming back from Chile and so I have to go."

"Chile?" Artemis repeated, and she and Diane both groaned knowingly.

"Another spoiled brat for whom the world is a Disneyland of exotic adventures."

"You could move in with me," said the god.

"No thanks," said Diane, winking at Artemis. Artemis grinned.

"I'm gonna have to move soon, too," Artemis said, "somewhere cheaper. Unless I find a really amazing job in the next week or two."

"We could move in together," said Diane. "I'll live anywhere. I can't move back in with my parents."

"How come you'd move in with her and not with me?" the god asked, hurt.

"Because," said Diane, smiling at Artemis the whole time, "I don't trust you. Besides, if you would lend me the money I need, I could move into the room coming up in this house."

"How much do you need?" Artemis asked.

Diane shook her head. "You don't want to be lending me money, babe."

Late afternoon found them walking along the high edge of a beach, shoes abandoned down by the picnic tables near the public latrine. Artemis kept her head down, not thinking of anything except the ocean. The sand felt warm as flesh, spreading her toes and oozing through the widened spaces like liquid, although here on the high edge of the beach it was as dry as parched lips. The sun was bright and she squinted to calm her stinging eyes. Diane walked ahead, taller, slimmer, with the relaxed, elegant stride of those who have lived in the West for a long time.

Artemis' legs were too short to keep up with that lanky stride. The hot sand burned her feet and the dry beach grass cut her legs. She would rather be walking the lip of the ocean, where the ground was firm and cool. She heard the blueness roaring in her ears, but caught only glimpses between the ends of the tremendous driftwood logs, large as the bodies of animals, that separated them from the ocean. A quiet menagerie of bones.

Diane came to a halt beside a giant trunk as thick as she was tall. The log could have been a lion, ghost white and still as death. Artemis caught up with her and paused, trying not to reveal that she was heaving for breath. She looked at Diane perhaps just a second too long.

"What's wrong with you?" Diane lowered her shades and warm brown lights flickered merrily behind her eyes.

"I was just thinking that you have the same kind of hair as me. And the same kind of eyes." The lion yawned lazily, and pawed the ground.

"Like we could almost be family?"

"Yeah. Well, no, not really. I mean, you're tall. I'm short. You have freckles. I don't. Your face is long, mine is kind of round. We couldn't really be family, but it's kind of nice, you know, having the same kind of hair." She giggled and then was afraid the giggles were childish.

"Boy, you're funny."

Diane slipped her foot into a cranny in the log. Her foot went where a hip bone seemed to turn in. She hoisted herself astride the creature's back. The high ocean wind ruffled her neat hair. She flashed her straight white teeth in a wide grin.

"You want to come up here?"

She offered a sturdy-looking hand. Artemis slipped her foot in the same hip-bone cranny and grabbed the hand. It felt warm in hers for moment as she hoisted herself astride the patient beast. It was not as windy as it had appeared from below.

Diane pulled a packet of Winstons from the pocket of her denim jacket. The paper packaging was crushed carelessly in a way that made Artemis think of worn jeans with a threadlined hole at the knee.

"Two more weeks and I'm out of here," said Diane, staring up at the wide blue sky as she held the open packet towards Artemis. Artemis fished a cigarette out of the narrow hole with her thumb and index finger, placed it between her dry lips and cupped her hands around the dancing flame her friend held towards her face. As she inhaled she was caught for a quick moment by the sharp odour of propane wafting off the lighter. Taking that breath was almost like breathing in Diane herself.

"Where are you going?"

"With my mother to Hong Kong."

"I thought you said you were broke."

"I am, but I just figured out where I'm going to get money."

"Where?"

"That guy you met this morning—his father is a collector. He collects antique clothing of all kinds, but specializes in the Far East."

"I didn't think you'd approve of that kind of thing."

"The guy's a total slime bag, no question about that. But if anyone's to make a profit off of him, it may as well be me."

"So what do you have that you're going to sell him?"

"Nothing yet, but I have a couple of ideas for where I can get a few things that should bring in enough for two plane tickets with enough left over for a couple of months of rent."

"Wouldn't your mother say something if she knew where the money came from?"

"I never tell her."

Diane leaned into Artemis' chest. Her smooth hair, with its fruity aroma of salon shampoo, was cool against Artemis' cheek. "I don't have very many women friends. It's funny how I feel so close to you even though I hardly know you."

Artemis put a tentative arm around her friend's waist, for a moment not sure what to say. She was aware of the sound of water moving stealthily towards them. "And now you're going away."

"Yeah, but not for two weeks. That's a long time." She looked off towards the horizon and then, as though she could read its appetite for sunlight, said, "We'd better get going before it gets dark." She squirmed out of Artemis' grip and fell to the ground with a soft thud.

Artemis looked down at her. She looked smaller. Artemis cast her eyes skyward and the blueness rushed through her skull. Then she too leapt to the ground.

They walked back along the cool lip of the tide that had risen by then to the brink of the driftwood line. The sand was damp with a chill that made Artemis think of the ground in another country.

They arrived back at the picnic tables. The greasy aroma of hot dogs and fries wafted from the direction of the snack bar.

"I'm hungry," said Diane, heading towards the tall boy with wire-rimmed glasses behind the counter. "You want anything?"

Artemis shook her head. She sat down at one of the picnic tables and began to brush the sand from her feet. When she looked up again, Diane had disappeared around the back of the snack bar to the public washrooms. Artemis pulled on her socks and jammed her feet into her sneakers, not bothering to do up the laces. She lay back on the seat of the picnic table and stared into the darkening sky.

"Hey, your sister's fries are ready!"

She turned towards the boy with the wire-rimmed glasses. "What?"

"Your sister's fries. They're here."

"Oh." She approached the counter. "She's not my sister. Just a friend."

He pushed the yellow cardboard container across the counter. "She looks like you. Ketchup?"

A moon twice the width of the highway balanced on top of a hill and threatened to plunge towards them as they drove away from the sun floundering in the blue depths and staining the water with blood and gold. Diane sped mercilessly down the highway with the window wide open and Tom Waits in the stereo all gutteral and rumbling. She held a half-smoked Winston firmly between her lips to keep the wind from carrying it away.

THROUGH THE CURTAINS of the sedan where I sat alone in a new red dress, I could see I was being carried through the neighbourhood of my childhood.

My father's old house came up on the right, but the place had all but vanished under tall grasses and overgrown trees. The top of the wall behind which I used to play just barely showed above the tops of weeds. I remembered that at the end of the road there was an abandoned house. It must once have been grand. The roofs of the pavilions beyond the high walls sloped with the kind of grace that can be obtained only with money. I had aways been afraid to go there. Neighbours used to whisper about fox spirits.

Something about the house fascinated me. And yet I never dared to approach it, until one dusk, some weeks after my mother had passed away. My father had been at his shop all day, or at least, he had not been home. Night was advancing quickly and the dinner I had prepared anticipating his arrival was getting cold. I put on a pair of his old shoes and an old coat, more comfortable than my own, and hurried out to find him. Instinct drove me to the end of the road. I walked with trepidation as I passed the last inhabited house on the road. The abandoned property was still a distant half-mile away. I walked that distance with wobbly knees. I found him there, standing among the tall yellowed grasses, calling her name through a chink in the broken wall.

As the four thick-armed sedan bearers carried me down this street now, dread welled up from the pit of my stomach. I didn't want to go near that house. In my head, I told myself it was still a long way off. Surely my new in-laws would be the inhabitants of one of the modest, comfortable houses that were rushing past. The faces of my childhood neighbours did not come easily to me, but perhaps I would recognize them when they greeted us. I imagined warm food smells and lamps blazing. Perhaps they would remember my father.

I recognized the gates of the last inhabited house as we drove by.

Even from a distance I could see the house at the end of the road. Bright lights streamed from the windows. As we approached, I could see that the hedges had been neatly clipped, grass mown, and trees pruned. The sweet odour of tree peonies filled the air. We alighted from the carriage and walked up to the gate. The iron handles were old and worn. But the sunken stone wall had been artfully returned to its original state. I had not thought such a thing to be possible. I remembered thinking, as a child, that the crumbled wall, the tattered gate, the sinking foundations had long since deteriorated beyond repair.

Under the bright lights of the front hall, we were greeted by the elder Li, a thin old man with a long trailing white beard like wisps of mist. He pressed his lips together and averted his eyes when he was introduced to me. But I was so astonished by the opulence of this house that I hardly noticed his rudeness. Lu Ch'iao stepped into the front hall, took my arm, and guided me down a long hallway and across a courtyard to her own quarters. With her own paints and powders she touched up my make-up. She adjusted my headdress and added to it a jade hairpin of her own. When the last traces of my long journey had been erased, she took a little silver bell from her dressing table and rang it. Four young girls in festive dress arrived within minutes.

"Mother-in-law and Father-in-law are greeting the guests now," she said. "I will signal you when it's time to come in."

In the distance, I could hear chatter and laughter and clinking glasses. Presently a deeper bell rang and two of the girls tugged at my elbows. They guided me back the way we had come, into the large dining hall, where we were to eat a celebratory feast. The young women pointed out my new parents-in-law and the important guests, urging me to bow deeply to each. Then they seated me squarely between my new mother-in-law and my new father-in-law, with my new husband seated just to his left. On his left sat Lu Ch'iao, smiling graciously. Of course, I felt terribly nervous, but still, I could not help looking around to take in the opulence of the hall.

There were screens printed with ibises, unearthly princesses, and peonies as detailed as though lit from within. There were couches covered with embroidered silk. There were mirrors and carvings of jade and rhinoceros horn. Many servants and attendants hurried about, heaping the table with food. Each dish was arranged in the shape of a fantastic animal, detailed down to wings and claws and eyes. I also noticed, however, that astonishing as the dishes were, there was not a single meat dish among them. I was not sure whether this was a strange custom of the Li family, or whether this was meant as an insult to me. The goblets were of a strange design, irregular in shape and engraved with the kinds of birds that appear in dreams. Between my fascination with them and my filial duty not to leave my parents-in-law without drink, I hardly averted my eyes from these cups all evening.

My father-in-law looked momentarily pleased when he learned that I was from the same neighbourhood. He even expressed a wish to have met my father. He asked nothing of my recent past, but his silence on that matter didn't register until later, when I was alone and shame could sneak in. I felt Lu Ch'iao's eyes on me the whole time, but I could not look back at her, so I did not know whether her gaze contained sympathy or resentment. I was glad when the evening closed and the three of us were free to return to the younger Li's section of the house.

The younger Li's resemblance to Lu Ch'iao was uncanny. I had thought so upon first meeting him, but now, alone with him on the wide sea of the bed, the likeness was utterly unsettling. He reached for me. I closed my eyes and imagined her face tilting towards mine. This was bearable for a moment, but then there were his hands. His hands were smooth, smoother than hers, smoother than any hands I had ever known, and cold. Not ice cold, but just a thought colder than comfortable, like the still-warm fingers of a man just moments dead. My teeth skated dry, top against bottom. His touch was flaccid, without substance. No warmth came to it even as the hours wore on. I thought of her lying in the next room, only a thin wall away. Was she sleeping, or was she lying awake counting the whispers of trees and trying not to hear our noises of pleasure and distress? It struck me later how similar not only the sounds but also the emotions could be. Pleasure and distress.

I tried keeping my eyes open. He so much resembled her that I could almost believe it was her, even with those cold hands. I kept my eyes open because it made my repulsion mounting to hatred bearable. Let the morning come soon.

In the morning, after he had left for his study, she called me. She sat on her bed in a loose green robe. Her hair had not been arranged, but flowed around her as it had on that full moon night only months ago. I realized I had never seen her in daylight before, had never noticed the creases beginning to form in the corners of her eyes or the strands of gray scattered among the locks of black hair. I gazed at her and she smiled at me, but there was an uncertainty or a weakness in her smile that was not present before. I looked at her, and in the length of time it takes for a mouth to open and begin speaking, something terrible happened. I looked into her eyes and in them our husband gazed back.

In a moment, he vanished and we were alone again. She reached out and brushed her warm fingers against my cheek, and I could feel the edges of the deep whorls of her fingertips, rough as sack, particular to her and only her.

Later in the week, to congratulate me on my freedom, an old client sent me two bolts of silk. One was raw, pink silk with a crimson undertone running through it that caught like hot jewels in certain light, the other as fine as human skin and as white as the moon. He was an aging minor official with a big heart and a talent for comic rhymes. We used to sit up late at night drinking and making light fun of the emperor's foreign policy. I realized I would miss him.

I was drinking tea when my husband came into the room.

"Don't tell my father about the silk," he told me.

"Why not?"

"One of those fancy goblets we drank from the other night is missing and he says it was you who took it."

"Because he thinks that my former profession was a dishonest one?"

"He says thieves and actresses are one and the same."

"I was never an actress."

"Still, if you begin wearing fancy new silk clothes, that will be just the evidence he wants. He will say you stole the goblet and sold it, and are now flaunting your dishonesty."

"And will you stand up for me?"

"What will I say?"

I flung the teacup to the ground in disgust and it smashed into white fragments on the stone floor.

The following evening Lu Ch'iao came into my room and set down a tray with a cup and a jug of cold water.

"No tea?"

"He says if you insist on breaking teacups then you will have to content yourself with water."

"That stingy old badger. I bet he's the one who pocketed his father's precious goblet."

But I was thirsty, so I poured some water and drank it. The cold rushed into my belly and I shivered. We played chess in silence. Armies moved voicelessly beneath our hands. The cold in my belly did not recede, but began to feel like a brick of ice chilling my vital organs. I lost the emperor too easily and she said my face was pale. She went to the bed and pulled back the quilts for me. I climbed in. She slipped in beside me and blew out the candle. The night had barely settled when his voice boomed down the hallway, calling her name. She lay silently for the longest moment possible before answering.

"I'll come see you first thing in the morning," she told me.

I dreamt of a snake sleeping beneath the foundations of the house turning its face away from the auspicious south. In the morning, I was heaved awake by a wave of nausea. I thought of the window and tried to get up, but the snake dream spilled out of my mouth before I could leave the bed.

Later, the doctor prised my lips apart, poked at my tongue, and declared me pregnant. I was ordered to lie in bed with the single occupation of tending the cold thing that grew inside me. Li assigned his old wet nurse to attend me. Entering the room for the first time, with an armful of fresh linen, she eyed me as though I were already planning to escape.

Every morning my mother-in-law came in to feel my stomach. Satisfied that it was growing, she ordered me, anew each day, not to leave my bed. As though the creature inside me would drop out the moment I stood upright. As though I were a dead thing housing something living. Then she would leave content, apparently not having noticed the chill that emanated from the centre of my belly, filling the room.

The old nurse noticed. She shovelled coal into the heater under the bed all day. But she was an old woman and at night she dropped off and the fire died.

Li came at night sometimes, but I discouraged him, telling him it upset his son. He always left.

Lu Ch'iao came less and less frequently too, without any explanation.

Thoughts of escape had not yet entered my mind, although I was slowly consumed by a restlessness that made my limbs twitch.

I watched the old nurse's head dipping between sleep and wakefulness as a shard of moon rose outside the window. On this night restlessness was my sole occupation. I could think of nothing else except that I needed to get out. I had been lying in bed for four months, rising only to urinate. I hadn't seen Lu Ch'iao in two. I wasn't sick. There was no reason for them to imprison me like this.

I was lucky that Li had left a set of his own clothing in this room, since none of my own clothes fit anymore. I dressed quickly and padded out of the house and into the garden. The air was redolent with the scent of pomegranate flowers that flooded down from the hills. As I stepped into a pool of shadow I glimpsed the figure of a man pulling a loose stone from the base of the north wall. Legs first, he slipped through the hole. On an impulse, I followed, although it took me some time to get through the narrow gap. I trailed him at a safe distance, hiding in the dry ditch beside the road until the man came to the door of the establishment where I used to work. He turned his head in my direction as he raised a closed hand to the door. I recognized none of these things. I did recognize the sound of her knock at the gate. But this time it was for someone else.

I waited for the length of time it took for the moon to move its own width across the sky. I knocked softly and the doorman let me in, smiling when he recognized my face and smiling even wider when he saw how big I was.

I raised a finger to my lips and he guided me to a spot in the shadows where there was a clear view of my old window. As I settled on a flat, well-placed stone, I realized that this was not the first time someone had thought this a convenient place to spy from. I turned to say something indignant to the doorman, but he was already hurrying soundlessly around the corner of the building and back to his post.

Lu Ch'iao reclined beside the window with the young acrobat from the south who had taken my room. The room blazed with the light of so many candles I couldn't count them all. In the

71

middle of the table sat a large golden goblet, from which they took turns drinking. I could hear their voices as clearly as if I too were in the room.

"When the invasion from the north comes, what will you do?"

"What can I do but wait and hope?"

"You could leave the city with me."

I stared into the open window as though there were no other window in the world. As soon as I was able, I got up from the rock and hurried home.

The same dread that had filled me on the first night riding the last half-mile after the last inhabited house filled me now as the pebbles crunched beneath my feet. I wanted to run, but was compelled to walk with a kind of nervous reverence towards the dark shape in the distance. There was a crumbling wall and a broken gate all overgrown with weeds and the drooping branches of willows. There were foxes at work here. A whole family of them, under the direction of the elder Li. It was the only way to explain the strange metamorphosis of the house. At a loss for what to make of this situation, I found myself still driven by panic. I had to get back into bed before my escape was discovered, before I found out any more secrets that I didn't want to know.

I followed the broken wall to the place where the stone could be pulled out and was relieved to find the stone still there. I was trying to dislodge it when there was a shriek from my belly. I felt something cold and fish-like turn inside. I fell back and the sky filled with a million pieces of broken moon, turning wildly at random like autumn leaves. My belly lurched.

Then Lu Ch'iao stood above me. There was a cool sticky trickle between my legs and my stomach was flat again. And warm. She held something towards me: human in form, clear and soft as jellyfish, with blue veins running through it.

A small wooden chest clattered over the wall.

"Now that you two conspiring ghosts have stolen my son, you can keep the rest of your stolen goods."

There was nothing for us to do but pick up the chest and walk back through town to the teahouse. We travelled slowly because of the dull ache between my legs that ran up to my belly. The first light of day spilled across her face, emphasizing the wrinkles and deep circles under her eyes. She took my hand and the fingertips burned in my palm. We walked.

"You knew they were foxes."

"Yes."

"Why didn't you tell me?"

"I wanted to free you."

 IT WALKED IN through the door in worn leather shoes, brushing gently against the warm wooden door frame and invading her sleep for once just a touch too casually. An every-morning smell, nothing to be surprised at, yet this morning the familiar smell of coffee surprised her. Or more precisely, struck her as strange. That it should be so ordinary. Artemis wondered what morning she had first woken up to this smell and thought to herself, hey, this is comfortable, cozy, familiar. She remembered for a moment how her father drank coffee, not regularly and usually in the afternoon, but then it was instant decaffeinated, not this heady European stuff.

This was different. A decidedly familiar smell. Warm. The air in the room was cold. She could feel it in the tip of her nose. The thick russet sheets smelled decidedly of them, of their skin, but also slightly stale, the way the smell of a person stays with his or her garments even if they haven't been worn in weeks. The sheets smelled of them, not of sex, but of sleep, dark and warm and motionless. They had been sleeping like this, side by side for months, but Eden never touched her while they lay there, although he took her for candlelight dinners and invited her to sleep over night after night. He kissed her sometimes in the daytime. Not on the mouth, but on her neck, or along the jawbone, tongue and teeth breathing her in, slowly, snake-lazy, wanting something but not sure what.

It had happened recently. Was it yesterday? A match flared in her mind's eye and his breath couldn't take her in the way it used to. Her blood did not spread like a wine stain on a white tablecloth the way it might have in the past, but gathered, pounding, in her chest.

In bed at night, the bed to which he had invited her, he lay beside her coolly, careful not to let a hand or knee brush accidentally against her taut skin. He lay closed and tight, turned away from her, snug up against the cool white wall as though it were an infinitely more desirable lover. She was conscious of it as a game now. The smell of Diane's hair burned in her nostrils. In the morning he made her good French coffee and she lay in bed and smelled its familiar smell and wondered why she kept coming back.

She lay in bed and smelled the smell that was almost like chocolate, only bloodier, that was almost like earth, only sweeter, and remembered with some consternation the night she tried to touch him.

It had been some six months ago, the weekend before Halloween. Enough of summer remained clinging to the trees that the air was still warm, although the thin blue odour of winter hovered around them all evening. She wore a mask he had made for her out of feathers and fake pearls that gleamed like a thousand tiny artificial moons, and fake emeralds that reminded her of the sea. The mask was shaped to make her look like a large jewelled pussycat. A gauzy dress billowed about her, suggesting the power of flight. Dressed as a bird with a long blue-green beak and great white wings folded gently against his back he walked beside her. They moved quickly away from the Yaletown warehouse party to where his car was parked. They smelled of sweat and cigarette smoke and the traces of vomit that stay with you hours after you've used a toilet where someone has been sick. They walked through the dark night, the thin blue hand of winter guiding them past their alcoholic blur towards the alley where the car was parked. She was cold. The diaphanous dress floated about her and she thought of a snowstorm in the mountains.

"Are you warm enough?" His voice broke the rushing silence of the night most unnaturally. It was not as though it were really all that quiet. The sounds of the city, traffic in the distance, streetlights humming, someone singing drunkenly several blocks away, were all part of the landscape but his voice broke the flow abruptly.

"Are you warm enough?" Because her mask was down, he couldn't see how her cheeks were pale as snow, not pink and ruddy the way the cheeks of some women go when they are cold. He couldn't see how pale her small, bony hands had become.

"Are you warm enough?"

"No," she said, "I'm cold."

He put the heat on in the car, but she didn't shiver or stamp her feet in an attempt to take it in.

"Stay at my place tonight. I'm too tired to drive you home."

He made hot chocolate the European way, grinding solid chunks in the coffee grinder and melting it into hot milk. She stood behind him. The broken black and white tiles on the kitchen floor felt cool, ragged and strangely pleasant against her bare feet. She had taken off her mask and left it on the coffee table in the living room, so she stood in her bare feet in that gauzy white dress and watched him.

"You look cold," he said. "This will make you feel better." He stirred the warm milky concoction that was just beginning to bubble. "Doesn't it smell good?"

She couldn't smell anything except the traces of unburnt natural gas that had escaped from the stove before the blue flame had a chance to catch them.

He took a wire whisk out of the second drawer. He sunk the rounded end into the pot and whisked gently, not noticing how the metal handle got hotter and hotter, until suddenly his hand burned and he dropped the utensil in shock. It sank to the bottom of the pot.

"Shit. Oh well, I think it's done anyway." He turned off the heat and pulled two matching ceramic mugs from the cupboard. Wrapping a grimy dishtowel around the handle of the pot in order to avoid burning himself a second time, he carefully poured some chocolate into her mug. He had already forgotten about the wire whisk, which tilted out of the pot and crashed to the floor.

She laughed affectionately.

He shook his head, chuckling at his own forgetfulness. He filled the other mug too and then handed the first one to her.

She took it from him and the warmth which emanated from its smooth irregular surface felt good against her cold hands. She held it for a few moments without even testing the temperature, so sure was she that it was too hot to drink.

Knowing that it was too hot to drink, he lifted it to his mouth. His nose and upper lip told him right away, *not yet, wait.* But his lower lip grasped the lip of the cup. The hot liquid entered his throat and he coughed and sputtered.

She laughed, still just holding her cup. Tentatively she raised it to her mouth and a sweet odour assailed her nostrils. She breathed it in, savouring, but something was not right. She continued to inhale gently, trying to ascertain the problem. It was not the smell of chocolate, but the iron and bleach odour of blood.

"Something wrong?"

"No. I guess I'm just tired. Okay with you if I drink this in bed?"

"Sure, I guess," he said, picking up last week's *Georgia Straight* and glancing through the contents to indicate he wouldn't be accompanying her just yet. Secretly relieved, she got up from her chair, holding the cup as far away from her as she could without alerting him to the fact that something was out of place.

She placed the cup on the bedside table, close to the wall, so that when she sat back, propping herself up on the buttery-soft down pillows, she couldn't see it. Still the odour of blood lingered insistently in her nostrils. From the floor she picked up two old issues of *Vogue* and an issue of *Elle* that a friend of his who worked in a salon had passed on to him for her benefit. She flipped through them absently with her cold fingers, looking at the pictures of slim beautiful white women in well-cut clothes posing in faraway locations. She wanted to go away. Maybe it was the cold that made her feel this way, she wasn't entirely sure. There was a series of photographs of a tall smooth-cheeked, blue-eyed model. Her brown hair was cut in a short bob and she wore long waistless dresses in pale colours on location in China. The model stood among a crowd of people in blue Mao suits, pushing bicycles. On the other side of the page she stood in a park among old women doing tai chi. There was something irritatingly delicate about the way she held her arms. Still, Artemis lingered over the pictures. Propped up on the pillows, with pictures of a brown-haired model in her lap and the bedside lamp glowing soft yellow, she began to doze.

She was melting into a smooth black sleep when the stench of blood invaded her lungs with a pungency and an urgency that overtook every other possible sensation. Her eyes were open and the room filled with interrogation-bright lights, white as a snowstorm. Almost invisible in the light's intensity, he stood in the corner, stepping out of his black Levi's. She squeezed her eyelids shut and reminded herself to keep breathing. She felt him walking close to her, reaching over to turn out the bedside lamp. He climbed over her to the other side of the bed. The odour raced through her brain. She thought she was shaking, but she was not even sure of that. She could barely discern how, far away on the other side of the bed, his breathing had already evened out, slow and shallow. She got out of bed and took the cup to the kitchen, holding it as far from her body as she could. She dumped the chocolate into the sink, stubbing her toe on a rough edge of broken tile.

Still cold, she slipped back into bed. He was still breathing slowly, the gentle rhythm punctuated every now and then by a dry, drawn-out gasp. She lay flat on her back with her eyes wide open, staring up at the ceiling, looking at the familiar brown water mark there shaped like a space ship.

I'll never be able to fall asleep, she thought to herself as she lay there with her eyes wide open. The smell of blood was gone by now. The water mark did nothing spectacular. In her wide-awake alertness, a kind of sleep began to come, the kind where you can never be sure if you are truly sleeping or not. She let herself drift slowly into it, an oarless boat slouching into a long watery tunnel. He breathed slowly and she noticed a warmth coming from his body. Something smelled like chocolate, ever so faintly, then stronger. She had a craving for something sweet. She rolled towards him, pressed against his back. In his sleep, he elbowed her in the ribs.

She put a hand on his belly.

Feigning deep sleep he pushed her away, as a baby might shove aside an unwanted blanket. Then, as though reconsidering his tactics, he turned over and his eyes froze hers like a deer through the sights of a rifle.

"It can't be like that between you and me."

"Tell me why we're here like this so often then." There was still the smell of good European chocolate. Her words were empty of desire, driven by a simpler need to unstring the tension that hung unspoken between them.

"Because we're good friends." His sincere gaze still wouldn't release her.

This morning he brought her coffee to her, sweet and milky. He knew she liked it this way. Just as he knew she wouldn't eat oranges until after her croissant. And as he knew there would be stray strands of black hair caught in the sheets if he was not careful to vacuum after she was gone. He leaned towards her neck, still warm and sour with sleep. As he leaned, he fell into the slit of light coming in through a narrow gap between the curtains. She caught him out of the corner of her eye.

"Don't," she said.

"What do you mean?"

She couldn't stand the thought of it, the heavy languid presence that would burn there promising nothing. "I just want to drink my coffee." She paused. "You got a cigarette?"

"You never smoke."

"I want to this morning." But she knew when she lit it that all she really wanted was to see the match flare briefly in the cup of her hand.

He got up and flung the curtains wide. The restless sunlight rushed in, flooding the bed and gushing over onto the floor.

"You never showed me any of those photographs."

"Which ones?"

"Of me and Diane."

"I didn't? I've sent out all the prints, I think. Might have a contact sheet around somewhere, though." He rummaged through the mountain of papers and prints on his desk. "Are you sure I didn't show you?"

"You've obviously had too many other things on your mind," she said, trying not to sound reproachful.

She knelt over the makeshift light table he had constructed from a piece of plexiglas and a wooden fruit box. He gave her a little magnifying glass embedded in a plastic cup, a loupe, he called it. A little circle that tightened around the image of her and Diane pouting ridiculously for the camera. In the one where Diane's hand burned against her thigh her face held a stupid, self-conscious smile, all teeth and embarrassment.

"I look terrible."

"Some of them are all right. You look almost like the real thing."

"I am the real thing. Except that the clothes don't belong to me."

"They should, shouldn't they?"

Something jerked inside her. She gave him an odd little smile.

"You know what? I'm going to give them to you."

"You don't want to do that."

"Of course I do."

"I was just being snarky. You shouldn't part with them so lightly."

"I think you should have them."

"What would your father say?"

"He's dead, isn't he?"

"What would I do with them? I can't exactly wear them on the street. Besides, have you any idea what they might be worth?"

"Do what you want with them. I think you should have them. Really." His eyes caught hers like a surveillance light. She struggled visibly to break free of his gaze.

"We shouldn't do this anymore."

"I know. It's weird isn't it?" He paused. "Maybe one of us should go away for a while."

"Yeah, but which one?"

"I don't know."

"That's the problem isn't it? We don't know what to do, so we just keep going."

"We're not so different from other couples . . ."

"Except that we're not a couple." She drained her coffee cup. She leaned into the cigarette and took a long drag, drawing her cheeks in as she pulled, so that he could make out the shape of her skull.

"Yeah. I don't know why I can't . . . why I don't want to, you know . . . I'm sure it means something."

She took a final puff of the cigarette and stubbed it out in the saucer of her coffee cup. She picked up her jeans from where she had modestly dropped them the night before and slid her legs into their clammy depths.

"You want a clean T-shirt?"

She shook her head. "I want to be on time for class. You coming?"

"I don't think so. Take good notes, okay?"

"You're such a scammer." She pulled her fingers through her hair a few times and tried unsuccessfully to avoid brushing against him as she made her way to the bathroom.

There was a matted clot of her own hair already caught in the drain of the copper-stained sink. It was cold and slimy against her fingers as she pulled it out and dropped it into the toilet. The hot water faucet didn't quite work properly, but she knew where to stand to avoid the initial spray that shot out between the washer and the turning mechanism before any water actually came out of the tap. She turned the cold on and let the water run until the temperature of each had thoroughly blended and then splashed her face a few times. She had to take two toothbrushes, his and hers, from the pink plastic cup before she could fill it. She brushed quickly and resisted the temptation to help herself to a dab of his cologne as she did on many of the too-frequent mornings she spent in this apartment. Not so long ago it was a scent that entranced her, leathery and pungent, calling up a kind of longing she didn't understand. She would have to remember from now on, she decided, to carry with her the bottle Diane had given her.

"Take a croissant with you," he said, holding one out, already slit open and stuffed with grape jelly the way he knew she liked. He himself thought grape jelly was a disgusting North American habit and had told her so on numerous occasions, reminding her each time of his aristocratic French mother. "And this," he said, proffering an elegant brown paper bag with straw handles from some upscale shoe store. The thing inside it had the weight of flesh.

She raised an eyebrow.

"The smocks."

"You're sure?"

He nodded. She stepped into her boots and walked out the door, which he held formally and strangely open.

In the bright spring sunshine, she hurried towards the bus stop, stuffing the croissant into her mouth as she walked. The bus pulled up behind her and she had to run to catch it. She didn't open the bag until she had settled down, finished the croissant, and licked the last sticky traces of jelly from her fingers. The smocks and matching pants lay in the bottom of the bag, carefully rolled, like little rabbit carcasses, quite limp and dead.

 IT IS A MIRACLE I have made it as far as I have. When I was young, foxes were a persecuted species, I can tell you. It is true that foxes don't enjoy the reputation they once did. Or perhaps *enjoy* is not the right word. *Suffer from*, more like. When I was a cub, foxes were thought of as a general evil, to be avoided at the best of times, smoked out of our holes, shot, or poisoned at the worst. The situation became even more dire after the invention of gunpowder, although by then I had learned to leap through trees and fly as fast as sound, so it wasn't so much of a worry for me as it was for later generations.

Now there are many who have forgotten about us altogether. It is a relief not to be so ill-regarded, although sometimes, I must admit, a little humiliating to be so much forgotten. I had once hoped for my own little temple, as in the old days, when the few who placed faith in us would build small shrines beside the road. But I have long since given up on that.

The summer my grandmother was killed by a merchant's son, my older cousin and I vowed revenge. At first we just picked off the family's chickens, and later stole their New Year's goose, but none of this was really satisfactory. I had yet to learn the key to a well-orchestrated haunting. At that point I did not yet have powers of transformation or any practical experience as to how it was done. My cousin said she knew a few easy tricks we could try. She had picked them up by trailing her mother into the village one night. I was scared to go with her, but she said not to worry. She would take care of everything.

On a full moon night we visited the merchant's wife in her chamber. My cousin leapt up onto the bed, crouched over her face, and blew cool air into her nostrils. Between each breath she muttered some strange words I didn't understand. I remained riveted to my place on the floor. When she had repeated this procedure for the third time, the woman vanished.

"She hasn't gone far," said my cousin as she slid into a crack between the wall and the floor. We found the woman asleep in an empty guest room on the far side of the complex.

Over the next few days we watched her through the windows of the house. She wandered about, muttering in a strange language. She said things that made my cousin giggle, but I understood none of them. She walked through closed doors and solid walls as though they weren't there at all, even in bright daylight. The merchant and his son were noticeably upset.

After a few days, though, the symptoms became less acute. She would say ordinary things about the weather or the house in conventional Chinese. She occasionally passed through walls, but more and more she would bang into them when she tried. By the end of the week she had given up and gone back to using doors in the same manner as everybody else.

"We have to go back," said my cousin.

"I'm afraid we'll get caught," said I.

"Nonsense."

The son and the cook slept in the same room as the mother now, each with a big cleaver close at hand. When I saw them I wanted to turn around but my cousin scoffed at me and called me a coward. "Think of it as a challenge," she said. "If you want to become an immortal, I'm sure you'll have to go through much worse than this."

When everyone in the room was sound asleep, we slipped in through the window. My cousin made me climb onto the woman's bed with her and blow cool air into her nostrils. She coached me through the strange sounds of the magic words. The first time it didn't work. I saw the boy stirring in his white cot and urged my cousin to abandon the project, but she made me try again. This time the woman vanished. My cousin, who was learning to see through walls, told me the woman was asleep in the cook's empty quarters, muttering and thrashing in a most satisfying way. We hurried out through a crack below the wall, me first, then my cousin. She emerged without her tail, blood gushing from the place where it had been. The merchant's son had chopped it off with one clean hack of the cleaver.

"Hurry!" she cried.

The merchant's son had to go through the door to get out. We saw him coming after us, but by then we had a good head start. We got away from him, and hid in a bamboo thicket until we were sure he had gone home.

After this incident I was much more patient and disciplined about my schooling. But my cousin's tail never grew back.

 IN LATE APRIL, Artemis and Diane planned a trip to the fairgrounds of the Pacific National Exhibition for the rides, which Artemis hated. Diane really wanted to go and Artemis wasn't sure later whether it was heart or nerve that she lacked to express her dislike for the place. Diane said she had to stop in at her parents' store, although Artemis couldn't help wondering afterwards if the detour was not more for Artemis' benefit than Diane would say. They got off somewhere on McGill and walked two blocks east and five blocks south, away from the water and the railway tracks. It was a hot day, and even though the streets were lined with thick chestnut trees and cedars casting a gentle shade, they sweated as they walked. The taps of Diane's cowboy boots clicked against the sidewalk.

"Wong's Sundries," the sign said, twice, once on the side that faced north and once on the side that faced west. On the north-facing side, there was a big gap between the "s" in Sundries and the rest of the word. In big red circles on the either side of the name was the Coca-Cola logo, the old-fashioned, handwritten one, not the one with the big chunky letters. It was hot inside the store, although not so bright as outside. Everything was dark-stained wood with a slightly reddish tinge. Thin streams of sunlight came in through the racks that partially obscured the windows. An old woman sat behind the counter, weighing spotty bananas for an old man in a suit. How he could bear it on a day like this, Artemis could not fathom. There was something wrong with the woman's eyes because she seemed to be looking at the far wall inside the shop, even as she concentrated on the change. Artemis couldn't remember what you call that, when the eye seems to be looking somewhere other than where it is. The woman wore a high-collared blouse with a small blue-and-gray floral pattern, Old World style.

"Ma Ma," said Diane, respectfully, and then to Artemis, "That's my grandmother. Father's side." Diane waved Artemis to the back of the shop. Diane's mother was in the storeroom cutting open crates of Kraft Dinner. Artemis stood in the doorway and smiled and said hello when the woman paused for a moment to nod at her. Diane reached into the back pocket of her cut-off shorts and pulled out an old Cancer Society envelope filled with cash and handed it to her mother. Her mother didn't say anything, but put the envelope into the front pocket of her pants.

"Where are you going?"

"The PNE."

"Hm. What for?"

"The rides."

Her mother didn't say anything else then, but turned away and went back to opening the crates.

MY COUSIN, the one we called Stump Tail, was incorrigible. She returned to the merchant's house without telling anyone and continued to terrorize the merchant's wife. She made friends with a more established fox family in the neighbourhood and became drinking pals with the eldest son. Together they bothered several families in the district, stealing eggs and secretly swapping vinegar for wine.

The merchant's neighbour had a penchant for gambling. My cousin and her new friend stole into his house one night and wrote spells under his pillow. His gambling habit grew more intense. At first he enjoyed it, but one night, feeling a little queasy on account of something he had eaten, he attempted to stop early, only to find that his hands kept counting the chips and tiles and his mouth kept egging his competitors on. He played mah jong for seventeen days straight, neither eating nor drinking, until he died of exhaustion. My cousin couldn't finish telling me the story, she was laughing so hard.

But the next night someone sold poisoned wine to her new friend. The two of them were found in the garden the following morning, stretched out stiff and dead as boards.

 WHITE BANNERS with bold characters brushed on in thick China ink fluttered with the fury of ghosts agitating to be released from the poles to which they had been fastened. The wide gravel space on the edge of Chinatown was packed with Chinese people, black hair making an ocean. Many of them had white bands tied around their arms. There had just been a huge massacre of students in a square just outside the Imperial Palace in Beijing.

The sun was bright, but it was cold for a day in June and Artemis hugged her jean jacket tightly to her body. The start-and-stop drone of the Main Street station skytrain interrupted the man on the makeshift stage reading a speech in Romanized Cantonese off a crumpled piece of paper. His accent was good, the accent of his childhood. She listened, letting the words flow through her, letting her body understand what her ears could not. When he finished the lot filled with a genteel clapping that almost blew away in the wind.

An Asian Studies professor took his place, cleverness gleaming from his egg-smooth forehead. He spoke confident Cantonese, unaware he was pitching his tones like an orchestra of tax accountants. She tried to imagine tanks rolling across the gravel here on the edge of Chinatown, but it seemed absurd. Not that something disastrous couldn't occur, only it might not happen here the way it does in China. Was that where the melancholy she felt sometimes came from? The possibility that she might not recognize an act of repression when it struck? Or did it come from tapping into a collective memory of all the deaths, abandonments, and slow stresses of war that have gone unspoken through the generations? Perhaps the precise stories and politics had been lost, but the emotional memory might move from one generation to the next as surely as any genetic trait. She imagined tanks rolling from the old Canadian National train station or across the power plant on the other side of the street. Rolling towards them, spitting, the plant going up in an orange burst, the thin blood smell of gunpowder, smoke billowing across the lot, and all these unfamiliar Chinese people collapsing around her.

A woman with a tray of hot tea in white styrofoam cups worked her way through the crowd. Artemis' throat dried in anticipation. A layer of cold fell over the crowd and she shivered. Someone draped a heavy black leather jacket over her shoulders. It was lined and the leather was soft and smelled of cattle, tanin, and fashion magazine men's cologne. She noticed these things in an instant and let the warmth from the jacket seep into her goose-bumpy arms, still watching the woman with the tray of hot tea, before turning her face to the jacket's owner. He was a tall man with chiselled features, skin the colour and luminosity of marble, brown curls strapped back into a ponytail, and eyes as green as bottle glass behind thick black-rimmed spectacles.

His face was familiar. The sea-green eyes made her think of a woman chained to a rock, the waves smashing up around her. Naked except for her hair, waiting for some terrible monster. He smiled. "For a minute I thought you were Diane."

"Well, I'm not."

"Yes, I can see that now. I'm sorry. Do you remember me?"

"No."

"My name is Saint."

"What?"

"Well, it's St. Clair, but everyone calls me Saint. We met at Diane's, remember?"

She looked at him slowly, his flushed cheeks and nervous eyes, and wondered how she could have imagined marble. "Oh yes, you weren't wearing glasses before."

He extended his hand gravely, an oddly formal gesture after the laying on of the coat. His hand was warm but unsteady. She moved to return the jacket, but he shook his head.

Up on the makeshift stage, a Chinese-Canadian man with radio-perfect English pushed his glasses back up his nose. "As Canadians we should encourage our government and our media to condemn the barbarous actions of the Chinese government. Those of us who immigrated to Canada did so because of the long-standing tradition of democracy in this country. We have made Canada our home and poured our life's work into increasing the wealth of our new country. Those of us who were born here have always had faith in our government. Now it is time for our country to do something for us . . ."

"They'll be only too happy to, you know," Saint observed.

"What?"

"Condemn the Chinese government. Politicians are always more than pleased to show how totalitarian other governments are and prove how democratic ours is. They love stuff about those nasty Communists."

"But don't you think it's important that countries keep an eye on each other for human rights abuses and stuff like that?"

"Sure, but that's not an objective thing in the context of Western imperialism in the Third World. They only tell the story in a way that gives Canada the moral high ground it can use to pressure for things that benefit Canada, and not the Chinese at all. Not Canada even, but white Canadian men of a particular class and occupation."

"I just don't see what else the options might be. I mean, if they're rolling in tanks and shooting people, what would you want our government to do? Pretend it wasn't happening?" She couldn't help admiring him for his ability to critique his own position, although she kept it to herself.

"Of course not. But there has to be honest reporting the whole time. About what the Chinese are doing when they're not shooting people. About genocides happening in Africa that we never hear about. Stories that don't go on about the hypocrisy of their capitalism while saying nothing about ours." He paused for a moment and looked down at her from those sea-green eyes. "This demonstration looks like it's going to wrap up. Why don't you come have a coffee with me and warm up? We could beat the crowd by leaving now."

She followed him through the ocean of dark heads across the gravel lot to the old Hong Kong Café with its high brown booths, arborite table tops, lime-green walls, low counters, and old-fashioned milk machines.

"Coffee?" asked the old waiter, turning over the thick white cups with their green rims and sloshing it in almost before they had a chance to nod.

"The apple tarts are good, if they haven't run out," said Saint. "So are the pork buns." She noticed his irises were ringed with a strange pale light, which she found discomfitting although she couldn't have said why.

"You come here often, hey?"

"It's a cool place. All the old Chinese bachelors have been coming here since the days of the Exclusion Act."

"Hey, Saint, you old sleezebag, is that you?" A woman's voice came from the other side of the booth's wall, behind Saint's head.

"What of it?" he demanded cheerfully, as a grinning, square-jawed face popped up over the wall that separated the booths, leaning over Saint's head and looking meaningfully at Artemis. A long black braid whipped up beside the face. It was the woman who had been carrying trays of tea through the crowds an hour earlier.

"I'm surprised it took such a long time for a sophisticated white boy like you to figure out this was a good place to come."

"Who are you calling sophisticated? I just like the apple tarts."

"Hmmmm. That's not what I hear."

"Yeah, well, what do you hear?"

"You think your reputation doesn't precede you?" She looked at Artemis the whole time she spoke. Artemis wasn't sure whether she meant to be friendly or not. Then the woman gave her a slow wink, the co-ordinated kind, where nothing on the person's face moves except for one eyelid going lazily down and up.

"Artemis," he said, letting his voice drop lower than normal, "I'd like you to meet Claude Chow. Claude, Artemis."

"Hi, sweetie," Claude said, as if they'd been best friends forever.

The waiter returned to take their order and Claude dropped back into her booth. Saint ordered two apple tarts, Artemis, a bacon-and-egg sandwich that arrived in a very short time on toasted white bread with the crusts cut off.

"People always give me a hard time because of my father," said Saint. "These days, anyway. I don't get it."

"What does he do, your father?"

"He's a collector."

"Diane told me, now that you mention it. What does he collect?"

"He calls them artifacts. I wish he wouldn't. Clothing, antique furniture, bowls, plates, sculpture. Anything, really. He's got a big enough house he can collect anything he wants. He specializes in the Far East."

"Oh?"

"You're not going to give me a hard time about it, are you? Of course, I could understand if he was stealing things, or depriving Eastern people of them in some way. But he buys them. He buys things people don't want. Or, at least, things that they're willing to sell."

"I see."

"Don't you have a position on it? Everyone else seems to."

"When a fox is fifty years old, it acquires the ability to change itself into a woman. At a hundred it can assume the shape of a beautiful girl, or that of a sorcerer . . . At that age the fox knows what is happening at a distance of a thousand miles, it can derange the human mind and reduce a person to an imbecile. When the fox is a thousand years old, it is in communication with Heaven, and is then called Heavenly Fox, t'ien-hu."

— HSUAN-CHUNG-CHI

I'M GOING to tell you the first story of my birthdays. Moon calendar birthdays. Soon I will reach my thousandth. A thousand years is a long time for a fox to live, especially now in the age of science, when it is common knowledge that canine life-spans average less than twenty European-style years. It has been a long wait and bus stop boring, especially for someone as restless as me. The worst part was the first fifty years, trapped in an aging dog's body. My hair started dropping out in clumps when I was about twenty-eight. Even the most feeble rabbits managed to escape my dull teeth. I ate mushrooms and moss and grew as thin as a Taoist ascetic and bald as a human baby.

My fiftieth birthday arrived in the cold dark, just when, hairless and blind, I thought I couldn't hold on any longer. My birthday enfolded me in human arms and granted me the first of my transformative powers, the ability to change into a woman. But I was given no choice as to what kind of woman. I was given a body discarded by an older fox who had just passed her hundredth year. There was nothing wrong with her, really. She was as young as the smell of fresh rain and newly tilled soil, but had the face of a poisonous mushroom, red with white spots and spongy. Her hair roped like the matted old man's beard that hung high and green in the leafless branches of swamp trees. Someone said to me later that there is nothing more beautiful than the modesty of the plain, but I think I had to live it first. In the meantime my sensibilities were driven by the same conceptions of beauty as everyone else's. And there would be no bargaining for chickens in the day market with a face like this.

At first, I refused to approach her. I spent much more time in my rickety canine body, so repulsed was I at the thought of becoming her. After a while, I discovered I could animate other corpses, not for long periods of time and seldom on more than one occasion. But in a more handsome body I could cause more trouble in a shorter period of time, so it was worth it. After a few winters had passed, however, my affection for her grew, the way the flavour of wood and sweet voices grows in young wine after it has been sitting in the barrel through the passage of several seasons. I discovered that she had a great capacity for mischief, or, rather, my own was greatly increased with her as my disguise. Howling like an attic ghost, we frightened rich families from their meals and I ate better than I had in forty years.

My fur grew back, red and thick as butter, and my eyes glittered again like resurrected stars. She put on weight, although she never appeared much healthier.

A blood-hot day in summer. The air is liquid and hard to breathe and I am filled with a restless frustration that burns along my spine. Whether I take animal or human form, the mosquitoes hover about me, a host of lesser angels. Each one lights a small fire on my skin that itches like hot peppers. I think of each spot swelling as big as a second head and bursting with pus and infection. I think of scratching the itch right down to the bone. I bite furiously at a particularly aggravating one at the base of my tail, biting harder and harder, trying to push pain into clouding over the all-consuming itch. What finally distracts me from the itch is an idea. Turning it over in my head like meat on a slow barbeque, I sleep off the hottest part of the afternoon.

The sun begins to drown in the liquid air, and the evening becomes cool enough to move through. I walk into the closest village, my unwashed hair smelling of complicated nightmares, and my red face puffy. My feet are bare and muddy and my clothes hang loose like scar tissue. I haven't yet found a place to steal new ones that will fit.

The first house on the edge of the village is a mansion surrounded by a high white wall. Beyond is a garden full of trees that can talk and flowers that smell of honey and spices. I speak to a man who guards the gate. He is small inside a clean but baggy uniform.

"I would like to speak to the lady of the house."

"She's too busy to speak to you."

"Then tell her that an old lady has a gift for her." The man calls through the gate and another man peeks through an eyehole. There is the whispering of leaves. The gate opens.

The second man leads me through the garden and the trees chat noisily. He doesn't answer them, and I don't want him to think I'm crazy, so I don't either.

The mistress of the house is sitting in the courtyard drinking tea and eating pastries.

"A few scraps for an old lady?"

"You lied about why you wanted to come in. Go away before my husband catches you and gives you a good beating."

The second house on the edge of the village sits on a small plot of land. A few meatless-looking chickens scattered about the yard peck disconsolately at the limp earth, as likely to get a gullet full of mud as of worms. For a moment, my mouth waters, more at the incredible good fortune of such an easy theft than at the kind of meal these birds would make. I coil my body, ready to spring, and then uncoil again, finding myself constrained by my own human limbs. I look at my hands, the well-articulated if warty fingers. The chickens will have to wait. I refocus my eyes and notice a woman has been sweeping the walkway for quite some time. She is thin and her arms are knotted. She might still be young, but there are thick streaks of gray in her hair, sprouting wiry, a warning from the gods. Her face is pale and her eyes are flooded with muddy tiredness, like a river delta after too much rain. She sweeps in brisk, sharp strokes.

"A few leftovers for an old woman?" I am careful not to come too close, in case she notices how ugly I really am.

"Please," she says, rushing to the broken wood gate to let me in. She takes me by the arm, oblivious to the smells of the forest in my hair.

It is no warmer inside the house than outside, but she loads the stove generously with wood from an almost-empty woodbox. From a large basin she fills a kettle with water and sets it on top of the stove. She waves me over to a warm spot, and disappears back out into the yard. I gather my bones into the warmth, allowing my body to sink into it. From outside where the mountains have swallowed the bleeding sun there is the sound of chickens babbling terrified nonsense, then a sudden silence. She comes back in, holding a lantern that floods the room with warm yellow light in one hand, and the limp body of a chicken in the other. It seems even scrawnier than when it was alive. She sets the lantern on the table. In the yellow light, feathers rise in a cloud around her hands and scatter at her feet like dirty snow. Her fingers move in a rapid, even motion, as though she were playing some strange instrument from a place far away. I dissolve into the music, let the open windows fly away.

The presence of a third party jolts me back. It is a tall woman, perhaps three or four years older than my host. Her hair is long, and black as the thick darkness gathering right up to the ledge of the windows. Her skin is smooth and translucent as a veil, but her eyes are lightless. I think I know her from somewhere, but I have never met a blind person before, so I dismiss the inkling.

"Your sister?"

"My late husband's concubine. She's blind."

"Yes."

"They say the blind have voices like angels."

"Is it true?"

"She sings like a peach tree in full bloom."

"How could your husband afford a concubine?"

"He couldn't. I stole my dowry back and bought her myself." She smiles as she sinks the featherless chicken into the kettle of boiling water. As the chicken cooks, the blind woman opens her mouth and a lilting tune like a cascade of ripe fruit pours out.

Although there are no spices in the chicken and rice she serves me, the intricate flavours of the blind woman's song makes these dishes suitable for much less humble immortals than myself. We eat quietly until the dishes are half empty.

"We don't get many visitors here," says my host.

"You have been very generous."

"I suppose you don't live in the village."

"Not exactly."

"Then you don't know what they say about us there." The blind woman kicks her under the table, accurately, by the look of things. "They say we murdered our husband."

"Did you?" I remember once coming across a man's body in the dump, the head hanging at an absurd angle. Not being human, I wasn't very much disturbed by him and continued scavenging.

"What do you think?"

"Don't listen to her," says the blind woman. "She's so excited that we have a guest that she doesn't know what she's saying. Sometimes she gets a little silly after dark. She's a great believer in ghosts. Go to bed, love, I'll clean up."

"I'm not silly! That's what they say. Go into the village and ask around if you don't believe me."

"Just ignore her," whispers the blind woman, and I could swear she's winking at me. "Won't you spend the night? I'll make a place for you by the stove."

The younger woman goes to bed. I watch the singer moving about the room, with the fluidity of intuition that no sighted person could match. She rummages through a chest for blankets, and as she begins the work of making a bed, I know why she seemed familiar. She is a well-practiced housewife. I want to ask her how she became blind, but don't dare.

"You married again," I said.

She raised an eyebrow. "Beg your pardon?"

Of course she wouldn't recognize me in my pimply body. "Weren't you once married to a man named Tam?"

"No." Too sharp to be true. "Never."

But she doesn't have to tell me.

I let her finish making a bed for me. Filled with chicken, rice, and music, there is a warm lethargy curdling in my bone marrow. Sleep caresses my tired back for perhaps an hour or two, until I am awakened by the sound of two women breathing in unison. I smile to think of them curled together on the narrow bed in the other room. When they are finally quiet and their breathing evens to the pace of sleep, I slip under the door of the bedroom like a gas. They are a tangle of limbs, still moist with sweat.

I look at them as little as possible, to respect their privacy, as I approach the basin of water in which they have washed. It smells of sweat, wood, cut grass, smoke, chicken feathers, and roses. I blow on it once and a gold sheen ripples across the surface suggesting seashell pink, blood crimson, midnight blue, peacock green, and then evens out again. I blow again and the water becomes viscous, pure gold but with the sticky, globby consistency of crude oil. I blow again and the basin is filled with small gold coins. Pleased, I revert to my four-legged self and leap out the window.

 ARTEMIS COULD HEAR the music booming before she even turned the key in the lock of the little bachelor suite where she had lived by herself for the last two years. With the music making its own company inside the apartment while she stood alone outside, she felt more than ever as though she didn't really live here. It was a problem she never could describe to anyone. How her own home never felt like hers. She was here almost every night now, as her nocturnal visits with Eden became less and less appealing. She would come in the front door and and wonder how to make it suit her better. It wasn't so plain as to be impersonal. There was lots of light in the main room, which did triple duty as a place to eat, sleep, and live. It was dominated by a double futon that folded into a couch during the day. Over it lay a piece of

Indian fabric in green and white. There were posters on the walls of bands that she listened but had no particular attachment to. Cotton dhurrie rugs in blues and greens were scattered across the worn hardwood floors. But none of these things grew on her. She had them merely because she did not know what else to put there. The only thing about the place that appealed to her was the assortment of objects scattered across her window sill, largely the products of her secret heists, containers and fragments of things, the fake box of the True Cross, the little ivory statuette she had bought the same day, a human shinbone, pictures of an Asian family she had bought at a garage sale, having no idea who any of them were, a small glass case with four brown, crumbling butterflies pinned to a green background she had lifted when the biology department was moving into new premises, a little pewter pillbox she had found one dawn with Eden in the ashes of a burnt house.

It was odd to come back to hear the place come alive without her. The moment she opened the door, the smell of hot oil wafted out. In retrospect, she realized she should have been more worried. It could have been any stranger in her house. Soul II Soul was on full blast, and someone was frying shrimp chips in the kitchen. Artemis dropped her knapsack and peered around the corner. Oblivious to her arrival, Diane was dancing and singing along with the tape as she dexterously wielded a pair of long chopsticks, moving from the pot of hot oil to the plate on which she was building a mound of large pink wavy chips layered with wads of paper towel to soak up the grease.

"How did you get in here?"

Diane danced over waving a fresh chip between her chopsticks and lowering it playfully to Artemis' mouth. "Climbed up the trellis and came through the window. You should really get locks for them, you know."

"You climbed up the trellis?"

"Those darn rose thorns got me pretty bad, but other than that it was easy." She was clearly pleased with her own daring.

Artemis was delighted in spite of herself. "You're so crazy." She slumped down at the kitchen table. Diane got a bowl, pushed some chips into it and set it down in front of her.

"Eden ever give you any of those pictures?"

"Yeah, last week. There's some for you too. I told him I'd pass them on." She got up and fished them out from a desk drawer, and put them on the table. "Watch out if your hands are greasy."

"I just want to look. Oh god, how goofy."

"It was kind of a goofy idea."

"I look like I'm in some kind of drag," said Diane. She leaned over an image of the two of them sitting back to back smoking long white cigarettes like truant schoolgirls. "Do you know where he got those costumes?"

"From his father."

"Does he have a lot of them?"

"I don't know. He says his father stashed a lot of stuff." Artemis could not have said later why she didn't tell Diane about Eden's recent gift.

"Bet they're worth a lot of money."

Artemis noticed something flare in the kitchen behind Diane. "The oil!"

Unattended, with the blue gas flame still raging beneath it, the oil Diane was using for deep frying had caught fire. The room filled with smoke. Diane rushed over to rescue it, jerking the pot off the stove. The burning liquid moved up in a long slow arc, slapping across her face. She dropped the pot automatically, her hand flying up to meet the burn. The pot fell over her, its contents splashing over her arm and chest and stomach. As she backed away from the stove, she slipped and fell to the floor. From the living room the music continued without missing a beat.

Artemis was at the sink. With cupped hands, she splashed water over her friend.

"You're supposed to use cream or cold oil." Diane's voice came out a raspy whisper.

"I've never heard that before." Artemis continued to throw water over the human heap on the floor until a pool of cold oil and water spread around Diane on the cracked tile. "I'll get you a towel. Do you think you need an ambulance?"

"No, it's not that serious." Diane rose slowly, wincing where burnt skin caught against the cabinets. She took the towel and dried herself slowly. "I should be going."

"You can't be serious. You should see yourself."

Diane ambled over to the hallway mirror. She examined the long red mark down the side of her face. She pulled the wet sleeve of her T-shirt away from her arm, surveying the streak's path down her shoulder. Water dripped from her hair and her clothes onto the floor. Artemis shut off the tape deck.

The only clean clothes Artemis could find were a pair of jeans she could no longer squeeze into and a never-worn T-shirt her parents had brought back from a tour of China the previous year. They had offered to take her, but she had courteously refused, saying the trip did not interest her. They brought the T-shirt back anyway, with two stone dragons facing each other on the front, and the name of the tour company on the back. She pressed them into Diane's hands and went into the kitchen to clean up and leave Diane her privacy.

In the narrow kitchen, she mopped the wet oily mess off the floor and dumped the pot into the sink. She scraped the plate of soggy chips into the garbage. Then she poured glasses of 7-Up, took the undamaged bowl from the table, and balancing carefully, juggled all this into the front room. The TV was on at a low volume. Diane sat cross-legged on the futon, wearing the clean, dry clothes and swaddled in the depths of the quilt that Artemis' birth mother had left for her.

"Where did you find that?"

"On the shelf in the closet up there. Is it okay?"

Artemis had completely forgotten she had stored the thing in her place at all. Her adoptive mother had made her take it when she moved out, although mercifully allowing her to store the chest and padded jackets in the house. The smell of mothballs wafted around the room. It bothered her. It called up myriad things she had no name for, and didn't particularly want to know about. But she couldn't think of a way to say so to Diane so she just nodded her head. "Of course."

On the television, a young Vietnamese girl wearing a transparent pink plastic raincoat rollerskated around a steaming bathtub in the middle of a large warehouse.

"Don't you ever wonder who your real parents were?" Diane asked.

"No. I don't."

"Not at all?"

"I guess I've never really thought about it. I never knew them. They didn't want me. So what's to wonder?"

"Don't you wonder about where you came from, who your . . . people were?"

"I know who my people are. My mother and father, Eden, you, my friend Mercy, I suppose, even if she drives me crazy sometimes."

"I mean the people who know your history. The people who will care about you even if they don't know you."

"I don't know. I really don't think about it. Look, here's some 7-Up. And these chips managed to escape the fracas." She paused. "Things move and change a lot from generation to generation. I am no less who I am for where I've ended up."

"I just don't understand how you can't be curious."

In a different scene, wearing a white vinyl coat with huge buttons and high black boots, the TV character walked into a record store. She carried a portfolio under her arm. She wandered down the middle aisle of the store, into the jazz section. Glancing furtively around to see that no one was looking, she slipped a record into the portfolio's secret sleeve. Some honey-rich voice trapped flat against black vinyl. As she moved towards the door, the clerk asked to see her portfolio. He drew back the cover, revealing photographs of the girl, stark naked, gazing precociously into the camera as her black hair swirled about her. He turned through several similar images until, red-faced, he could look no more, and then handed it back to her, even though he was sure he had seen her slip a record somewhere between the heavy leather covers.

 IN 1258 I fell in love with the Chinese princess who was sent as a tribute to the Prince of Persia. She let me touch her foot. I held it in my hand, fragile inside a tiny embroidered shoe, shorter than the length of my palm. The secretive shoe was enough to make me pack my bags and pursue her across the reaches of the new Mongol empire. She was interested in me, but not half as interested as she was in being tragic.

When it was cold in the mountains, I blew warm breath into her hands. When it was hot in the desert, I blew cool air into her ears. We passed a carving of Buddha as big as a whole village. We passed dark caves where thousands of sutras were hidden. We were almost accosted by bandits except that I smelled the sweat of the thrill before attack on the wind and rushed the whole retinue into hiding. After two years and the deaths of seven horses, we arrived at Jamal al-Din's marvellous astronomical observatory at Maragha, perhaps six months from our destination. There were astronomers there from all over the Empire, some with strange pale faces and light hair, some with the bulky bodies and thick beards of the northern tribes, some clearly from the south, who were so small that beside them the little princess became a towering giantess. One of these small men sat down with us and late into the night explained the mathematics of the Cowherd and the Weaver. Everyone nodded off except me, being a nocturnal type myself, and very much interested in the mechanics of the stars.

The princess had long since become bored of our simple camaraderie. She talked passionately of her plan to run away. She would not meet this prince, never mind how much shame it might bring upon her father. The following evening she climbed the highest wall of the observatory and jumped. To her surprise and consternation, a young starwatcher below caught her. He thought a goddess had descended from the heavens. She had fainted dead away and thus could not inform him otherwise. When she came to perhaps an hour later, he was sorely disappointed to learn that he had caught not a goddess but a mere princess in his arms. In embarrassment, we cut our visit short and began the last stretch of our journey the following day.

She decided she would settle for the melancholy life of a captive in a foreign land. It wasn't as good as dying as it required considerably more patience. But when we arrived in the Persian capital almost a full three years after our departure from Khanbalik, the prince himself had passed away. His son was a practical man, more interested in silk, gunpowder, and paper than he was in women. The gift of a Chinese princess was refused. She was to embark for home as soon as fresh horses could be found.

 HE TOLD HER about his evenings as if they were something magical, a journey into a forbidden country. It started after a man called Angel hanged himself. Eden had seen him just two nights before at the bar with his boyfriend. After Angel died, Eden started cruising the strip on Homer Street where young men sold themselves. He would go and talk to them, and sometimes they would sit with him in his car and touch him, and not even charge, so Eden said, because he was young and handsome just like them.

She saw them sometimes in the early evening before the sun went down, if she was walking up from downtown to cross the Granville Street Bridge. There was one who was there all the time. He was tall and lanky with a lean face and glazed eyes that scanned the street restlessly up and down. Intent on his work, he did not see her at all as she marched past, stealing surreptitious glances.

She believed that Eden could make the night into something she herself could not. A place of magic and illicit secrets that revealed themselves only to him. It created a well of longing in her she could not understand, nor make an object of, the way he seemed able to. But the seams in the illusion they had built for themselves were beginning to give.

"Come to the bar with me tonight."

"But it's men's night."

"We'll fix you up. Come on. It'll be fun to see if we can get away with it."

They cut a sheet into strips and flattened her small breasts against her chest. He slicked her hair back and tucked it under a skull cap. Loose jeans, a baggy T-shirt, and men's shoes her size he had picked up at some fancy vintage clothing store.

"Well, you don't look too sexy, but you do look like a boy," he said.

"They're going to be able to tell if they just look at my arms," she protested holding out a skinny wrist, fist clenched.

"Lots of Oriental boys are very slender. They won't bat an eyelash."

She looked uncertain.

"Bet you anything some rice queen tries to pick you up!"

The doorman gave her a slow once-over that made her cheeks flush. He nodded at her, and she had the distinct feeling he knew but had decided not to say anything. The bar was packed and redolent with the animal smell of men. They towered above her. She never felt tall walking down the street, but here she felt like a dwarf in the land of giants. There was not the mediating presence of women to make a gradation between them and her.

They pushed their way to a table at the back where Eden had some friends. Tom, who had come to her place with Eden for drinks once, recognized her and winked. She winked back. Eden pushed her a bottle of beer and someone offered her a cigarette, which she was about to take when Eden leaned over and whispered, "Don't. Your hands will give you away." It was true. She looked at them and marvelled at their smallness, like a child's. She had never really thought them extraordinary before, but now, looking at her companions' large hands as they drank and smoked and gesticulated, her own seemed wonderful and strange.

Eden pulled her onto the dance floor, and some of the other guys from the table came too. Under the pulsing lights she melted into the music, closed her eyes, imagined her body as boyish as she could and hoped her hips wouldn't give her away. When she opened her eyes there was a man staring right into them. She stared back crossly, but instead of being embarrassed the man just smiled and continued to stare.

"Someone better teach you how to cruise fags properly," yelled Tom above the music, "or you're going to find yourself in trouble."

"Yeah, no shit. So what do I do?"

"Well, that guy is going to be over here any second now. I'm sure you'll think of something."

"Tom, come on. This isn't funny."

"You don't think so?"

She couldn't read his eyes. Was he amused, or was he angry that she had invaded a territory not meant for her and wanted to see her get her comeuppance? She looked around for Eden but he had gone off a song and a half earlier with a man who looked like Rutger Hauer. The man with the stare was manoeuvring slowly through the crowd towards her, inching, sussing out the situation. She glanced nervously at him from moment to moment, wanting to know where he was, where she could run to.

"Don't keep looking," said Tom. "He'll think you're interested."

The man crossed the path of an old friend, who grabbed him playfully from behind and they danced together the way old pals do, hamming heat and passion with a kind of affection that has long since moved beyond those things. Not that they didn't look for action elsewhere. In the meantime, Eden resurfaced.

"Can we go now?" Artemis asked.

"She's chickening out," said Tom.

"Were you giving her a hard time?" Eden asked him, getting protective.

"Of course not, Daddio."

They moved on to a bar that had once been gay, but had slowly been infringed upon by heterosexuals until gay people stopped going there, at least for the most part. The man who looked like Rutger Hauer came with them. In the back seat of the car, modestly concealing her activity beneath her coat, she unbound her breasts and shook her hair loose.

It was hard to find a table, but after several turns around the bar, they finally found a spot at the counter overlooking the dance floor. A waitress came by and Eden bought a round of beer. As he pushed a pint down the table to his new friend, there was a look in his eyes that made Artemis disappear entirely from the room so that she was shocked by her own absence. A look of longing. A look of conspiracy. Caught up in her own sudden invisibility, Artemis did not feel the gaze of the woman dancing on top of one of the four pillars that delineated the dance floor. If she had cared to look she might have seen a well-muscled stomach undulating smooth as water beneath a little T-shirt cut off at the midriff, and small dark eyes watching her every move. Small nose twitching.

Someone else was watching too from across the dance floor — a young man with dyed black hair offsetting his pale face. She looked back with ease because it was so much less complicated than the man who had thought she was a man. She only half welcomed it. The unnatural darkness of his hair, while appealingly glamorous, concealed its true colour, and she thought of it more as a lie than as a secret. As he approached her, a kind of relief flooded her veins.

"Dance?" A single word tossed up in the smoky air.

She laughed because no one did that anymore at this bar, asking you to dance. If you wanted to dance you just got up and did it. She was not sure if he knew this and was flying rebelliously in the face of the not-so-new convention, or if he was a recent arrival from the suburbs who was still living light years behind. There wasn't any point sitting here with Eden and old Rutger, she thought, so she followed him to a place under the black lights.

At two o'clock, when the lights went up just as surely as Cinderella's coach turned into a pumpkin, he handed her a matchbook with his name and phone number on it. "Call me for coffee?" Under the strident yellow lights, his skin looked sallow. His eyes were red and the dark hair greasy.

Diane called several days later. A week had passed since the burning incident.

"It's all peeling. Looks disgusting."

"Will you come see me?"

"Doctor says to stay home and rest. He thinks the accident was the result of some nervous disorder."

"That's ridiculous."

"That's what he says."

She didn't call the matchbook man until a week later. She and Eden had made plans for dinner and she called at the appointed time, but Eden wasn't there. He had been doing that a lot lately, making dates with her and then standing her up. Exasperated and restless, she dialled the number on the matchbook.

He lived in the basement of his mother's house. He was waiting at the door when she arrived.

"Don't mind the posters and stuff. My mom's into some hippy feminist shit. She thinks she's cool, but she's kind of crazy." There was a poster for the Vancouver Folk Music Festival, and a number for demonstrations and conferences on the walls. In the kitchen was a calendar with bright full-colour photographs of bare-breasted brown-skinned women with an explanation in tiny letters underneath saying what they were doing and where this activity fit in the cycle of their lives. She followed him down the stairs beside the fridge.

"I used to live on my own, but a poor person can't support himself out there these days, you know. Only the capitalist pig dogs."

"Yeah, I know," she said.

"My mom's all right. She's a little crazy, but she doesn't hurt anybody."

The basement was sparsely decorated and cold. There were two guitars on stands in a prominent place against the front window. There were posters on the walls of bands like The Gang of

Four, the Clash, Art Bergman. The futon lay open and unmade. There was nowhere else to sit, so she sat there.

"You want a beer?" He had a little bar fridge containing nothing but. He handed her one and then came and sat next to her, put his hand on her breast and tried to kiss her ear.

"Hey, not so fast."

"Isn't this what you've come here for?"

"No. I don't know. Not like this."

"Like how, then?"

"I don't know. I thought we could talk, maybe."

"What do you want to talk about?"

Later she couldn't have said why she felt compelled to tell him things she had never spoken of before. But they tumbled from her lips as if of their own accord: the unexplainable airless nights on Eden's bed, her fascination with his disappearances, the feeling that she was being watched but never seeing by whom or from where, the whole mess with Diane, the burning, the old quilt with its thick odour of mothballs, the single, never-again-mentioned kiss, and how Diane was beginning to drift away. And then the man in the men's bar and not understanding what had driven her to go there in the first place, except that it was more than a vicarious curiosity about Eden's life.

"You ever sleep with a woman?"

"No. Why?"

"Maybe you should try it." He leaned towards her and kissed her mouth. His breath was thick. His hands were cold and clumsy. Only his dark hair was reassuring, but when he undressed his pubes and armpit hair were a brilliant and alien golden-red that glinted in the pale beam of the streetlight coming through the squat window.

She left him without waiting for morning to come. Truth in the dark was one thing, under the scrutiny of the sun it was something else again. She didn't want to wake and gaze down the length of their bodies, to observe her own blue bony limbs flush against his sallow ones with their fine coat of red down. She did not want to breathe in the stale smell of the night's contact or feel the sweat of his sleep running between her breasts. She returned to her own apartment, where the ghost of Diane lingered, even though almost three weeks had passed since the burning accident.

I HAVE big feet. In this century, I'm glad to have them. It makes it a lot easier to balance in these heels I've got, shiny red leather dreamt into a perfect shape. For a while, it was a problem. I spent weeks on end in the graveyards waiting for lily-footed dainties to pass away before their time. I could go nowhere with the long paddles left to me by the poetess, although they served her perfectly well in her own time. But starting with the courts of the khans up until very recently, I might as well have worn an olisboi beneath my skirts as gone about on my obscenely masculine feet. It fact, it was around the time of that first visit by the young Venetian and his two uncles that I stopped visiting male scholars except in those very temporary bodies I found in the hills and managed to animate for a night or two. I focussed my attention instead on the courtesans who wrote beside the river under the full moon, or the nuns who sat out in the courtyards with their ink blocks after the rest of the clergy had gone to bed. They were puzzled by my lean, squarish jaw and plain dark robes that betrayed nothing but my amusement with the game of dressing. What seemed to relieve and reassure them was the sight of my feet, their phallic length. And then it was "Tea, elder brother?" Or "A game of rhymes, perhaps?" If they discovered later that I was a woman after all, by then it did not matter so much.

But occasionally I made errors. One night, passing through a neighbourhood near the Western market, I noticed a young woman sitting by a candle in the window, brush poised in her elegant hand. I was tired and hungry, on my way, in fact, to visit the Saracen cloth trader who kept a yard full of plump chickens. The old rooster, great grandfather to the eldest of the hens, was randy again. I could hear his unfortunate love of the moment squawking in consternation. The woman glanced every now and then out the window, and the longing in her eyes was more than I could resist. I reknotted my hair, smoothed my robes and approached the door.

"Oh!" she exclaimed, evidently surprised to see me. "Are you his brother?"

I was puzzled for a moment, until I realized that she was not the lonely scholar of this sad little house, but merely some prostitute or courtesan, waiting for a man to return. Of course, I was disappointed, but then I should have known to trust my knowledge of this city by now. I knew every scholar, every priest, and every nun of every faith that was practiced in Chang'an. There were many, believe me. Some strange ones imported from way beyond the Gobi Desert. The priests worshipped their god as though he were the only one that existed, in spite of the evidence to the contrary right in their own neighbourhoods. I could never understand this, but humans are often a peculiar lot. And then I thought, if she holds a brush, she can write. What does it matter if she doesn't own this little house? It was a pleasant and convenient place to haunt, old as the city itself and covered in climbing trellises.

"His brother, yes, exactly," I said, so as not to disappoint her.

"You'd better sit down, then. I'll get you some tea." Tea was all these people ever drank anymore. I don't know whatever happened to good old barley water, but I suppose tastes change with the times. It was much too hot and nearly burned my nose, which remains sensitive to sun even until this day. I was more than a little surprised when she noticed. Most humans do not have such a keen eye.

"Perhaps you would prefer to drink wine?"

I nodded gratefully. She took a bottle and two cups from the cupboard and poured generously.

"Are you clever with couplets?" she asked.

"Not as good as my brother," I answered. I have never been particularly given to modesty, but in this case I thought it might round out my disguise. Especially given her uncannily keen eye.

"Well," she said, "my work is not so sophisticated that you should have trouble." She pushed the scroll towards me. On it was written:

> *The order of nature is never fixed*
> *The west is moving, the east cannot be still.*

Clearly she was disturbed by the visitors in the court of the khan. It was true he listened too willingly to their advice and bestowed too many gifts upon them. His scholars met their priests, who spoke of the one god as though it were a bag into which they wished to stuff everything they had learned of the Middle Kingdom.

I picked up the brush and after considerable thought wrote:

The nature of order is never still
It moves not with the wind but with the will.

"Very good," said she, "although that end rhyme smacks suspiciously of Western influence."

"I have lived in their company for much longer than you," I said.

She shook her head. "You should not pass judgement on things about which you know nothing."

This remark made me raise an eyebrow. With her literary skill, there was already more to this woman than met the eye. But how extraordinary was she?

She smoothed the fine hairs of the nib against the ink block, added a few drops of water and worked them through the ink until the brush was saturated again. Then she wrote:

A strange guest visits the walled city

and pushed it back. This was clearly a test of some sort, although I couldn't be sure what she was testing for.

I wrote:

Ordinary ghosts roam the streets.

"Ah," she said, "are you afraid of death?"
"Not at all," I replied.

The sheets are white, the streets are quiet.

The guest is more afraid of wine than spirits.

It took me a while to finish this one, but when I was done, I made the last stroke with a grand flourish and accidentally dropped the brush. Quick as a fox I was under the table to retrieve it, brushing my hand against her dainty three-inch foot as I did so. She was still blushing when I surfaced above the table again. She giggled when I leaned forward to kiss her, took my hand, and guided me towards the bed.

"I hope my brother does not come back soon."

"If he does, I hope he will have the good sense to hide himself among the trellises for a while."

I cannot tell you now what made this such a hurried thing, since I am usually a creature of breath and careful pacing. But at the same moment we placed our hands in that telltale place between the legs and I discovered that she had something that I had not, and she discovered, since I had no olisboi with me that night, that I lacked something which she had. Being good natured creatures, we both fell to laughing and went on with what we were doing.

When I finally got up to leave, she gave me her dainty embroidered shoe as a token of the evening, and I went home dreaming of all the possible disguises the future held.

∅

"I haven't heard from you in weeks."

"It hasn't been weeks, just ten days or so.
I've been busy. What have you been doing?"

"Reading. Playing Space Invaders."

"You should try to get out. Meet people. Ming says
that people who stay home all the time are more
prone to high blood pressure when they get older."

"Who's Ming?"

"It's not her real name. Her real name is—uh,
I forget—Charity or Patience or something awful.
She says being called Ming makes her nervous,
but it suits her so much better, don't you think?"

"How would I know? I've never met her."

ARTEMIS GREW AFRAID that Diane would disappear altogether into Ming's world and never come out. Instead of looking for a summer job, she spent the long afternoons in the games arcade playing Space Invaders. As the aliens rained down on her head, she imagined Diane trapped under debris in a fort below the screen, and fired heroically from the gunner's position all afternoon. Sometimes it was the church she stepped inside, slumping into one of the back pews and breathing holy air. Christianity did not particularly interest her, but she imagined the church to be a stone temple from the time of the Greeks with light streaming in through the high windows, and a marble altar with a stone bowl for the blood of the sacrifice.

Once, standing in front of the altar, she imagined a man's blood gushing over her hands. She hurried out into the wet street with cars rushing by. She heard the long sigh of bus doors closing. She ran to catch the bus. The driver opened just one of the folding doors to let her in and then pulled quickly away from the curb while she stood at the fare box counting change. She counted a dollar twenty and had to do the last five cents in pennies while her wallet threatened to spill its entire contents onto the floor. Finally, she had the right coins, dropped them down the chute, snapped her wallet shut and turned to scan the bus for a seat. There might be one in the back. She wobbled towards it, knees bent like a skateboarder's, when the driver suddenly slammed on the brakes, cursing under his breath at two cyclists who cut in front of him. Artemis lurched forward and fell into the soft lap of an Asian woman who was growing out her dyed blonde hair. The dark roots reached her ears, and from there her hair was blonde to the chin. Artemis was sure she had seen the woman before. She didn't know where, but the sensation of that last act of looking came to her so vividly that she said, "Hello," before apologizing for her loss of balance. The woman smiled, and in a rich voice that was almost other-worldly she said, "Don't worry about it," as her warm hand half-lifted Artemis back to standing. Artemis thought she smelled chicken on the woman's breath, but she couldn't be sure.

Diane was sitting on the front steps of Artemis' apartment building with a knapsack and two stuffed shopping bags beside her. A bedraggled but defiant Diane, with a long red streak from which skin was peeling still marring her perfect face. "I got kicked out of the house. Ming would have taken me in, but it was too awkward to ask her mother. Do you think I could stay with you for a while?"

"Why did they kick you out?" Artemis asked, trying to conceal her feelings of delight mixed with relief.

"I couldn't pay the rent. I don't know what the big deal was. It was just a sublet. Stupid white girls can afford it. So what do you say?"

"Of course, come on in." Artemis picked up both shopping bags and they climbed the stairs to her little one-room suite. She would have Diane to herself now. She didn't even stop to feel hurt that Diane had asked Ming first.

Diane curled up on the bench in the seat by the window, and her thin body became small, no longer a young woman's but a child's. Artemis put rice on the stove, crushed garlic, took sui choy out of the fridge, and began cutting. This was what she could do now to keep Diane's attention, and it was easy, meditative. The cabbage fell easily in long diagonal slices under her hand. It felt both familiar and foreign at the same time. As a young teenager, she had hated these tasks. Her mother had made a point of teaching her to cook Chinese. She had always resisted those lessons. She resented them. Her hand had been clumsy beside her mother's practiced one. "Teach me lasagne instead. Teach me chicken pot pie," she would complain, but to no avail.

From the window seat, Diane watched, murmured approvingly as Artemis plunged into the serious act of cooking, slivering beef into paper-thin slices like flower petals of flesh and pouring on sherry and soy sauce so it would be tender when cooked. She threw the crushed garlic into a small puddle of hot oil in the cast-iron pan. From the corner of her eye she tossed a quick glance in Diane's direction, ready to absorb the comfort she felt seeing Diane curled so small and fragile against the window. But Diane was not there. Above the hissing of the oil, Artemis could hear her, laughing with Ming on the phone. Diane was still on the phone when Artemis had finished cooking, and laid each artfully arranged dish on the table. She stuck her head into the main room.

"Dinner," she said in her mother's voice to the back of Diane's head, which faced away from the kitchen towards the entrance. Diane threw up a hand, at once an acknowledgement and a dismissal. It was a good fifteen minutes before she came to the table. She heaped her plate with food, not really looking at it, and ate hungrily.

"Ming and I are going to a women's bar tonight." She did not extend the invitation.

"Your first time?"

"We went last week. There's a woman there who likes me."

"Oh?"

"I guess you're studying again tonight, huh?"

They used bookshelves to divide the room. On her side, Diane tacked up a poster of Tracy Chapman posed in the conscious act of thinking, promotional posters for a couple of recently produced independent films, and some snapshots of friends. Her futon lay unmade, the shape of her restless sleep demarcated by the indentation in the mattress and the human curves of the crumpled sleeping-bag-turned-quilt with its batik cover. She was seldom home, but her presence filled the apartment now, the way nothing up to that point ever had. Artemis' little heap of talismans on the window sill diminished against the bright summer light that poured through the panes. She found herself always alert for the sound of Diane's key in the lock, even late at night as she sank into sleep.

One night, alone with the flicker of the television, she took the smocks Eden had given to her down from their hiding place high up on the closet shelf. She shook the red smock Diane had worn out to its full length. It wavered in the air neither dead nor alive. The smoothness of the fabric as she held it at arm's length from her body suddenly made her skin crawl. She rolled it up quickly and returned it to the bag. She pushed the whole bundle back into its place on the shelf.

She came home late on a sunny afternoon, having spent so long sitting in the back pew of the church that the pastor appeared and invited her to Sunday's sermon. She had muttered an embarrassed refusal and hurried home.

She pushed the door open and nearly knocked over Diane, who was posing in front of the mirror on the bathroom door. Diane had on a short black crushed-velvet frock that fit her torso closely and then flared out in a short skirt.

"Do you like this dress? Ming gave it to me." She sashayed into the living room and back towards the door with a grin that was both self-mocking and self-satisfied at the same time. And innocent too, something that pulled on Artemis' wrists where the pulse was making her feel less afraid of abandonment than she might have otherwise, and somehow protective. Diane was almost back at the front door when she stumbled and fell, clutching her stomach and gasping for air.

"What's wrong?" Artemis threw down her bag and flew to where Diane had collapsed.

"Nothing, I'll be fine."

"You don't look fine. Let me help you to bed." Artemis touched her arm.

"No, leave me. I just need to lie here."

"What is it?"

"Trouble with my stomach. It's nothing. Don't worry." She got up and half-crawled, half staggered to her bed and collapsed there. Artemis thought she noticed some bruising along the inside of Diane's legs.

"Why don't I call an ambulance?"

"No. Don't." She doubled over again, and suppressed something loud and animal that rose visibly from her belly to her throat. Her expression, combined with the burn scars that lingered on her face, created a forlorn whole.

"Diane, for fuck's sake. Tell me what's wrong."

"A miscarriage," she whispered. "I had a miscarriage this afternoon and Saint gave me the dress because he felt guilty. Don't tell Ming. Don't tell anyone. My family can't find out."

The following morning Diane was up early, frying bacon and brewing coffee. Artemis got up and ate with her, and so they wiled away the morning the way they might have mere weeks ago, before Ming had appeared.

"My rasta friend Tony is coming by later to drop off some weed. Hope that's okay with you," said Diane.

"Have I met him before?"

"Well, he's not really my friend. He's not really a rasta either. Too white, too upper class. Never been to the Caribbean and can't get the Britsh Properties out of his accent. But be nice to him, okay?"

"Why?"

"He gives me a good price."

Tony arrived in the early afternoon, enveloped in a cloud of marijuana smoke and patchouli. Artemis slouched over the kitchen table as she had since breakfast, reading a novel set in an Italian villa. Tony plunked himself down beside her.

"What are you reading?"

"It's called *Alope's Robe*. It's about the discovery of an ancient moon temple in a small Italian town."

Diane pulled up a chair. "I don't know why she wants to read that stuff."

"There are worse things, girl. Jah say we should read what moves us."

"Somehow I'm not surprised to hear you say that, Tony," Diane retorted.

"Girl, sometime you should listen to what I tell you. Wouldn't do you no harm."

"Doubtless. Did you bring any weed?"

"We'll get to that, child. Did I tell you about the time Ronnie get busted for growing hydroponic in his mother basement?" He didn't wait for an answer. "Well, Ronnie mother go to London for six month to see she new boyfriend. Ronnie think that plenty time to get a crop going and she have such a fine dry basement . . ."

Diane looked out the window while he talked. She played with her hair. Tony rambled on with no signs of stopping. After fifteen minutes of Tony's unbroken chatter, Diane gave Artemis a strangely conspiratorial look, excused herself from the table and left the house altogether. Tony did not stop his story to acknowledge her departure, but merely shifted his address to Artemis. He had her cornered for the rest of the afternoon.

He was still there when supper time rolled around and Artemis' stomach started to rumble. She didn't know how to be rude.

"You hungry?" she asked.

"No, girl. I should be going."

"Suit yourself."

There was a knock at the door. Perhaps Diane had forgotten her keys? It was Saint. "Diane in?"

"Saint, my man!"

"Get out of here, Tony. Hasn't your mother got supper on?"

"Diane took off," said Artemis.

"She said she might have some things to interest my father. I think she was hard up for cash."

"Diane don't have nothing to sell anyone," said Tony. "She broke though. I can tell you that."

"I might have some things to interest your father." Artemis immediately wondered whether she was being too impulsive, but it was out now, and what use would she have for those creepy smocks anyway?

"I'm on my way there now," said Saint.

Artemis went to the closet and took the bag out without bothering to look inside.

I'll come with you.

"Great," said Saint.

Tony said, "I guess I should be going anyway."

The house was set back from the road and largely hidden by a tall hedge of shiny green leaves over which a profusion of morning glories climbed, the innocence of white cups disguising their intention to choke their host. Saint spoke into a voice box beside the gate, and after a moment the wrought-iron gate, with spokes that curved and curled between straight iron bars and ended in sharp, unexpected points, swung open. Artemis knew it was some simple electronic mechanism that allowed a person inside the house to open them by remote control, but there was something about the hedge and gate that transported them to another place in another century, so that the swinging could just as easily have been a result of magic as of science. The grounds were not as meticulously kept as she might have expected. Roses that had passed their peak of perfection some time ago now hung sadly from thorny limbs, the hip eyes at their centres just beginning to glow. To some, a few bright petals still clung weakly. But every flicker of colour that remained, no matter how feeble, burned with life against the backdrop of the massive house itself, which towered like a tremendous stone in unsettling jet black. It seemed to have risen out of the earth, neither natural nor unnatural, its turrets pushing up out of the trees that surrounded it, as if competing with them for sunlight. The house was immense, all spires and gables, trimmed with curls and circular engravings. In the two black turrets were long stained-glass windows, indicating two circular rooms with high ceilings. The lines of the glass circumscribed yet more roses, pink, yellow, and blood red.

"Don't mind my old man," said Saint. "Collecting is his life. He runs an auction once a month—it's the most talking he does. So he talks very fast. If you don't understand what he says, just ask me. I'll do what I can."

Artemis walked on flagstones up to the door, reverently, as though something were sleeping inside. She gripped the straw handles of the shopping bag. The smocks rested there, uncomplaining.

"Don't let him talk your ear off," said Saint. "He'll try."

A woman answered the door, evidently the housekeeper. She was a large woman, with a dignified face, the most prominent feature of which was a sizeable but nonetheless elegant nose. "Mr. Hawkesworth is waiting for you in his study."

The foyer had once been grand. Two staircases angled off in opposite directions, reversed their courses at the first landing and met again at a balcony that overlooked the door. The balustrades were elegantly carved of some dark wood, which Artemis could not identify. Against every possible wall leaned various antique tables with elegantly carved legs, scattered with small curious objects. Each table had a theme. One contained miniature dollhouse chairs, each worked in meticulous detail, some daintily carved wood, others richly upholstered in brocades embroidered with the teeniest leaves and flowers. The chairs were not of the same proportions; some were meant for larger dollhouses, some were so small they could have collectively furnished a walnut shell. Another table overflowed with objects of deception. A papier-mâché elephant that opened at the neck to reveal a candy box, a tiny slipper that was actually a hatpin holder, from which spiked long silver pins that ended with a bright jewel or a baby's head carved from ivory. Yet another table was covered with clocks ticking away the hours of history as they had for god only knew how long; others had stopped, clinging to some distant moment of glory or sorrow in the past that was now remembered only with numbers, five after nine or that dubious minute before midnight. Still another was adorned with the exoskeletons of various rare and exotic marine creatures—turtles, oysters, and corals in odd geometric patterns, all browns, yellows, off-whites, pale autumn colours suggesting red here and there only in the faintest whispers. Artemis could have examined these things for hours but the silent pause in the foyer had already grown far too long.

Saint took her hand. "Don't let the old lady catch you gawking."

They walked into a cavernous study.

The floor was strewn with flowering carpets that absorbed the sound of their footsteps as though with the intention to erase their presence. Among the leaves and petals, tigers prowled, snakes slithered, and little people galloped on horseback, ancient instruments of war taut in their ready hands. The walls were papered in scenes of old China, mandarins and courtesans reclining under breezy pagodas while gardeners trimmed peonies and labourers lugged twin buckets of water on poles across their backs. Above the visitors, from wall mounts, the heads of exotic animals presided, stunned eyes staring down at them with the sagacity of the dead. The place positively hummed with artificial life, objects ordinary enough in themselves made strange through the act of collection.

Among these things sat Mr. Hawkesworth, a tiny man with large water-blue eyes and thin lips from which proceeded a constant stream of words and numbers. He sat perched behind a carved oak desk against the study's far wall.

The volume of old Hawkesworth's mutter increased slightly. Artemis could not make out a single word.

"He's asking you what you have," said Saint.

Artemis felt suddenly sorry for the little rolls of fabric in her bag, as though they were alive, as though she were delivering them to an unknown and unpleasant fate. Reluctantly she drew the smaller one out of the bag and unfurled it before the old man's eyes. He beckoned her closer. He took the garment in his long bony hands and scrutinized it with an almost pornographic gaze that made her shiver. The mutter rose again.

"He wants to see the rest," said Saint.

If she had dared she would have turned and run, but she remained frozen where she was, and scooped the second garment out, along with the accompanying pants. He took them in those hawk's hands. She cast her eyes to the flowered carpet so as not to see the long fingers wandering over the fabric, the small bright eyes missing nothing.

"He says they are excellent examples of their type," said Saint. "He wonders if you come from an aristocratic family."

"They were given to me by a friend."

"He says the quality and condition are exceptional. He would like to offer you nine hundred dollars for everything."

She gasped at the amount. She had had really no idea what to expect. "Is that good?"

"I think so. Of course, he wants to be able to make a profit if he decides to sell them, but it seems as though he intends to keep them for his own collection. He has quite an impressive wardrobe of Oriental garments. One robe used to belong to the last emperor's concubine."

"I see."

More than anything she just wanted to get out of the airless room and forget about what she was leaving behind altogether. She looked the old man in the eye and nodded agreement.

Later, walking back down the garden path, with a cheque in Hawkesworth's looping, twisting hand burning in her pocket, she wondered how such an ordinary man as Saint could have proceeded from the body of that man and any woman.

He parked the car in front of her apartment building. She thanked him for his help, and was about to step out of the car when he grabbed her wrist. "Invite me up."

"I'm afraid Diane will be sleeping."

"If she's there, I'll go."

"Maybe another time."

The door was quiet as she inserted her key into the lock. It clicked open loudly. The blinds were up. The apartment was empty. Or rather, all of Diane's things were gone from it, the futon, the posters, the books, the strewn clothes. Her shape did not linger, not in the bedclothes, nor in the faint soap and lemon smells of the bathroom, nor even as a ghost in the full-length hallway mirror. She was gone. On the walls a few of Artemis' own uncomfortable posters remained. Here and there were furnishings that she had bought, the things that never seemed to belong to her.

The only thing of significance left was the old blue quilt her birth mother had left for her. It had been fluffed out, neatly folded and left in the window seat. She sat down there. She tugged at the even folds and pulled the quilt around her, letting the smell of mothballs waft into her lungs. For the first time the pungent odour was comforting.

∅

"Saint. She's gone. Do you know where she is?"

"I haven't seen her."

"It's so empty here."

"Do you want me to come by?"

☎

She let him lie down beside her. She let him touch her because the same hands had touched Diane, carried a part of her with him now. Buttons and zippers slowly came undone. A heap of clothing built gradually on the floor. They held each other in unfocused arms. Rocked back and forth like a wooden horse with stunned eyes. On the verge of sleep, she came, her mind fixed on the image of an old sleeping bag on a sagging futon, preserving a curved indentation, the curling question mark of the spine.

∅

"The Garden of Eden. Adam speaking."
"Very funny. Is Eden there?"
"He's sick. He ate a rotten apple."
"Ha, ha. Will you put him on, please? It's important."
"As long as you're nice to him. He really isn't well."
"Hello."
"You sound terrible."
"It's just a hangover."
"I called to say you were right."
"About what?"
"About one of us leaving. It's going to be me. I'm going to Hong Kong next week for the rest of the summer. My father got me a job in his friend's import/export business."
"You can't leave."
"Why not?"
"Because—because so much is happening right now."
"Yeah, and I need to get away from it."
"Come and see me before you go."
"I don't know if there will be time. I'm giving up my apartment and putting everything into storage. I have to pack."
"Will you write me?"

☎

 ON A RETURN trip to China via Hong Kong, I spot Artemis in the market, and realize for the first time that her gait is measured and cautious the way the Poetess's was nine hundred years ago, when she stepped outside her aging father's gate for the last time.

The ones who are born overseas are always obvious. She thinks that as long as she doesn't speak, releasing a poor accent, or wordless open-mouthed silence, she is safe, invisible. But her eyes betray her terror of being spoken to. In the mornings she is already on the bus when I get on. I feel her eyes snare me as I drop my coins into the fare box, so I purposely take a seat directly across the aisle from her. Now she will have to look at me. Her eyes go down, and she does not look up again until I ring for my stop, get up from my seat, and leave through the rear doors. She gets off at the stop right after mine and trudges up to her office.

It's not so much that she is small as that she walks as though she were. Having lived so long in the land of giants, perhaps it's hard to adjust. In fact, she's of average height compared to the citizens of this city of tall buildings and high finance. At least, that's what kind of city it is to them. To her, the tall buildings and shiny cars are mere overgrowth, a disguise concealing the past. This she glimpses when she peers into the backs of shops, or steals up certain side streets where the cobblestones have not yet been paved over. Her eyes are like mine, quick and dark. She has learned how to conceal in their depths anything they take in. A woman with a prominent dowager's hump hobbling up the street in an old-style suit. The brown, calloused hands of a vegetable peddlar. She knows these are the things that a Western tourist would see. This disturbs her. Is she trying to prove to herself how quaint and archaic these people are, even the ones who have managed to disguise themselves in three-piece suits and well-cut dresses? Or is she merely looking for shadows of herself, glimpses of a truth beyond the dull surface mirage of twentieth-century life in any city? She does not know that beneath every mirage is another mirage.

The search for shadows makes her hungry. Always keen for a hunt.

This makes her dangerous, at least to me, an old Fox of the once firmly established Hu family of Chang'an, the capital of old China, now living in the cold outreaches of the British colonial legacy. Especially now that I am alone and tired of my solitude.

And here in Hong Kong, less than ten years before the colony returns to China, who is to say which of us is more out of place—she whose parents knew these streets as children, or I who have not been here for five hundred years?

At lunch time she comes out onto the steaming streets with other office workers and goes to the noodle shop or else the Japanese bakery in the basement of the Matsuzakaya mall. This time it's the noodle shop. She orders wonton or fish-ball noodles in a clumsy accent. Once when she went for lunch late, the restaurant was nearly empty and a group of bored waiters gathered around her and asked, "Japanese?" "Korean?" She said, "Ga la dai yun," and they all reached out to marvel at her hair as black as theirs.

Today she is buying mangoes in the street market from an old woman in a straw hat. She knows how to choose them, pressing the yellow skin gently, testing for the right balance of firmness and tenderness. The old woman tells her she looks like her lost daughter and gives her a special price even though she doesn't understand a word. In the street she slits the yellow skin with her pocket knife, and peels it back like a banana. Oblivious to whether or not anyone is paying attention, she bites into the sweet flesh and lets the juice run past the side of her mouth.

I get careless and let her catch a glimpse of me in the hawker's market. Perhaps she knows I'm watching for her and is watching for me too. She's rummaging through a cart of clothes with Liz Claiborne labels, holding a denim skirt up to her body and tugging on the elastic to see if it will go around her waist. I cross the street a block away, cutting across her field of vision. She looks up. Later, going behind the hawkers' stalls in an alley, I hear her speaking grammatically jumbled Cantonese with a watch seller, but I stay hidden until she's gone.

 ARTEMIS TAKES an elevator to the top of one of those fancy hotels. She gets out at the revolving restaurant at the very top and is seated by a harried waitress struggling to be polite, at a lonely table by the window. The man she intended to meet is dead—an old tea merchant who had been friends with her adoptive father when he was a young man studying ancient trade routes in Asia. She will meet his daughter and his blind wife, who used to sing tragic roles when she was younger. The old woman has lost her voice now. The body has fallen out of it, leaving only a ridiculous falsetto that her old ears can barely hear. They arrive just minutes later, the daughter pushing an empty wheelchair, the old woman hobbling on a cane. She stumbles over the crack between the moving and the stationary sections of the restaurant floor.

"She won't use the wheelchair. She loves all the new hi-tech things, except the ones that will actually improve her life." And then, sheepish at this blurted-out display of emotion, the daughter tries again in a more even, amiable voice. "Hi, I'm Leda."

The old woman says something in Chinese, as the waitress helps her sit down.

"She wants to welcome you back," says Leda.

"Back?"

"She knows you've never been here before. But she means it as a compliment." Like her namesake, interposing her body between the human and the divine, Leda spans the gap between cultures. "She says the West is a very strange place. She hopes you will find life here more ordinary."

"More ordinary by the day," Artemis assures them.

Leda offers to take Artemis to a resort in the New Territories. Artemis meets Leda, her cousin Shirley, and two of Shirley's co-workers at the Star Ferry. She is happy because they all speak English. Inside the ferry terminal, they follow smooth hallways to the subway station. She likes the way the seats are built for people her size, even though she has to stand this time because the train is so crowded. At one station many men and women in business suits crowd onto the train. At another there's a large group of factory workers. She finds herself thinking things she thought she would never think. "No wonder the government is so strict about border control . . ." She wishes she could forget that she is Chinese too.

She gets wedged up against the glass at the front of the car. Voices flood like water into her ears, displacing air. The steel pole she clutches is beginning to sweat. She imagines long fingers wriggling through her ribcage to grab her lungs and squeeze. A thin breath dribbles out of her lungs and she gasps to snatch it back, but the greedy fingers squeeze tighter and all that goes in are the familiar voices she doesn't understand. She is growing pale. The fingers snake into her belly. Grow double heads. Maybe forked tongues too. They writhe. She leans forward. A clot of vomit rushes into her mouth, but at that moment the train stops, the doors open, and the people rush out.

They flood through the brown doors of a brown train station in the hills.

It would have been nice, an American-style bathroom, white

tile floors so well disinfected you could lick them, a claw-foot tub waiting like a porcelain womb, a wide-basin sink with hot and cold water running crystal clear as a mountain spring in the land of the immortals. And a pristine white sitting toilet that could flush away all those messy bodily unmentionables. The single bob of a handle and it all swirls away to some unknown, unthought of, and unremembered place, to be replaced by clear, lovely water.

But this is almost China, soon to become China again. One of those nearly forgotten places in the hills. Unlike those fancy hotels for Westerners, the rich, and the overseas Chinese, there is no gray woman mopping away the parts of people that they themselves are afraid to discuss, or holding out white towels smelling of lemons. There is just a dry sink, a bare lightbulb, a wet floor, and a hole in the ground that smells unhappy.

When Artemis comes out, Leda says, "Maybe your digestive system hasn't adjusted to being in a foreign country yet," laughing kindly behind an accent as perfect as American denim.

Artemis smiles and says, "I guess not." They have missed a bus waiting for her, but no one seems the least bit reproachful. Still, she finds herself feeling bad, and the night is hanging by a thin thread, threatening to tumble out of the sky at any moment. They stand together on the curb outside the station talking about Shirley's new boyfriend, who has just bought a motorcycle.

"Crazy, the way traffic is these days," says Leda.

Shirley laughs. "I'm not that serious about him anyway. If he dies in an accident I'll just go find another one. There's lots where he came from!" She looks at Artemis. "You got one?"

She has just received a letter from Eden detailing his various summer flirtations. "Sort of," she says, "but not really."

It's cool inside the bus, air rushing through the open windows as the serviceable but hardly elegant vehicle bumps over pot-holes two or more at a time. By the time they reach the resort the eroded hills have drunk all but the last drops of blue from the sky.

It's the way she imagines a nunnery to be. She knows that it's too plain to resemble one really, five identical buildings with undecorated high white walls and a slanted roof made of long black bamboo poles. They are led into one building by a perky young woman with short hair wearing a green polo shirt. There are thirty beds in the big hall laid out in three rows of ten each. She's glad there are still beds left by the window.

When they get to the dining hall, it's already packed full of office workers and their families. She recognizes a man her father's age as a draftsman who works on the floor above her. She nods her head in his direction. "First holiday in twenty years," he tells her later. She finds it strange to sit around a table with strangers and share a meal with them, poking chopsticks into the same dishes of rice noodles or pork and vegetables, but at least they belong to the same profession.

 THERE WILL BE a thunderstorm tonight, and I will pay the first of many visits. The dark is heavy as she walks back towards the building. Although it's cooler than in the daytime, the air is viscous as honey and the night is as dark and smooth as hair. She has no choice but to take it into her lungs and let it flood through her bloodstream. With each inward breath her blood grows thicker, until it is as rich and dense as the dark. The night ripens. The first drops of water descend just as they reach the door of their building.

By the time she has washed and climbed into bed, it is raining steadily. Thunder muttering in the distance. In the sleeping hall the air is still tight. It is hot, and mosquitoes buzz incessantly except when they stop to insert a tiny pin into her skin, take a single drop of blood, and leave her feeling hot and itchy and irritated. She tries to seal her entire body, heavy with night air, inside the sheet, except for a tiny hole to the side where she puts her nose. Sleep is just passing a gentle hand over her face when the first flash comes. The room is startled blue for an instant. The growl that follows doesn't come until perhaps ten seconds later, trembling over the hills and smashing into her ears. How could everyone else be sleeping? A whole room full of women and no one stirs.

The next bolt bites closer. I feel more confident now, strong enough to nudge sleep aside and lean gently against her back, careful not to conjure up memories of the train ride, as she tries to curl away from the storm.

Either she doesn't notice me or she pretends not to. A torrent of rain passes over like a wide-winged angel and moves on to the next hill, black blades pounding. The air is thicker than ever. If she doesn't come out from under the sheet, she will choke on it. The next bolt of electricity explodes right over her head, banging in her ears like the Mongol army galloping into China's ancient capital. I put my hand on her shoulder and gently pass it over her body in a gesture of comfort. The sky is descending in liquid torrents.

A memory rushes at her, arcing through the dark. It comes from when she must have been two or three years old. Lying on a white camping cot in an empty house, lightning came to her for the first time. It struck the gigantic oak right outside her window, setting it ablaze for a moment, until the rain came and the flames were lost in a hissing fizzle of steam and smoke. She lay still the whole time, fingering the satin border of a pink blanket, which would eventually fray from an excess of touch.

Outside the wide-open windows the rain washes her memory away. I put my hand on her belly and she rolls over and looks at me. There is no surprise in her eyes. It is as though she expected me to be here, and is pleased. Or perhaps she knew the whole time that I was there, and was stringing me along, the way some humans can, in spite of their naïve appearance. I stroke the soft skin on her belly, feel the sharp bones of her hips, move my hand up the centre of her ribcage and let it rest between her breasts. She reaches her hand up behind my head and pulls me towards her. If she is surprised that my body has weight the way a human woman's body does, she doesn't say anything. Her mouth opens, revealing the first hollow of her body. Her tongue is small and pointed. Her breath comes from a warm place inside the earth. We fly close to the ground and let the thunder come back.

PART 3

Degrees of Recognition

HAVE I ALREADY mentioned that we foxes are generally predisposed towards intellectual types? It is both our curse and our blessing. Artemis is not so much a woman of action as a woman of reason. She always sticks her head into a book for answers, eschewing the problematic world of experience. This is a fact that brings on the contempt of more than a few—people who have big hopes for the world. But who am I to make excuses for her? I am drawn to the magnetic coils of her mind, wound neatly as a headful of snakes. I haven't decided if my predisposition is genetic or merely practical. In my tradition we've generally gone for scholars and priests on account of their vivid imaginations and propensities for solitude. Priests or other holy people—in my case nuns, which is slightly unusual, but hardly unheard of.

You wouldn't, for instance, catch me haunting a welder. All those bright toxic lights and foul-smelling gases would entirely obfuscate the more subtle kinds of ambience I like to generate. You wouldn't catch me following dancers or acrobats around either. People who don't keep still are hard to surprise. Some foxes would say they are hard to seduce, but me, I'm a creature of poetry. I stay away from such loaded terms. You wouldn't catch me trailing political activists or arts administrators either. They'd be too preoccupied and bleary-eyed to notice.

Unlike the Poetess, who suspected my motives long before I myself was aware of them, this one denies my existence alto-gether. Oh, it is fine when I come through the window at night in a fine green velvet riding jacket or when I fall through the late-night television screen—a trick I've found quite effective since she started subscribing to the Chinese cable channel, with its plethora of martial arts movies and serials about ghosts, foxes and other spirits. In the state between sleep and waking she's as receptive and suggestive as a lake in a hurricane. As soft as night sifting down through the clouds.

The Poetess, who had already become a Taoist nun by the time I began visiting, accepted me simply. I appeared on her doorstep in the rain perhaps a year after her companion Lu Ch'iao ran away with an acrobat.

"I have been expecting spirits for some time now," she said to me the first time, "so you may as well come in."

I stepped through the stone arch into the main room of the temple. My gauzy white dress, the conventional habit for hauntings at the time, was drenched and clung to my body like a shroud. She passed me an old silk robe from which the embroidered phoenixes were unravelling.

"It's clean," she said. "Haven't had the money for anything new in quite some time." She paused. "What are you?"

I considered lying. I could have called myself a courtesan, a prostitute, or a dancer, and most people would have been none the wiser. But there was a deep intelligence simmering behind her eyes that I dared not deceive.

"A Fox," I said.

"I thought so," said she. "You know I'm mad, don't you?"

My turn to be bewildered. The parameters of human insanity never made much sense to me.

"Have you come just to keep me company or are you here to cause mischief?"

Her forthrightness was terribly disarming. I began to fear I'd made a serious mistake. Had she been a Taoist priest I would have left as soon as possible, keeping my eyes open for ropes or knives or poison pills in the meantime. Not to mention bottles with good stoppers on them, as I've heard plenty of stories of bearded men smelling rankly of their own skin and bones still having the power to reduce foxes to trails of gray smoke and force them down the necks of bottles. Once the fox smoke was inside, these old codgers would seal the bottle over with a bit of pig's bladder. Hardly an ending I could go to with pride and dignity.

I had come up against a difficulty, you see—one my mother had warned me of in her final admonishment of me before I left the den forever. "Male scholars and Taoist novices are ideal for haunting. Young female corpses are suitable for animation. Old priests will do you in. If you must take on this lifestyle," she had said, "remember these few simple things."

In the company of this young nun, not yet two dozen years old, what could I expect? She had the eyes of an old woman. I had thought that at most she might have glanced through a few scrolls of the Taoist teachings on sex and immortality, but I now suspected she'd mastered a legion of spells that would make her an opponent to be reckoned with, should she choose to take an adversarial position.

But I wasn't looking for an opponent. Opposition was never something that interested me.

She was still waiting for an answer.

"Just to keep you company," I said.

Her eyes shot briefly to the corner of the room, and as they did, a faint light flared there, revealing what rested on the stone floor. A row of brown glass bottles and a pig's bladder all gray, shrivelled, and wrinkly like a discarded womb.

"You needn't lie to me. I know why you've come."

It was a clear declaration of war. I suppose I resented it. For the first time I was forced to stare my true nature in the face. It had been easy to pretend that my pursuit was merely an act of love, and she, a Taoist priestess, of all things, should surely have a little patience with illusions. But my hundredth birthday was coming and this was more than a mere haunting. She knew it and I knew it.

"Just remember it was you who brought it to this," I said.

She shrugged her shoulders. "What do you know of the future?"

"That you shall die and live again through me."

She got up, went to the corner of the room and picked up one of the brown bottles. I flinched, but she didn't pay me any heed. From a cupboard above them she took two cups, and set them on the table. She tilted the bottle into the cups and from its mouth, to my utter surprise, since I was almost sure the bottle had been empty, flowed a stream of wine, red as pig's blood. I looked at the brimming cups dubiously. My cousin was poisoned by an aspiring Taoist priest and I was reluctant to drink.

"What are you afraid of?" she asked. "You have just said that I will die and you will live." She drained her cup in a single draught and I followed her.

Soon we were both warm and glowing from the inside. Though she poured continuously and generously from the bottle, the wine never seemed to flow any less freely.

When the candle had burned down to a stump and the wick was beginning to sputter in a pool of wax, she rose and went to the cupboard in the corner. She took out a piece of paper, laid it on the table, and cut it into the shape of the moon with a sharp butcher's knife. This she pinned to the wall above the table, sat down, and refilled my cup and her own. Presently, the room was bathed in a cool silvery light. We could imagine ourselves two sages sitting by the river in the moonlight.

She picked up a chopstick and flung it at the paper moon. It seemed to sail into the distance, tumbling over itself as it flew through the air. It smacked against the surface of the moon. Something came rolling back — a barrel-shaped drum. And then, turning through the air as the chopstick had, a drummer, growing larger and larger as she approached. Drum and drummer slid across the table and tumbled onto the floor. The drummer picked herself up and then the drum, drew a stick from her side as one would a sword, and began to beat. There was the sound of horses. It surrounded the temple as though the entire imperial cavalry had suddenly taken a great interest in our little soirée.

The Poetess saw the terror in my eyes and laughed. "They will come," she said, "but not yet."

I hadn't been watching the moon. It had swollen to twice its original size and was getting bigger. Its curved surface jutted prominently towards us, no longer a flat piece of paper, but a burgeoning satellite. It swelled and swelled until it filled our entire field of vision and pushed us right up against the walls of the temple. The sound of galloping horses crashed in our ears the whole time. Then the temple was gone and we were perched precariously on the lip of a moon turning slowly through space, with the sound of heaven's cavalry in our ears. I am afraid of heights and have a tendency to motion sickness. I clung for dear life, although had we fallen, I don't know where we would have fallen to. There was nothing but dark sky out there, not even a single star. I was mesmerized by the sound of horses. I didn't expect to see them, but then there they were, kicking up great clouds of dust on the horizon. They swept over us. Miraculously, neither of us was trampled to death. I raised my head and breathed in the air of the future.

"This is a prophecy," she said. All around us in the field, men and horses lay dying. Severed limbs, crumpled bodies, and unattached heads such as I had often seen at the execution grounds in my youth, rolled about here and there. Some of the faces could have been those of the villagers of nearby towns, some were strange—broad and bearded like those of the horse sellers in the Western market. But still we clung to the now grassy, bloody surface of the planet like cicadas clinging to a leaf, with the dark sky turning below us. From a dead man's chest a lotus flower sprouted. A young woman stepped out of it and danced gracefully as a reed in the wind. A soldier came and picked the flower and put it through his buttonhole. The dancer fell down and shrank to the size of a cricket.

"Hmmmph," said the Poetess.

I lost my grip on the planet and tumbled through the sky, turning over and over. I thought I was going to be sick, but then I landed smack on the cold temple floor. It nearly knocked the wind out of me. When I caught my breath, I looked up to see her crossly removing the paper circle from the wall and crumpling it into a ball.

"What happened?" I asked.

"Everything they did and none of it matters."

"What are you talking about?"

"When I was very young, all the non-Chinese religions were made illegal in an attempt to keep foreign influences at bay. The Manicheans and Nestorians, the Mazdaists and the Buddhists all had their temples forcibly closed and their priests and nuns turned out onto the streets. But they didn't forbid the breeding of horses."

"What have horses got to do with it?" I asked. I like horses. I like their brown eyes and the way steam rises from their nostrils as they graze in the fields on cold days.

"Horses are war machines."

"Is that what we saw?"

I recalled that the dancing girl had had bound feet like the dancers I had once spotted during Autumn Festival.

"And the man who picked the flower?"

"Did you notice his ghostly complexion? A man from the city of canals even farther to the west than the Island of the Dead."

"How will it turn out?"

She knelt and picked a chopstick up from the floor.

"You will find out," she said, and pointed to a mat in the corner where I could spend the night.

 THERE WAS NOTHING familiar about the woman who sat beside the only unoccupied seat in the bus from Seattle to Vancouver—the last leg of Artemis' journey back from Asia. The woman's black hair was shaved down to within a millimetre of her scalp. Her black leather jacket, worn soft at the elbows, sat loosely around her shoulders. Her eyes were hard but unfocussed and acknowledged no one who came down the aisle.

Artemis was tired, since she had not been able to sleep at all in the whole nine-hour stretch returning to Seattle from Hong Kong. She eased nervously into the empty seat. Her limbs were still cramped from the plane ride, her eyes hazy with the confusion of day turning to night at the wrong hour. She did not look at the woman again, although curiosity burned down the outside of her right arm, the insistent desire to scrutinize more closely. After half an hour on the darkening road, she ventured to turn her head. The hard eyes were closed, the woman leaned back in her seat. Through the corners of her eyes Artemis explored the woman's face. It was familiar. Jowly.

"Mercy!"

The woman opened her eyes. She looked at Artemis. A little light of recognition flickered in the depths of her pupils and then vanished. "Everyone calls me Ming now."

"Ming?" The name jarred her as familiar, but she wasn't sure why.

"It means 'bright.' "

"Like shimmering. Shimmering Ming." Artemis grinned.

"Laugh if you want. A lot has happened since we used to talk."

"You look so different. When did you cut your hair?"

"After . . . what happened. You never came to see me." With this accusation, an intimacy swung between them like the pendulum of a clock.

"I did. In the church."

"But you didn't really want to know what I was going through. You couldn't get out of there fast enough."

"You weren't exactly friendly yourself."

The bus pulled in to customs. The bus driver instructed everyone to pick up their bags and walk through the customs building. He would meet them on the other side.

After the hypnotic darkness of the road, the lights inside the customs building were strident. The passengers lined up behind two booths. One of the customs officers was a white man in his fifties, heavy and smelling strongly of drugstore deodorant. He had probably been doing this since he was twenty. He pumped the questions out brusquely, not for a moment doubting his ability to inspire terror.

"Where have you been? What was the purpose of your visit? How long were you there? What is the total value of the goods you purchased in the U.S.? Are you bringing any restricted substances into Canada?"

The other customs officer was a young woman, sturdy-looking in her blue uniform. It was she whom Artemis and Ming chose, and as she questioned them one after the other, she smiled with the conspiratorial smile of someone who understands this ordeal the same way they do. Artemis payed a small amount of tax on the two suitcases she carried, jammed with an assortment of clothes and electronics.

The line-up was dwindling when the older officer ordered everyone out of the waiting room and back to the American side of the barrier, where they were to wait until further notice.

"What's going on?" Ming's eyes darted about nervously.

"Drugs," said a bored man in a lumber jacket.

"What kind?" asked Ming.

"Who knows? Who cares?" said the man. "They probably found a roach on the floor and feel like having a little excitement tonight."

The customs officer crossed over to the corner where the driver stood talking quietly with the newlyweds who had been sitting in the front seat. He consulted with them briefly. There were hisses and occasional gruff, cynical laughter. The bus driver gesticulated in an exaggerated way that betrayed his nervousness.

The customs officer walked back towards the quiet crowd. The man in the lumber jacket looked so bored he might pass out at any moment.

"You and you," said the officer, pointing at Artemis and Ming.

"What?" said Artemis.

They stepped into a long narrow room behind translucent glass. It was empty except for a computer terminal and a long steel counter.

"We're not travelling together, you know," said Ming. "We just met."

"Just get into the room."

They stepped in.

"Bags on the counter."

Artemis put down her knapsack. Ming hoisted her small black suitcase onto the counter. "You first," the officer went on, looking at Artemis. She unzipped the suitcases and unpacked them, item by item: a battery-operated clock, cheap cotton underwear, T-shirts, a padded vest, jeans, spare glasses, a note pad, a small radio, a toiletry bag containing soap and toothpaste, and sanitary napkins wrapped in discreet pink plastic, which the officer poked through with an annoyed look on his face as though *she* were subjecting him to some kind of unreasonable farce.

"You next," he grunted to Ming. Ming's eyes were glazed with bravado, or was it fear? *What if she really was guilty?* Artemis thought to herself for a moment. Ming unzipped the suitcase. A black leather portfolio lay across the top. The rest seemed to be clothes. The man opened the portfolio and roughly fingered photographs in heightened primary colours, pictures of women's bodies savaged and strewn across a landscape of steel railings, barbed wire, and smashed concrete.

"What are these?"

"I'm an artist," said Ming.

The officer shook his head with the tired disgust of a man who has seen it all. "I'll hang on to this."

"You can't. Those are my originals. I've got negatives in there."

"Unpack the rest of your bag."

She turned it over. Jeans, T-shirts, sweaters, socks, and underwear tumbled out onto the table. The man rifled through them, and then undid the zippered pocket at the top. Inside was an envelope full of receipts and a package of cigarette papers.

"These wouldn't be for rolling joints, now, would they?"

"No, sir."

"So you smoke roll-your-owns, then?"

"Yes, sir."

"Better show me the tobacco, then, or I won't believe you."

Reluctantly she reached into the inside pocket of her leather jacket and produced a ziplock bag stuffed with fresh tobacco. The officer opened it, pinched up a bit and smelled it. "Good American tobacco, this is. You wouldn't happen to have disposed of the tin and tried to avoid paying duty on it, by any chance?"

Ming was about to shake her head.

"Don't lie to me, now."

"Yes, sir," she said.

"Pack up," he said, "and go see the young lady at the counter outside. Here're your photographs. You know there's a fine, don't you, for evading the proper payment of customs duties?"

She started to stuff her clothes back into the suitcase.

"And when you're done, go back to the waiting room with the others. No one is getting out of here until someone fesses up."

Ming lingered at the other customs officer's counter for a long time, sorting out what she owed. The bus driver and the burly customs officer had returned to their mumbling corner and Artemis was sitting slouched in one of the uncomfortable blue plastic bucket seats when Ming came back. A small man with a pock-marked face and ice-blue eyes strode over to where the customs officer was standing. The bus driver quickly rounded up the other passengers and herded them onto the bus.

"It had to be one of you, or else him," said the lumber jacket in that same bored voice. "I was wondering how long it was going to take."

———

The fabric was unreal in the photograph. In the photograph Artemis' cheek pressed tight against Diane's in a gesture of sisterhood. The now-vanished smocks clung to their bodies the way bright wings clung to the strange carapaces of the white moths that flapped against the window. Eden had gotten the photograph published in some upstart new art magazine. She was staying with him while she looked for part-time work and a place to live, and geared up for her fall classes. She slept on the couch in his living room. He wasn't around much, which was just as well. She liked her solitude.

In her absence, Eden had become quite the urban socialite. His walls were plastered with photographs of interesting people he had met or solicited, drag queens in outrageous feathers, actors, models, street kids with long unhealthy faces and wild hair, mimes, jazz musicians, buskers, leathermen, jewellery vendors, boy prostitutes, video artists, performance poets, an English Ph.D. who could crank cappuccinos faster than anyone he had ever seen, a fourteen-year-old girl with studs in her tongue. He had gone into a hospital emergency ward for a few nights in a row and photographed bleeding accident victims, a man who had lost his eye in a fight, an anorexic girl who was so thin you could see the sharp borders of her eye sockets and cheekbones, a young man with lesions on his face who refused any emotion but mirth, a woman whose legs had been claimed by cancer and mind by some unnamed demon that loved playing solitaire even with an incomplete pack. There were photographs of animals too. He liked strays, especially the injured kind. There was a dog with only one ear. There was a cat that was so fat its head had almost disappeared inside its body. Over the summer, an elephant had escaped from its trailer waiting for the circus's stint in town to end. Its act had been banned as a result of protests by animal rights activists. It must have been bored, waiting out the week while its human counterparts monopolized the ring. Somehow it got away, and Eden had photographed it wandering lonely and out of place under the Burrard Street Bridge. The shot had been taken from above, probably with a telephoto lens, so that you could make out only the round body, the triangular head. Trunk and legs were obscured in the downward gaze. A bright blanket in patchwork colours hung lopsided off its back.

It was a wonder she could sleep, surrounded by all these people and creatures with their passionate faces and questioning eyes. Once, when he didn't come home at night, she had dragged her sleeping bag out of the living room to his neglected bed, but the stale smell reminded her of a time she didn't want to remember. She had staggered back out to the couch with its uneven springs and lumpy cushions.

Tonight there was a note on the fridge. "Call your mother."

"I don't know how to tell you this."

"I'm grown now, Mom, I can take it."

"Are you? I'm not so sure."

"You called to tell me something."

"Your biological mother contacted me this week.
She wants to meet you."

"You don't like the idea."

"It makes me nervous."

"Me too."

☎

Afterwards, Artemis couldn't sleep, turning the problem around in her head like a math problem with no solution. Eden stumbled in at 3 a.m. smelling of scotch and cigarettes. He flung the lights on before he realized she was there on the couch.

"I forgot you were there. Shit. I'm piss drunk."

"Never mind. I wasn't sleeping."

He came and sat at the foot of the couch. "I saw Mercy tonight. She asked about you. I told her I'd get you to call."

"She calls herself Ming now."

"Yeah, well. Call her, okay. Don't make a liar out of me."

"I talked to my mother tonight. My real mother is looking for me."

"You have a real mother. What do you need another one for? Oh Christ, I'm going to pass out."

"Do you think I should let her find me?"

He slumped gracelessly over the coffee table.

"She hasn't had anything to do with me for twenty years. Why should I be interested?"

The slumped figure heaved. Sighing, Artemis pulled back the covers, sat up, and placing a hand under each of his arms, helped him to stand. She guided him across the creaky wood floor that groaned with their weight, a rough, clumsy noise against the cool silence of three in the morning. She led him into the bathroom and helped him kneel over the toilet, where he violently and copiously vomited. The tile was cold on her feet. She did not mutter soothing words or stroke his hair as she might have in the past, but sat on the edge of the tub watching, as though from a great distance. When he was done, she filled the toothbrush cup with lukewarm water and handed it to him to rinse.

 A STRANGER in the supermarket told me I was beautiful. A man with a bushy mustache rather like my own tail and millions of freckles. I met him in the fish section. He was buying prawns at twenty-three dollars a kilogram.

"For a special Thai dish," he said.

"Seems awfully expensive for something you're going to spice the flavour out of." His mustache was lovely, the way the fine hairs lay just so against one another and fluttered a little in the minuscule breezes generated by the meat cooler.

"Oh, but the spices don't diminish the flavour at all. They enhance it."

I shrugged and pretended to look at a pair of trout laid head to tail against black styrofoam. But their eyes were dull, and even through the clear cellophane wrap I could smell that they weren't too fresh. I passed them over in favour of a special on free-range chicken.

But afterwards, I wondered what he meant by "beautiful." In my human form I may seem compellingly real to most people, but I am careful to avoid mirrors. For you see, I have no reflection. I assume I'm no more or less attractive than most. People don't cut circles around me in public, or give me that pitying eye the way they used to long ago in the Western market when I occupied that good-hearted but hideous body.

Beside a shoe store I spotted one of those instant photo booths. To be honest, I've always been a little afraid of photographs. I hate the bright lights, the funny chemical smells. But the man with the mustache had sparked my curiosity. I glanced surreptitiously about before stepping behind the little blue curtain and sitting in front of the hazy mirror. Of course there was no reflection. I dropped in coins that I had filched from Artemis' travel bag when she wasn't looking, and then stared into the glass, keeping as still as possible. The lights flashed four times, nearly blinding me. Then I stepped out of the booth, feeling foolish as I waited the five minutes for the photos to drop out of the little slot.

No luck. All I got were four identical pictures of the back-drop: white clouds on a blue background.

 A BATHHOUSE seemed an odd place to meet someone with whom you were trying to repair a flagging friendship, but Ming insisted on it. "Nothing in my life has ever been ordinary, but now I'm in control of it," was all she offered by way of justification. The bathhouse was a modest Victorian three-storey walkup that had once been the property of the now-derelict church next door.

"One kind of cleansing to another," said Artemis, glancing over the plaque beside the front door that gave a brief history.

Ming scowled, taking the remark as a dig at her religious past, which, Artemis discovered, had become a touchy subject.

"I heard it was once used as a halfway house for—what was it they used to call them?—'fallen' women."

They left their coats on brass hooks in the foyer and paid their seven dollars admission, which Artemis found stiff. The walls in the front room were pale pink and lit by lamps that protruded from mounts on the walls, casting a soothing light. It made her think of the hotel restroom where she and Diane had celebrated their little heist and Diane had cut up the credit card half a year earlier. The brick floor was pleasantly heated, warm against her bare feet after she removed her shoes. Against one wall was a rack of cubicles in which women stored their belongings; there were no lockers.

Ming undressed quickly, feigning nonchalance. There were tattoos on her arms, tattoos that revealed her road to her rein-vention of herself—a dragon and phoenix, a yin-yang symbol, a lotus flower in full colour, delicate pink and yellow. Tattoos that American sailors docking at Tsim Sha Tsui for the first time would get, Artemis thought. Ming's body was long and thin except for the belly, which bulged out in a low curve, as though there were a cantaloupe weighing in the bottom, like the bodies of courtesans in pornographic Ming dynasty paintings. Her legs were short, but smooth and well shaped, rounding out at the calf. In spite of Ming's bravado, there was a nervousness in her movements that made Artemis wonder if Ming knew just how obvious it was she had been brought up to use closed dressing stalls if available and a judiciously placed towel if not.

Politely attempting not to look, and yet looking just the same, Artemis had a moment of recognition that had nothing to do with Ming's appearance. It was the name.

"Are you the same Ming that Diane used to talk about ?"

"She told you about me?"

"Just a bit." She turned her back to Ming, more nervous than she had thought she would be about shedding her clothes in front of an old friend. But then, this was no longer the same girl.

"She told me about you too."

"What did she say?" They moved into the next room to shower. The hiss of water and steam drew the conversation to a halt for a while, as they washed with the medicinal-smelling pink soap that came out from the plastic wall-mounted dispensers when the plastic lever was pushed back.

The hot tub was square and almost filled the whole room, except for the border of blue and white tiles just wide enough to walk along. A number of women lounged in the swirling depths. Steam rose from the surface, obscuring their faces. Ming sank her body in directly, slowly but with a firm determination. Artemis stuck a toe in, then sat down on the lip of the tub, letting her feet grow accustomed to the temperature.

"So what did Diane say? She just disappeared, you know." Artemis suspected it might not be a good idea to pursue this further, but it was too late.

"She said you stole her guy and ran off with the dresses that she was going to sell to get her mother to Hong Kong. She said you knew how important it was that her mother make it there for her own father's funeral."

The steam rising off the pool had rendered her limbs languid. It was impossible to feel outrage at the accusation. She looked at Ming dumbly, as though she had been drugged. "What? But the smocks were mine. Eden gave them to me."

"You stole them after she gave you the idea."

"That's crazy."

"She said you would probably lie about it afterwards."

Across the pool, an Asian woman rose from the water. A woman with long black hair with the remains of a blonde dye-job trailing at the ends. Her little nose twitched once, giving her away, should Artemis have cared to notice, which she didn't. The woman rose to standing, then kept rising, the hair billowing about her. She hovered above them for a moment and then rose through the ceiling.

"And how do you account for sleeping with her boyfriend?"

"I had no idea she thought of him in those terms. Besides, for all either of us knew, she had left town when it happened. She had vanished from our lives." A long black strand wafted through the water and tangled in Artemis' toes. She pulled her feet out and picked it off with disgust. "Diane has a lot of problems, you know. Her brother disappeared and then was killed. Not that that gives her any right to go around making up stories."

"What happened to her brother?"

"He was murdered in High Park in Toronto."

"How horrible."

"Yes, well . . ."

There was the wet sound of footsteps. Another woman entered the room. Ming turned her head to see who it was, then grabbed Artemis and pulled her into the water.

"What are you doing, for fuck's sake? It's hot."

"Quick. Hide your head."

She said it with such urgency that Artemis' action was automatic. "What?" she whispered.

"It's her. I don't want her to see me with you."

Artemis raised her head to catch sight of a woman, who was almost decidedly Diane, stepping through the far doors into the next room.

"If she saw us, she saw us."

"Shit," said Ming.

They sat in silence for an uncomfortably long minute. Finally Ming said, "I've got to go."

"But we just got here."

"Stay if you want. I'm just saying, I've got to go." Her body was flushed red as she pulled herself out of the hot water. The dragons pulsed. "You coming?"

"I just paid seven bucks. I think I'll stay for a bit."

"Suit yourself. You can call me if you want." She tried to walk off jauntily, but her flat feet flapped against the tiles.

It was too hot in the pool to be hurt or disturbed by this turn of events, although Artemis suspected she would be both a little later. She sank down into the bubbling depths, comfortable now that she had adapted to the temperature.

"You must have done something nasty," said a voice through the fog. She squinted her eyes to focus on the hazy figure in the direction of the voice. At right angles to her a little way down a woman floated horizontally across the surface of the water.

"None of your business," she snapped.

"Sorry. I couldn't help overhearing. And knowing the party in question—"

"What do you know?"

"That Diane is a gifted twister of the truth."

"What happened between Diane and I wasn't at all what Ming implied."

"Although the facts do have some basis in reality."

"Yes. But it wasn't how she said."

A silence fell awkwardly between them. Neither of them could relax, even in the moist, soothing heat.

Artemis pulled out of the hot tub, wrapped herself in a towel, opened the glass double doors, and stepped out into the open-air patio where women sunbathed in the summer. It hadn't been swept that day, and the gray flagstones were littered with lacy leaves in orange and brown. It was starting to rain. There was no one else out there. She sat down on one of the long wooden benches that surrounded the courtyard, and propped her chin in her hands. A cool breeze rushed through her. The glass doors clicked open again. It was the woman who had floated in the hot tub.

"I don't know if you remember me. I'm Claude."

"Artemis. We met in the spring."

"Yes. In Chinatown. You were with that man." She paused. The silence began to get tense.

"The smocks were mine to do what I wanted with. They were given to me. And Saint, she didn't want anything to do with him. I didn't either, really. It was just one of those things, you know."

"You don't want to go home with all that buzzing through your head. Why don't you come for coffee with me?"

In her street clothes Claude seemed softer, more ordinary. The clean smell of soap wafted off her skin.

They stepped into the Pofi Bar up the street, a small Italian-run café with bright orange arborite seats and pine veneer tables. The air was thick with cigarette smoke and the smell of wet wool from all the chess players with tied-back hair, budding goatees, and Ecuadorean sweaters. Claude ordered a cappuccino. Artemis ordered decaf. The chess players, for some reason, preferred the artificially lit tables along the inside wall to those by the windows. Maybe it was warmer there. The two women slid into seats at the only table available, a long one beside the window.

"Have you ever felt as though you were just on the brink of learning something important about yourself, and then had it all fall away in an instant?"

"It hasn't fallen away."

"How could you know?"

But Claude could know. One could tell by the way she listened. Her eyes were the kind that one could be sure of, attentive and open. Artemis looked at her in a way she had not been able to at the bathhouse, out of self-consciousness and also distraction with Ming's story. Her body was broad, somewhat muscular. Her grace was that of a dancer, although she had none of a dancer's slenderness, but took up space comfortably, without worrying how much of it she occupied.

"What's bothering you?" Claude asked. "It's more than this business with Diane, isn't it?"

The gray sky got grayer and they finished their second cups of coffee and still did not want to break the stream of talk that bound them together like fishing line, almost invisible and yet able to bear whole, live wriggling things without strain.

"Come to my house with me," said Claude finally. "I'll make you a bowl of noodles."

No one had offered her noodles since her falling-out with Diane. Diane was good at it, arranging the vegetables, green onion, slices of barbequed pork, and boiled-egg halves artfully on top of the dry noodles before pouring the soup on so that the condiments floated, just beneath the surface.

When they stepped outside, it was still drizzling but was not quite dark yet. They walked back down to the bookstore in front of which Claude had locked her bike.

"Double you." Claude said it like a dare.

"How's your balance?"

"You won't fall."

Artemis sat side-saddle on the aluminum rack above the rear fender, holding Claude's waist as they wheeled silently through the wet dark. The road went on forever and the darkness belonged to just the two of them. Even though the bike wobbled a little under the extra weight, it didn't feel unwieldy. The echoes of childhood scoldings for the dangerous act of riding double were barely audible.

The apartment was a ground floor suite with the entrance at the back of the house. They used to call this kind of apartment a basement suite, but with housing prices rising and landlords trying to make a buck, it became "ground floor." The door opened into a tidy kitchen with a low ceiling. It was small but had enough room for a kitchen table. Claude wheeled the bike into the hallway and propped it up against the radiator. Artemis hung her wet coat on one of the hooks behind the door, pulled one of the padded vinyl chairs out from the kitchen table and sat down. Claude was already rummaging in the fridge for things to go with the noodles.

"What do you know about this woman you said is trying to find you?" asked Claude as she tossed half a daikon and a styrofoam take-out box up onto the counter. They could hear the wind pick up outside and the rain come harder.

"My mother. God, I just can't think of her that way. I know she's into Greek stuff, Homer and Plato and all that. That's how I got the name. It's hard to decide who to resent more for having made a little living breathing colony of me as a child."

"You think you were colonized?"

"I don't know. Diane once said something to that effect, but I didn't know what she meant. Now I'm trying to make sense of it, but there isn't much to make sense of. Do you have a normal family?"

"What's normal? My dad's a crochety old bugger who works as a mechanic. My mum owns a little French restaurant."

"French? Why not Chinese?"

"Because French makes more money. But the food isn't very good, except the *fois gras*."

"How can you say that?"

"Easy. It's true. Want some goose liver?"

She rustled in the fridge for a cellophane-wrapped package

and nudged it onto a plate. The water she had put on the stove began to boil. She dropped in noodles and slices of daikon.

"You have siblings?" Claude asked.

"Naw. I'm an only. You?"

"I have a brother. He's an actor. He plays gangsters and nerdy intellectuals and shit like that. His best role so far was a cop who gets shot in the first five minutes of a two-hour B-movie. I hate him."

"Why?"

"Tell you about it later, maybe."

There was a long pause, then, for some reason, they both began to laugh. It started with a little smirk on Claude's part, then a thin giggle on Artemis', and then the dam burst and they laughed until they shook.

"It's a relief to be here with you."

They slurped up the noodles and downed the thin slices of pork and translucent disks of daikon. Outside the rain descended in huge drops, the wind smashing it into the side of the house. Artemis scarfed down the last noodle just as all the lights in the house crackled and went out.

"Got some candles in here somewhere," said Claude, getting up to rustle through the kitchen drawers. "I love power outages. They make life real again."

"I should go before it gets any worse."

"You don't want to go out in that, do you? Look, here, candles!"

She lit the way into the middle room, which doubled as a bedroom and a living room. The whole apartment was dark. Claude firmly skewered the candles onto a seven-headed candelabra. The room did not blaze but hung in a cozy darkness that made them feel glad to be inside. The futon lay flat open and was covered with a quilt. Tiny patchwork stars against a white background.

"My grandmother made this," said Claude. "She was a big fan of Little House on the Prairie." But Artemis didn't laugh, because the storm outside and the candlelight made the room ghostly and serious.

"Tell me why you hate your brother."

"Have a drink first." She got up again and came back with ice cubes in two heavy tumblers. Into these she poured a generous inch from a half-full bottle of Johnny Walker. "Cheers."

"Cheers. Your brother?"

"It's a harsh story. Are you sure you want to hear it?"

"I didn't mean to pressure you."

"It's not that I mind telling you, it's just that, well, I'll have to ask you to keep it a secret. And it will be a secret that weighs on you."

"I don't know what to say . . . Use your discretion, I guess."

Claude breathed in a lungful of the night. "I'll tell you because I trust you." She put down her glass of scotch and placed her hands in her lap. "I used to love my brother. He's two years older than me. He used to be my protector, when we were going through school. Kids couldn't call me names or beat on me because my brother would shred them. He was solid, like a boxer. He was strong and his punches were accurate.

"We used to kiss each other, starting when we were very small, like we were boyfriend and girlfriend. When I was five and he was seven, it was really cute, everybody thought so. They didn't know we were still kissing when I was twelve and he was fourteen. Then one day he caught me making out with this girl in the cloakroom. I remember we were lying on this heap of coats and it was warm and we were engrossed. I don't know how long he stood there watching. That night he had two friends sleeping over. They were restless and raucous all evening, talking about the different kinds of guns that can be legally obtained in Canada, and how to go about purchasing models that are not. In the middle of the night they came into my room. They held me down and stripped me. And then they each took a turn. There was blood all over the place. I sat up on the wall watching myself being pounded into nothing. You know that feeling? I was only thirteen. I couldn't tell my mother because it would have broken her heart. He used to come in the night quite a bit after that, until he moved away for university. And he was growing. He grew bigger and bigger, like an ox. He's the biggest man I know and strong. For all I know, he is still growing."

"God, Claude, shit. Shit."

"I told you you might not want to know."

"No. I'm glad you told me." She looked at Claude steadily. Claude looked back, wide-eyed, a little sad, a little defiant. What happened next was something that often happens after open-hearted confessions. It started with warm breath that became a kiss. A kiss that became gentle hands, breasts and bellies, a rhythmic walking into the sounds of the night. The walking became something much more aggressive, something greedy. Fucking the way horses or other large creatures fuck, Claude's many broad fingers inside Artemis' hollow, sucking cunt and the wind outside wailing. There was something about the largeness of it that was gentle. Their bodies filled the room. And somewhere, at a low level like a sound so deep you can't hear it, there was a violence that travelled from one to the other as surely as violence always passes between those who love each other.

DEAR HSUAN-CHI,

We have the same hands. I wonder what you used to do with them, the fires you've lit, the vegetables you've peeled, the fabrics you've considered, the poems you've written. I wonder about other hands you've touched, some smooth as rose petals, others rough as pumice, and with what intentions. You wonder about someone's life when they've occupied the same body as you do, but a thousand years and many journeys lie between us, so nobody's memory will serve either of us half as well as the dreams that come to me sometimes at night in the rain.

There is this dream I have and it begins with another language flying into my mouth like a flock of familiar crows, wings black as my hair has remained even after all these years. They fly into my mouth screaming words in a language so close to me that its rhythm matches my heartbeat, their wings flapping as though to generate a monster wind that will send waves washing up from the shore to enfold entire cities, drowning them in blue. The language settles gently as a silk dress, quiet and warm as skin against skin and the mind in my belly understands and swallows. I am on a journey somewhere, swimming in warm salt water, perhaps with a few companions, who understand when a stray crow occasionally flies from my mouth, and my words make sense to them and I feel safe. Sometimes one of the companions is my mother and even the crows understand the words she speaks, smoother than their black wings and without the awkwardness of material substance.

These are crows that understand things like time and immi-

gration. I swim in the blood-warm ocean and they fly out of the past and sometimes the future, bringing twigs, scraps of fabric, strands of hair. They fly into my mouth, nest on my tongue, and tumble out again in spring, unrolling tapestries of woven and embroidered stories, each silken petal and bird's eye winking in colours bright as precious stones. It is these details that make me feel wanted, as though I belong somewhere.

In dreams, this is how I know you. In the stories the crows build. When I wake the memory of that warmth remains, but the details go crashing into a bottomless ocean, and no details remain in my conscious mind. When I dream, I am all heart and belly.

I have waited for you for a long time. I had never expected to feel sorrow, not like this, welling up like desire or an unexpected premonition of one's own death. I have waited. I knew for a long time that it would be you and not anybody else. I don't know how I knew. Nobody told me, and, in fact, I had seen you before on only three occasions, from which I built my expectations.

You must have been about eight years old the first time. Your hair was cut into a bob with wide bangs. It had snowed that winter, and on that particular day the whole countryside was covered in a cool white blanket like the shed down of a bloodless angel. Very few human figures dotted the landscape, and smoke poured furiously from the chimneys of houses that could afford wood. But you were outdoors. I saw you as I cut through the trees in the woods behind your house, the weight of your small body pushing a huge ball across the yard as you forged horses out of snow. You wore a thick padded cotton jacket and mittens, but your head was bare and your bright cheeks stood out against the darkness of your hair. I could hear you chatting to your horses as you built them, oblivious to the cold and the way the goddess of snow whirled about you with a threatening kind of love, her gauzy sleeves trailing. I remember hunger gnawing somewhere between my heart and my stomach as I stood watching you, but I was unwilling to move, mesmerized by the cavalry of white horses that grew beneath your small hands.

Eventually, the sky descended and the snow moved through shades of blue and crimson and mauve, descending into a crisp, chilly black. You and your horses melted into the darkness and I padded quietly away, somewhat irked at myself over having used up my share of daylight without obtaining dinner.

You had already begun to smell of cinnamon, calling to mind the moon's fabled grove of that spice, the second time I saw you, perhaps a year after you became a nun. The temple had hired a troupe of acrobats. You and the guests sat watching, charmed by the flexibility, balance and daring of the young women in bright satin suits. Nimble as citizens from the country of monkeys, they stacked themselves into a crooked tower, with chairs and bodies jutting out at the most terrifyingly irregular angles. Near the top, a young woman hanging perilously to one side by an arm and a leg caught your eye. You watched her, oblivious to the other performers, so that she moved through the air and hung there all on her own like an angel without wings. In the gentle evening breeze, blue satin nudged her legs.

A metal sound from the kitchen warned me I'd best be on my way, but just as I was leaving, I saw you lean towards a friend's ear and whisper something about that particular acrobat.

Two weeks before your death I stumbled across you sleeping at the base of the cassia tree at the foot of a hill. The night was dark and an odd combination of smells floated on the air—the scent of your blood racing though your body, and someone else's soaked into the earth. Near that tree, the air always smells of cinnamon, but on this night it reeked of the spice. The air was so thick with it, it wrapped around me like a second fur.

The odour made the new moon night an even darker blanket than usual so I had to hover over you sniffing, trying to determine what had happened from the other smells in the air. Men, cotton, garlic, steel, breath . . . I hovered like a small guardian angel until a thin yellow light hissed up from the ground, telling me that, somewhere beyond the forest, morning was coming. Then I could see you had a black eye. Your clothes were torn and there were bruises all over your body, but especially on the elbows and knees. Your ribcage heaved unevenly up and down, as though your lungs were fighting back the sweet odours of the forest that must be replacing all the oxygen in your blood.

I wondered then if you had done something wrong. The smell of another woman's spilled blood soared high on the cool morning air and somewhere far away there were birds.

On that day I was sure you would be coming to me soon. Still, I wasn't curious about your life, nor whether you might have to go through something dreadful on your journey towards me.

As I look at you now I remember my sister telling me how there had been many men at your house in the past week. She had also said it was easier than usual to steal this week because the townspeople were distracted, excited as they were about an execution. All I knew was that you were coming.

I realize this is the first time I've seen you this still. From a distance you seemed beautiful, your skin smooth and perfect. Now I can make out a few acne scars to the side of your nose and on your forehead, and how the mole beneath your eye which seemed elegant from a distance is not perfectly round. Your hair, although abundant and black as the sea at night, is brittle and smells unwashed.

I look at you for a long time in the blue light, trying to imagine you whole, your spine long and supple. The bruises I had noticed two weeks ago are somewhat faded, but there are fresh ones, and I can't ignore the fact that there is dried blood flaking off your neck and chest and face like iron rust. Having been buried for several days, you have the sweet aroma of earth and germination about you, but you still reek of the sour smells of stale sweat, urine, blood, and dying. It might be a hard smell to stay with if I hadn't been looking forward to this for such a long time. Still, your crumpled body is not much more than a smelly clot of earth. There is something as banal as leftover rice and wilted vegetables about this. I try to stop up the gaps where disappointment seeps into my soul like dirty floodwater.

As I watch you, I notice the odour of cinnamon has intensified to the brink of solidity. It makes me a little dizzy, and then altogether queasy, as though I had eaten rotten meat. Your body seems to be spinning away from me and I am gripped by the terror of losing you. You are growing smaller and smaller, diminishing to a tiny ship on the horizon. I try to steady myself for a moment. I reach out to touch you, to place my hand on your chest. I reach out and my fingers wrap around your heart beating madly like small bird caught in the trap of your ribcage. Beating. Your heart is beating. I am aware that somewhere far away, my own body is falling into a black bowl spattered with stars like the intelligent eyes of animals, but that falling is happening so far away and your heart is beating, pounding against my palm, harder and faster, an overripe papaya, its heady aroma almost overwhelming. Your heart beats even faster, grows larger still, until I am engulfed in its pulse, life flooding the night and spilling right over onto the edge of morning. Sunlight rushes up like the tide to meet it, pouring cool yellow and blue over the mountainside. Sleep finds me quietly, slipping underneath the commotion like smoke beneath a closed door.

My first urge when I wake on the cold lumpy ground is to return to the warm earth, disappearing down an old fox hole dug by my grandmother. I place my hand on my chest to feel my heart, which is still beating. But the hand is a human hand. The earth feels unpleasantly cold against my back. How could the earth feel unpleasant? I touch my face, the irregular mole. A human face. Your face. My knees and elbows ache.

 ON THE THIRD FLOOR in the cold, musty stacks of the university library, in a well-thumbed volume, Artemis found her name. She had planned this search, hoping it might give her a clue to the temperament and motivations of the woman who had abandoned her twenty years ago and recently changed her mind. The virgin huntress — Did she want me to be lonely, or was it self-sufficiency she hoped to invoke with this stilted, archaic name that no one uses anymore? No one except immigrants who don't know better, she thought.

In her mind's eye she saw a crib in a small room, with streaks of light coming through the slats of a venetian blind. Over the crib leaned a thin young woman with a pale face, tired eyes, and long black hair. The woman paused over the crib, then turned and left the room, closing the door softly behind her.

Eden's studio sat at the halfway point between the library and the bus stop. Light poured cheerfully from the windows. As she approached, her first thought was to go in and surprise him. Her feet were cold and all her clothes were damp with the constant moisture that hung in the air now, at this turning point of the seasons. She would welcome the warmth of the studio. But as she grasped the cool steel knob of the door, she found her hand reluctant to turn it. She told herself it was respect for his privacy that was making her think twice. But she knew this wasn't quite true.

Pondering over the meaning of her reluctance, she didn't notice Ming striding towards the studio from the opposite direction, dressed in leather from top to toe, with a black cap perched at a jaunty angle on her head. A cigarette with a long cylinder of ashes that refused to fall perched on her lower lip. Smoke wafted from her nostrils.

"Ming! What are you doing here?"

"Going to see Eden. He's supposed to do a shoot with me."

"I wanted to ask you . . . about what happened at the baths last time."

"What of it?"

"What's the story with Diane?"

"Don't let it bother you."

"But it does. It does bother me."

Ming shrugged. "What books have you got?"

"I was looking up the origins of my name."

"Why?"

"I don't know. Curiosity. Is Diane telling stories about me to lots of people or just you?"

"I don't know why I should say anything about it to you."

"So she *is* spreading stories around."

"I wish you two wouldn't force me to take sides."

Inside the building someone clattered down the stairs. Eden opened the door. A large lock of hair swung into his eyes as he stuck his head out. He pushed it back casually. "Ming! I thought I heard your voice! And here's Artemis too. I never see you. Want to come up and help with a shoot?"

"I think I'd better get going."

"It's my birthday on Friday. There'll be a party at the house, and you're invited."

"I hope so. I'm still sleeping there, in case you'd forgotten."

Artemis started house hunting in earnest. On Friday, she came across the first real possibility—the bottom floor of an old house on East 4th Avenue. The outside was dirty cheap gray stucco. There was a flight of stairs that led to the front door of both the upper and lower apartments. The apartment was wide and spacious, although a little on the dark side. The ceilings were low, and a tattered gray carpet clung to the floor.

"It's hardwood underneath," said Marlina."You could easily

remove it." She beamed encouragingly at her prospective new tenant. Artemis smiled down at her, taking her in. Marlina was tiny. It must be hard to get people to take you seriously when you are that small, Artemis thought to herself, having had some experience of that herself. But the acid-washed jeans, frilly white shirt, and denim vest with large denim flowers flopping over the front panels didn't help. "Any repairs you want, within reason, my father-in-law will take care of them," said Marlina. Her voice was her saving grace, firm, friendly, and businesslike.

The apartment smelled of stale marijuana and cheap incense. But the only other possibility was a basement suite Artemis had seen two days before, owned by an ex-military official who wanted to teach her chi gung. She had looked at other apartments, including one in the same building she had lived in with Diane, but the new manager of that building didn't offer her the suite. Artemis didn't complain, but the woman volunteered, "I don't call it discrimination. I just call it selection. I have a responsibility to my existing tenants to ensure that I let good people in."

So she told Marlina she would think about it and hurried up the street to buy a gift for Eden's birthday party that evening.

Eden was drunk and high on cocaine and giggling like a new bride. He was whirling around the house with a girl called Manon. They disappeared into the bathroom to do more lines. When they came out Artemis hugged him, said happy birthday, and went into the kitchen to fix herself a drink.

Diane stood in the corner by the photo of the lost elephant, in deep conversation with a slender Black man. Artemis caught her eye, but Diane scowled. When Artemis looked again, she was gone.

A tall woman with white-blonde hair nudged her arm and passed her a joint. Artemis was fairly sure it was the woman she had done make-up on for one of Eden's first shoots half a year ago. She bobbed her head thank-you and took a drag.

"Speak English?" the woman asked.

She nodded, her lungs full of smoke.

"I don't think she understood me," said the woman, turning to an equally tall, equally blonde friend.

Artemis let the smoke out of her lungs.

"*Nee ho ma?*" asked the woman politely.

Artemis gave her a rude glare and walked off. Unfortunately, there wasn't really anywhere to go. The small apartment was packed with people. She decided right then to take Marlina's place.

"You check everything out," said Marlina. "Anything that doesn't work, you let me know. My father-in-law will come and fix it." Then, "Since you are Chinese I'll let you have it for five hundred dollars, instead of five hundred and fifty."

"Five hundred? The old tenant told me she paid four twenty-five."

"Our expenses have gone up," said Marlina's husband, Feltham, clutching his cell phone. His gray wool pants were several inches too short, revealing gray socks sagging around skinny ankles. "You know, hydro and so on. You want it or not?"

Joanne, the woman who moved in upstairs the same month, loved plants. She brought them from her previous apartment in long planters and placed them on her narrow balcony. Salmon-pink impatiens, blue trailing verbena, and little purple clusters of lobelia cascaded through the wood railing. Beyond them, closer to the house, sat little terra cotta pots of herbs and foliage, and a porcelain planter containing a small kumquat tree. But that was where the niceties stopped. Like Ming, only more successfully, Joanne cultivated a tough-girl image. Her hair had been shaved down to a blue-purple scalp. Thick rings of surgical steel shot through her lower lip and left eyebrow. A switchblade and a recipe for Molotov cocktails hung out of her back pocket. Oddly, she was also studying part-time to be a lawyer. "To beat those fuckers at their own game," she told Artemis later.

Joanne greeted Artemis eagerly. "You be careful of those two. They're pretty sly. And if they ever ask you about the two cedars out front, tell them you absolutely love them. I'm almost positive they're scheming to cut them down."

"Is that your boyfriend?" Joanne asked when Eden jumped out of the cab of their rented truck. Joanne helped him carry the couch through the narrow front door. Artemis invited her to dinner. Joanne offered to make sushi.

They sat on the couch and used the boxes for a table. Joanne rolled the maki expertly. Artemis laid out trays of take-out food they had ordered in: Singapore fried noodles, butterfly shrimp, almond guy ding.

"I'm sure," said Joanne, "that Feltham and Marlina have got something up their sneaky little sleeves. They ever try to pull a fast one on you, just let me know. I'll straighten them out."

"Thanks," said Artemis, not sure what else she could say. Eden tossed her a nervous look.

"Landlords are scum," Joanne continued, "all of them, doesn't matter where they come from. Next time I move, though, I'm gonna make sure the landlord is white. At least I'll be sure they understand the law, then."

Still no one said anything.

After they were gone, Artemis settled into the place. She began to feel at home here, pots and pans in the cupboards, a bar of soap by the tub, housewarming flowers shedding petals all over the window sill. Ming had helped find furniture for her—in the alleys or discards from other friends. Eden brought an old black-and-white TV he no longer used. Candle wax collected in little solid pools on the counter and window sill, where she had stuck candles before dinner.

The next morning she went to the phone company, and that was when she found out about the phone bill. She owed over four hundred dollars that she knew she hadn't spent. It could only have been Diane.

Now, as she walked down the street to Eden's house to use his phone, Artemis noticed a weakness in her knees. It travelled through the perimeters of her body, down her legs and arms, so that a whining buzz came from them like electricity on the wires out of a power plant.

Eden answered the door in his bathrobe.

"I need to use your phone."

"I knew you wouldn't last long out there on your own."

"Just let me use the phone."

"You know you don't need to ask. Whatever's mine is yours. What happened, anyway?"

"Diane racked up a bunch of charges on my phone bill."

"What?"

"Look, can I do this first and explain it to you after? Before I lose my nerve." She tested her voice before picking up the receiver while Eden looked on.

"What are you scared for? You should give her hell. She's the one who should be scared."

"I know. I can't help it. I don't know why I feel this way." She took a deep breath and picked up the receiver.

"Hi, Diane. What are you up to these days?" She strained to keep her voice even, with the unfortunate result that it came out an octave higher than usual.

"I'm working. In a department store. When did you get back?" Diane was unflapped.

"About six weeks ago."

"I don't talk to anyone about you unless they ask, you know," Diane said. "And then I just say we lost touch."

"I don't talk to anyone about you either."

"Is that right? Don't pretend you don't know what you did."

"What I did? Look, I'm calling you about a phone bill—"

"Those dresses you stole."

"I didn't steal anything. They were given to me."

"Don't lie to me. Because I know."

She found herself wondering whether she had taken them without Eden's knowledge. She closed her eyes, tried to envision him handing her the bag, to feel its live weight. For her trouble, all she felt was an inexplicably deep certainty that it had been a dream, that it hadn't happened. She turned to him for reassurance, but he had left the room.

"And I won't even mention the business about Saint."

"It wasn't like that."

"Just stay away from me, okay?"

Claude came to visit, coming in from the October rain with a bottle of wine in one hand and a box of cake in the other. "Why did you move into a place that was for sale?" she asked.

"I didn't."

"But there's a big for sale sign in the front yard. Aren't you worried—"

"It wasn't there this morning," said Artemis, looking out. Sure enough, there it was, stuck deep into the ground by a firm hand. "I can't believe it. It must have happened in the last hour or two."

"You haven't called me."

"Things have been kind of crazy."

"I was hoping you would call, that's all."

"The move has been stressful. I have to go to school. And I just had this awful phone conversation with Diane." She explained, slowly, hoping it had really happened the way she said.

Claude shook her head. "Don't worry. It's not you that's crazy. She's the one with paranoid delusions. I call it victim one-upmanship."

"One-downwomanship."

They laughed until they both felt guilty and then Claude opened the wine.

"What about your mother?"

"I don't know. It scares me. What if she's like Diane? And also, my mother—the woman who brought me up—it makes her unhappy, you know? I know she's a white woman, and maybe her motives for wanting me were a little questionable, but I don't want to hurt her."

"You and your mother come from different sides of the fence at least as far as the colonial history goes. It must feel weird."

"It doesn't. It feels perfectly normal. I mean, it's the only thing I know. And your mother?"

Claude's laugh was good-natured. "Touché. Still makes the best *foie gras* ever."

When Artemis pointed out the for sale sign to Joanne, Joanne didn't say a word to her but picked up the phone to yell at Feltham. "How could you put the house on the market and not even tell me? You asshole. I'm going to take you to court."

"It's all perfectly legal," Feltham said. "Besides, we didn't know when we rented to you that we were going to sell it."

"How could you not know? It's been two bloody weeks. I'm calling a lawyer."

At 7:30 the next morning the front windows of the house next door shattered. Bleary-eyed, Artemis looked out the window and saw that a demolition team had arrived and was busy swinging into the exterior walls. Upstairs she heard Joanne cursing them.

"Those dickheads! Landlords and developers are all jerks! All of them. Capitalist pigs!"

Artemis phoned the tenants' rights association, but they said the for sale sign was legal, unless she had a lease, which, of course, she didn't. The house next door sank to its knees.

A yellow Miata pulled up, and a man got out first. He was tall with finely chiselled features and long dark hair. A blonde woman in a smart grey suit with wide cuffs on the sleeves and pant legs stepped out of the other side. Albert, the real estate agent, pulled up behind then. Marlina was with him.

"I hope we're not disturbing you," said Marlina.

The blonde woman walked up the front stairs. "Lots of potential," she said.

"I guess you could look at it that way," said Artemis.

Joanne was on the doorstep in a flash.

Albert pointed out the new sink in the kitchen.

"We could do a lot with it, don't you think, Jane?" said the man.

"Are you planning to renovate?" Artemis asked.

"Yes," said Jane. "I'm an artist. We could take down this wall and make a large studio."

"Albert told me yesterday," Artemis said to Marlina, "that the new owners would almost certainly continue my tenancy. Doesn't look like he worked too hard to find that kind of people."

Marlina didn't say anything.

"You know," Joanne said to Jane, whom she had been trailing closely, "there are some structural problems. The roof isn't too sound."

"Really?" said Jane.

"Yes," said Joanne. "Also, there are mice. The wind comes through the bedroom wall at night." Jane didn't say anything, so Artemis added, "Also, the plumbing isn't in the best of shape. The toilet overflows all the time, and the bathroom sink leaks."

Marlina gave her a remorseful look.

Joanne kept going. "I noticed a couple of cockroaches yesterday. I wonder if there are any more?"

Eventually the couple left. Albert, too, drove off with a worried look on his face.

"You know, I really am sorry about doing this to you," said Marlina. "We didn't want to do it. My mother's visa application was rejected when we applied in the family category, so we have to invest in a business in order to bring her here. This is the only way we can raise the money. She's not ill yet, but she's very lonely since my father recently died. I don't want to leave her in Hong Kong all by herself . . . Don't tell my husband I told you this. He'll be very embarrassed."

The red car that pulled up in front of the house later that evening looked familiar. A fancy new Camry with a fender job. This Camry was the sort of car a young bully businessman would drive —a man like Feltham. It was not Feltham who stepped out, however, but an old man with a stooped back. Out of the passenger side climbed a young boy, may be eight or ten years old.

Artemis didn't answer the doorbell right away. But as soon as she did, the boy began his spiel, like a lesson he might recite for school:

"I am the son of Feltham Chan. This is my grandfather, Mr. Chan. He would like to give you something." The old man said something to the boy in Chinese that Artemis didn't understand.

"Please do not tell my father," said the boy.

The old man handed her a thick envelope.

"*Mmm goi,*" she said, badly, "thank-you."

The man said something to her in Chinese and she said, "Yes, I promise I won't tell." They went back down the steps and into the red car. Inside the envelope was five hundred dollars, in twenty-dollar bills.

The next day Albert came on his own, with a South Asian family. When they were gone, Joanne hung a string of tiny Canadian flags across the porch. Unaware of its traditional use, she pinned Chinese "ghost" money to the front door with the side that said "Hell Dollars" showing. From her window, Artemis saw her write "No Pakis" on the bannister, but when she asked Joanne about it, Joanne she said it wasn't her. "Maybe Marlina did it," she said.

But as it turned out, no one took an interest in the house until a few months later.

I AM HAUNTED by the ghosts of the living.

She is so quiet and contained. She does not know how restless her spirit is, how it waits for me at every street corner and sometimes starts out of doorways with famished eyes.

There are days when her ghost won't leave. Thirsty days when the wind is high and small vacuums all over the city suck words from people's lips and spill them in the most unlikely places. She comes to knock over pots, push books from shelves, turn milk sour in its cardboard carton. She finds her way under the floorboards to make them creak or inside walls, where she scuttles like an army of rats. At least on those days she is too restless to touch me, although when night comes she refuses to let me sleep, flicking light switches or scattering rice across the kitchen floor.

I rack my brains for stories to appease her, to entice a little peace, but they always end up different from how I intended. There are stories for beginnings and there are stories for endings. There are stories meant for healing and stories meant to cause harm. There are stories for explaining, meant to talk away the things that cannot be healed over. There are stories meant for company when a pebble soul calls out into the empty, owlless night. There are stories meant to quench the thirst of the heart. There are stories told by parents to children. There are stories told by children to parents. Family stories are especially strange because the louder they are told the less they are heard, because then the gap in interpretation between teller and listener is often so wide as to be insurmountable. There are stories told by lovers. Sometimes they are instructional. Sometimes the stories are not told with the mouth, but with the whole body, arcing across skin, shooting history into veins. Stories set into motion the moment they spill, stories that cannot be turned back and started over. They can be told and told again, but with each telling an older rhythm reasserts itself and there is never any taking the story back.

This is a story to be told with the weight of memory. It was told to me by a fox perhaps two hundred years my senior. This is what she said:

THE OWL

My mother was an owl. She built a home in the dark and fed me live mice, all hot blood and crisp bones. That is where my passion comes from, the daily acquaintance with all that matters in the world, life and death and how easily one can spiral into the other.

I was fourteen years old when I heard the emperor was coming in a grand carriage down the street where I lived. I sat behind the flower-latticed window in the courtyard combing my hair. Usually, I never left my room without it being thoroughly coiffed and bound. I did not look up for fear of giving away my intentions, but my mother said he was frail as a chopstick.

The horses and chariots that came to take me away mere weeks later sent my mother flying high up into the trees from which she refused ever to come down, although at night I can still hear her combing her hair. Sometimes she weeps. But for me it was never a matter of sorrow. The strong lean horses were a sign of good things to come.

The emperor's hands were cold and his body pale and wrinkled, but I basked in his love because it meant possibilities. He kept me company for a fortnight and then vanished into a political intrigue or the arms of another woman.

I was fourteen years old when he abandoned me. I spent another fourteen years waiting for a second chance. There were many other young women to keep me company but we were all competing for one thing and we elbowed each other mercilessly. How can I tell you of fourteen long years in one breath? The dull weight of them, one pressing into the next. Occasionally the emperor would find favour with someone I knew. It was a chance for the rest of us to mince her like the mice I longed for. A little taste of blood, hardly sufficient in the midst of all this timid food. Women would sometimes brush up against each other for comfort over the long nights in winter, women whose empty hearts could be filled for a moment with chaff or gold without having any idea of the difference. There was one who took my fancy for a brief time. Her hair was blacker than any I have ever seen, so black the moonless night hurt my eyes if I turned to it too quickly after breathing in her hair. I knew her only in the dark, beside the trickling of an artificial stream. As luck would have it, the emperor took an interest in her very shortly after I did, and, of course, there was no competition. She died from eating mouse poison concealed in a moon cake. Perhaps I had something to do with it, perhaps I didn't. I knew better than to give over very much of myself to any of these women whose futures were not shaped yet, whose alliances I might want or have to shun on pain of death, and I wasn't going to take any chances. What does it matter? History books will record that part of my life in one sentence if at all.

The sky offered me a chance. The planet Venus appeared in

the daytime for a number of days in a row. The emperor was alarmed and asked the court astrologer what it meant. The astrologer told him it meant a woman would become emperor, taking the place of the sons of heaven.

The emperor remembered me only on his deathbed. My name escaped his feeble lips like something from boyhood. I don't think he knew as he was dying that I dragged the last embers of life from his body into mine. They warmed me slowly, heat funnelling down my throat into the pit of my stomach. The fire fed on itself and grew so large I was afraid I could not contain it.

The crown prince's face showed concern, but I would not have called it a look of grief. Not then. There was something like triumph in his eyes. In the night an owl called and the prince said he needed to relieve himself and asked for a woman to attend him. I got up and followed.

Piss in the stone basin. Water on rock. A man pissing always sounds different from a woman. The water has farther to travel. Pissing away the world, the relief of it, to feel air travel to a forbidden place. I sat behind him listening and an intimacy sprouted between us, green leaves shining in the sun, where before there had been only a tiny seed.

As I offered him a bowl of water to rinse his hands, he splashed water in my face. Water on rock. Usually water is thought of as the female element, easily moved, slow to heat up and slow to cool. The old poets would have talked about the parting of clouds and the downpour of rain. But I will tell you simply it was not a passionate thing we did, but a thing of the gray space that comes before mourning and immense power. His hands were strong and his breath hot and vital and I could only hope that there would be no child this time.

We walked back to the emperor's rooms as though nothing had happened, but I knew that, for a while at least, the gods were scheming in my favour.

As the old man breathed his last there was grief in the eyes of the crown prince, and that was how I knew I had him.

After the old emperor's death, all of his consorts were sent to become nuns at the Ganye Monastery.

Just before I left, something happened that I think helped me later. A hairpin fell from the head of the prince's wife, not yet declared empress, as she crossed the courtyard. None of her attendants noticed. I hurried to where it had fallen, a delicate thing of jade and gold pulsing with leaves and birds. I picked it up and turned it over once in my palm. It was still warm from the heat of her hair. At the risk of looking undignifed I scurried after them, saying as loudly as I dared to one of the attendants, "The empress dropped this." I did not think she would be so easily flattered, but she turned to thank me and there was pleasure in her eyes.

I was not afraid of the razor. My hair is thick and grows back quickly. The sun bled a quick red as I stood on one of the outer walkways of the temple and cut with sharp sewing scissors. A lifetime's growth falling in snake-thick coils to the stone floor. I must have looked like a teenage boy gone mad before I stepped into the main temple where the head nun shaved off the last of the short pieces. I was very sure after that to keep my face clean. Without hair and without makeup, there is only one's face to rely on. It had better be a clean, strong face.

One of the sisters told me I had patient eyes. I smiled at her and said nothing. He came soon enough, the new emperor. He doubtless had many things to pray for. I was there, to provide incense and a small torch to light it. He looked into my eyes once. I hope he saw more than patience.

The stories came back as quickly as the tide. I was pleased and relieved to hear them. It meant they were spreading like wildfire in the palace and would reach many helpful ears in no time. The emperor was infatuated with a young nun at the Ganye temple.

It was his wife, now empress, however, who made the difference. She came to me disguised as a gardener under cover of night with a wig and one of her own robes.

"Do you remember me?" she asked, so humbly I had to restrain myself from laughing. I could only nod in response. "The emperor takes no advice from me anymore. It is the concubine Xiao who dictates all policy into his flapping ears. I am afraid that soon it will be her, not him, that rules the empire. Nothing could distract him from her until he came here and met you. I think you have a duty to your country."

I took the wig and the robe and put them on. In the dark

basin of water where I washed a holy face for the last time, I stared long and hard at my reflection and prayed for charm.

She clasped my hand tightly as we hurried back to the palace. Later the legal concerns were dealt with, a little tricky because of my relations with his father and because I was a nun. I didn't let myself worry about those too much. The emperor was a man who enjoyed all kinds of positions, who liked observers and mirrors. No wonder his empress had a hard time keeping him. The emperor was a man who probably preferred boys, soldiers or the sons of soldiers. We tussled through the night, all limbs and crevices, laughing like wild animals without worldly concerns.

She laid two fabrics before me one day. "Which is finer?"

"Neither is fine enough for you," I said, "they are nothing but silk. You should ask the imperial weavers to weave threads of real gold into fabric for your use."

"And which of these hairpins?" She showed me four or five like the one she had dropped the day we first met, each one alive in translucent green. I chose one. "It's yours," she said.

It was then I started listening to the walls. This is what they said:

"The empress didn't compliment my cooking."

"The empress said I was lazy."

"The empress said I have a dark face."

I still had an owl's wings. I took these people under them and they told me things. Sometimes at night, his thick body glistening with sweat, the emperor would ask me for advice.

"I am worried that the treasury is being depleted."

"Taxes should be decreased, people are starting to get restless," I told him.

"The empress says the same, except she worries about how the army will be able to maintain control if their budget is cut any further."

"She should talk, the money she wastes on fabric for her robes."

My son was born in the year of the Dog. His eyes were bright and he giggled when tickled. I knew a boy child would never love his mother. Horses would take him in search of money and power and he would forget all about me soon enough. For all I knew, he might kill me before my time if he needed to discredit a rival by accusing him of some heinous deed. Still, I tickled him.

She brought sweets when she came to see him, fat round cakes stuffed full of red bean paste and egg yolks rich and full as the moon. She went into the nursery to tickle the baby and I could hear him laughing like a stupid hyena. Fickle, foolish child! I slipped into his room as soon as she was gone, checked the windows and doors, outside of which sat two silly fourteen-year-old maids who were supposed to be his nurses. It was only afternoon, but the room was filled with evening light. A thin breeze came through the gauze mosquito screen. With a thin dagger I burst his tiny lungs and slipped out a side door.

It is something I will never forget, and yet something I don't quite remember. A lifelike dream to make fate go in the direction it was meant to.

The emperor came to see me a short time later. I smiled at him and touched his face and held his cold hands in my warm ones. When he asked to see his son, his face was almost that of a child. Still holding his hand, I guided him past the nursery doors to where the child lay quiet as though sleeping. A red stain was spreading across his tiny back. I screamed only a second before the emperor himself opened his martial mouth and let out a loud bellow of grief. The two maids at the door could only say that the empress had paid the most recent visit.

My wise husband had the murderer immediately stripped of her title and thrown in prison. I made sure, with a little help, that the concubine Xiao's part in the whole affair did not go unnoticed. She soon joined the ex-empress in her dark cell. A familiar feeling of relief washed over me. The little girl who had languished in anonymity for fourteen years washed away with the tide. We made love under bright sunlight, surrounded by mirrors, and I became empress in the year 655.

Little did I know then that he continued to visit these lowly nameless women in that hole of a prison where they lived. On a sentimental whim, he issued an order that they be released. Imagine, allowing cold-blooded murderers to wander the palace freely. My rage could not be contained. Fortunately, there were men among the prison guards who could move more quickly than the emperor's plodding bureaucracy. They were only too happy to remove the prisoners' eight unnecessary and meddling limbs and place the schemers in large clay jars. I hear it took them four days to die.

"In the underworld I will change into a cat!" This is what they told me the concubine said before she died. "And she will be a mouse and I shall make a snack of her bones!"

I ruled the empire on the whole with an even hand. Anybody will tell you that. Everything I did in my life was for the good of the kingdom. What we do in our personal lives does not matter so much, as long as it makes us happy. So what if I kept a pretty powdered boy running freely about the palace for my own pleasure? If there were fifty years between us it is because I was still a robust and healthy woman at seventy. I ran a tolerant but not undisciplined ship. The only thing I wouldn't have in the palace was cats.

 ARTEMIS THREW a handful of bath salts into the water and undressed quickly. Her clothes fell in a heap more round and stationary than the scattered garment trails of lovers. She lit candles and melted into the blood-warm water. The sensation of heat was addictive, drew memory, pus, and other bodily impurities to the surface, sucking them out, like poisons from a wound. They say when a snake bites, you must suck the poisons out with your mouth and spit, being careful not to swallow. Just so with the expiation of memory. She closed her eyes against the soothing heat and the flicker of candle shadows against the wall, and felt Claude's index finger tracing her collarbone on the last ferry of the day between Tsawwassen and Schwartz Bay.

They had stood on the deck, the dark feeling strange and invaded by the light gushing from the windows of the boat, illuminating the crowd of travellers inside. The crowd was so brightly lit and clearly visible it was hard for the two of them to imagine themselves alone, except that the whole garden of stars blossoming above their heads assured them they were. Claude's breath was a warm blanket enveloping Artemis like a cloak of invisibility. Out on the water, the Gulf Islands floated by like impossibly large animals, silent, breathing, and calm as the sea itself. In the distance, a ferry going in the opposite direction glowed with strident artificial light, illuminating the quiet sea. For a moment Artemis was drawn towards it, and she shivered. But Claude's breath took her in gently and her hands were warm and quiet and slow as the ocean.

Now, in the bath, she was afraid that the water might not wash the memories away after all, but fuse them to her bones.

The trust between them had begun to decay imperceptibly. It started with the canoe that used to belong to Claude's father.

"My father's a crochety old bastard," said Claude. "Always yelling and scolding for the stupidest reasons. The only time I like him is when he's in a boat."

They were on the beach at English Bay, unloading the old fiberglas canoe from the roof of Claude's station wagon. "He' s a good boatman," said Claude. "He used to fish and sail in all kinds of boats when he was a little kid in China. The old scumbag." She hoisted one end of the canoe onto her shoulder and instructed Artemis to do the same.

"You shouldn't talk about your dad like that."

"Why not, the stingy old ratface? He was never very nice to me."

"Because . . . he's your father."

"And loves his kids too, even though he's mean as piss to us, the old badger," said Claude, grinning, clearly pleased to have an audience for her inventive insults.

They put the canoe down with its nose in the water. Claude instructed Artemis to sit in front, then she pushed the boat all the way in and climbed into the rear seat, from which she steered with a deft hand. The sun was high and the water was calm. They paddled with a dreamy, gentle rhythm around the curve of the Stanley Park seawall.

"You want to steer?"

"Not really. I don't know how."

"It's easy. I'll teach you. We have to trade places, though."

"So should we pull up somewhere?"

"If we're really careful we should be able to do it without having to."

"But we don't have life jackets."

"Just turn around and come to the middle of the boat."

Artemis slid her paddle into the belly of the boat and turned, resting her weight on one knee for just a moment. The canoe listed heavily to one side. "This is too dangerous."

"No, it's not. Come on." And Claude counterbalanced her as she moved in the opposite direction towards the prow. Somehow, they changed places without the thing capsizing. "Okay, now just turn the paddle the direction you want to go."

"What do you mean? Like this?"

"That's right. Now let's cross the Narrows."

"What if a ship comes?"

"Don't worry."

One did come. It didn't cut particularly close to them, but its wake was enough to set the little canoe bobbing crazily up and down.

"Are you sure this is safe?"

"Don't be such a wimp. Aren't you having fun?"

They paddled along the North Shore and by mid-afternoon had made it to Lighthouse Park. It took a long time because Artemis' steering made the boat fishtail back and forth, and Claude complained loudly. "Not so sharp. Your judgement isn't so great, is it?"

The water got choppy as the bay widened. Artemis got more nervous, Claude, more irritable. A speedboat flew by, tossing the canoe high in its wake. They didn't tip, although Artemis would describe it later as "almost tipping." She pulled in her paddle.

"What are you doing, idiot? Steer!" yelled Claude. "Last time I take *you* out canoeing."

Artemis chastised herself for being so gutless. She decided that this would be a learning experience and steeled her nerves. If Claude noticed, she said nothing, but hurried Artemis along impatiently. By the time they got back to the car, the sun was going down and Artemis' arms ached. She did not, however, want to admit this, being embarrassed about how little she could take. They lugged the canoe back to the car and hoisted it onto the roof. Artemis made space for her backpack and her wet coat in the back, thinking about a bath or margaritas on a sundeck somewhere. Then there was warm breath and gentle teeth along her neck and kisses in her ear, and a whisper, "Let's go for drinks, I'm buying."

This was the first time, so Artemis didn't think about it much, was merely glad that the strange unpleasantness of the canoe trip had vanished and that she was treasured again. They sat out under the last red rays of the sun in air that was, for perhaps the first time that year, balmy with the burnt-sugar smell of summer. They drank margaritas in childish flavours, blackberry, kiwi, and then watermelon, and talked about that first day in the rain. At the next table, drinking by herself, was a woman Artemis thought she recognized, but she couldn't think from where. Her hair was blonde with dark roots and she wore a single long diaphanous scarf around her neck in sky blue.

The dogs made it worse. There were only two at first, brother and sister with brown furry faces and pointy lop-sided ears. Claude picked them up from the SPCA and called them Samson and Delilah. (Claude professed a secret passion for those old biblical movies that they used to show on CTV when she was growing up.) Artemis thought they should have Chinese names, especially since they looked so much like the street dogs she had seen in photographs of China: their tails curled over the top, almost making a complete spiral, and the fur on their faces was uneven and stuck out all over the place. But they were Claude's dogs and those were the names she picked. These dogs Artemis did not mind. She would even say, if asked, that she liked them. They followed her around the apartment begging for food, and licked her hands when she held them out empty. It was annoying sometimes, but other times their simple-minded and unequivocal affection was a relief from the uncertainty she felt with people, even those she cared about, like Claude.

The Rottweiler was another story altogether. His name was Uzi, but it should have been M16. God knows who had trained him, or what for, but it couldn't have been anything very pleasant. Apparently, he got out of hand even for them. Claude had found him at the pound, surprised that someone would discard such a fascinating and valuable beast. The pound people said that if no one claimed him that day, he would be put down. He'd been there a month already. Claude felt sorry for him and led him into her station wagon. He got along fine with Samson and Delilah. They ate together, chased each other around the small apartment, teased each other with playful nips, yelped joyously, and slept in a heap under the kitchen table at night. Sometimes they slept with Claude in her bed, but not when Artemis was there.

The big problem with Uzi was when he went out. He would fly off his choke chain like a hawk with metal clippers for teeth and shoot straight for the throat of any dog in his path. The list of dog owners to whom Claude owed serious apologies and boxes of chocolates for fear of being sued grew rapidly.

"You've got to get rid of this dog," said Artemis.

"And then where will he go? Who will want him but me?"

"He should be put down."

"You are so cruel. You would say the same thing about me, wouldn't you?"

And then one night, carelessly letting the screen door hang open as she paused in the doorway to call good-bye, Artemis inadvertently let Uzi fly by. Like a shot he was out in the night. The baleful cries of the summer crickets and the shock of his sudden disappearance overwhelmed her like gale force winds after a nuclear explosion.

"How could you be so stupid? Have you any idea what you've unleashed?"

"I didn't mean to."

"You better get out there and start looking." Claude grabbed the choke chain off its hook and pushed past her. Artemis followed, afraid that the night held something much worse than just a vicious dog.

The look on Claude's face was half scared and half furious when she came back to the house fifteen minutes later with the dog whining on a tight choke chain. Artemis stepped out of the darkness from the opposite direction.

"I can't trust you with shit," said Claude. "Go home, why don't you."

"I can't," came the response, raspy. "I just missed the last bus."

"Jesus." Claude walked back up the front lawn to the side of the house, while Artemis just stood there, unsure of whether or not to follow. "Well, come on, then."

But later in the night her hands were warm and gentle and the crickets sang as they breathed each other to a place beside water. This breathing was no small thing. It was the kind of breath that comes from deep below the earth. In the breath and in the warmth that moved from hand to belly, history itself passed between them. Impossible that they should be here like this, in this place where they were meant to compete for white people's attention, for white people's money and knowledge. They talked about it as a defiance of gender and racial expectations, and this made their passion illicit and dangerous, which in turn made it weigh more like a water-heavy melon, bursting with sugar about to turn.

"I don't know why I let this happen, I don't know why," Claude whispered late at night on the brink of sleep, half to herself, half to Artemis' hair. Artemis had no idea what she meant.

Ø

"Are you busy?"
"I'm on my way to class. What's wrong?"
"Delilah got hit by a car."
"Is she hurt?"
"Broken leg."
"You should take her to the vet."
"That's what I'm calling about. I have a previous engagement."
"So tell them you'll be late."
"I can't."
"So you want me to take Delilah to the vet."
"Would you mind?"
"I guess I could always borrow Eden's notes.
If you really can't break your date."
"I can't. I suppose Delilah could wait, but then again,
you can never tell what other damage has been done
until the vet checks it out."

☎

Claude was gone when Artemis arrived. The car keys and a piece of paper with the address sat on the kitchen table and Delilah herself sat under it, licking at a warm pool of her own vomit. Samson and Uzi were asleep on the bed in the living room. Artemis coaxed the dog away from the pool of barf and shooed her into the car. She hated driving this car. The gearshift was rough and sticky and the brakes were going. She had to slam on them to get the thing to roll to a slow stop. Why Claude should choose a vet so far from where she lived, Artemis couldn't fathom. Cars honked at her because she had trouble getting the car from first to second.

With all the stop signs and lights through downtown this happened often. But she was thankful the dog didn't puke again in the car.

The waiting room smelled like a barn. A row of dogs and dog owners sat patiently against the wall. One of the dogs had a wounded eye from which pus ran freely, but he just sat there with his thick tongue hanging out of his mouth, looking stupid. Maybe the gates of hell are guarded by dogs like these and their dough-brained owners, she thought. Two of them sat in the corner talking frankly about the merits of dried versus canned food.

The vet's office looked like a surgery ward. The vet's assistant, a short-haired young woman in overalls and a white coat, lifted Delilah onto the steel table. The vet talked to the dog the way you would to a small child. Delilah didn't trust him at all and growled. The assistant had to hold her down while the vet poked and prodded, gave her an injection of anaesthetic and began to push her leg bones into place. Just then the receptionist called Artemis to the phone.

Artemis looked at Delilah's stunned eyes, hesitant to leave.

"It's all right," said the vet. "She'll be fine."

Artemis left and took the phone. It was Claude.

"Can you come pick me up?"

"Where are you?"

"At Café Elysium."

"What are you doing all the way out there?"

"Diane took me here."

"Diane."

"Yeah. I don't know how to tell you this but—Do you think you could come and get me and then we can talk?"

"What about your dog?"

"I'll wait."

Café Elysium was one of those new American-style espresso bars out on the West side, miles from where Claude, Artemis, or Diane lived. All forest green, eggshell, and shiny chrome. One Claude had said a number of times that she hated. The car stalled twice on the way, and the gear shifts got rougher and rougher. Delilah whined the whole time and tossed Artemis almost human glances of resentment. Artemis drove as fast as she could, half out of hurt and anger and half just wanting to avoid as many red lights as possible so she wouldn't have to gear down and then up again.

Claude was sitting in the window blowing clouds of tobacco smoke. Artemis saw her as she leaned on the brakes to turn onto a side road, but the brakes weren't engaging. She swung sharply onto the side road, narrowly missing the car that came up that road in the opposite direction, and yanked on the hand brake.

Then Claude was there, tapping on the window on the passenger side.

"What have you done to my car?"

"Your fucking car nearly killed me. The brakes are shot."

"There's nothing wrong with it when I drive it." An irritated four o'clock driver swerved around them.

"Just help me push it out of the way."

"I'll drive it," said Claude. Artemis got out of the driver's seat and held the door for her. Claude drove, angling the car gracefully to the side of the road and throwing the hand brake just in time. Without looking at Artemis she stepped out of the driver's seat and slammed the car door hard behind her.

"Where are you going?"

"To call a tow truck."

When she came back, Artemis said, "You can't use this business of the car to pretend that something more serious isn't happening." She was proud of herself for the clarity of her position. It was something she'd figured out after many dealings with Diane, who had a great talent for hijacking any crisis with one of her own in such a way as to make the other person's look trivial by comparison. Anyway, Claude wasn't half as smooth.

"I wasn't trying to. It's just, you know, the car had to be dealt with and you didn't seem to have a handle on it. Do you want to go inside and have a coffee while we wait?"

"I didn't bring my wallet."

"I'm buying."

"No thanks. I'd rather sit out here. Tell me about Diane."

"Now?" Claude's face suddenly seemed very young, like a child too large for her age being scolded for bullying a smaller one.

Artemis looked at her expectantly.

"It's complicated."

"What is that supposed to mean?"

"Look, it doesn't really matter anymore because Diane went out to get cigarettes almost two hours ago and never came back."

"There was something going on between you."

173

"No. I mean, there used to be. Before I met you. But not anymore."

"So why didn't you tell me when you called the first time?"

"You didn't ask. I didn't think you needed to know."

"I can't believe you're doing this to me."

"You can't go through life assuming the role of the victim in every difficult situation. You play everything with this wide-eyed innocence and you think it means you don't have to be responsible for anything."

"Ask me about Delilah."

"Is it serious?"

"They pinned her down on a steel table and gave her an injection. The vet tried to make a jigsaw puzzle out of her broken bones."

"What are you trying to tell me?"

"I thought there was more trust between us than there seems to be now."

"Diane is complicated."

"Diane is a bitch."

"I should have told you. I don't know what I was thinking. I've known her for a long time, you know. She lived with me for a short time before I met you, but then she got involved with some guy. She's so smart. Her politics were so sharp. She could take apart anyone that had ever hurt her with such clarity. Her teachers, her brother, her father. Our stories were so close. Or at least, I thought they were. It was addictive almost." It was starting to rain.

"She knows how to hook people in."

"Well, I don't feel sorry for her anymore."

"Are you sure?"

" I thought you'd rant and curse at her."

"I will, trust me. But later. You're not off the hook yet."

"I said I was sorry."

"Sorry or not, that damage is done." Artemis found herself reaching for Claude's hand, but it was with a sorrow she had not felt before. The sorrow of knowing that people can hurt each other and still keep going. Their clothes were starting to soak through when the tow truck pulled up. The driver declared that the brakes were indeed shot and agreed to tow the car to Claude's mechanic back on the East Side.

"You may as well come for the ride," Claude said to Artemis. She scooped the dog out from the back seat of the car. Artemis opened the passenger door of the truck.

"I'll take the bus."

"Come on, the mechanic's is close to your house." Claude deposited Delilah squarely in the middle of the front seat.

"It isn't, really."

There was a nervous pause while the tow truck driver finished hitching the car up. When he was done, Claude climbed in beside the dog. Artemis crossed the street and stood in the rain at the bus stop, hoping the bus wouldn't take too long to come.

 I KEEP A BOTTLE of arsenic from the time I worked as a courtesan. It was the gift of a young Persian merchant who had a shop in the Western quarter of Chang'an. "Women from the Far West use this," he told me, "to keep their skin white. Just a little drop at a time to maintain a look of elegant pallor." I would make use of this gift every now and then. It tasted bitter and smoky, the way I imagined the future would taste on nights when I felt less hopeful than usual.

Lu Ch'iao left me for the acrobat, but gave me a number of pieces of jade and gold as a parting gift. I sold them and bought this temple. It had been deserted for some time. Local rumour had it that foxes had taken over. Some people said I was crazy. Others said that I myself was enchanted and that was why I wanted to move in. I liked the way it sat on a hill, just outside of town, shielded from others by a grove of bamboo.

My first visitor was an official in charge of expurgating foreign religions. I thought I had nothing to fear, having declared myself a follower of Taoism, one of the oldest indigenous religions. He was a handsome man, and in exchange for my company, he made many handsome donations to the temple. One night, grasping my hand in the bell tower, he told me the coins he had donated were all cast from bronze obtained from the melted bells and statuettes that had once filled Buddhist places of worship. I remembered the day, as a child in my father's house, all the nuns and monks of a nearby temple had streamed out into the street, awkward in their secular clothes and suddenly homeless. Looking up at my own temple's great brass bell, he asked me if I was superstitious. I shook my head. He asked to stay the night, and I shook my head again. When he tried to force me, I grabbed the clapper cord and hoisted myself up to where he couldn't reach me. There I swung, back and forth above his head, and the bell thundered above us the whole while. Soon there were neighbours' footsteps at the front gate and he was forced to flee.

The second visitor to come and stay shaved her head before she arrived. Even without her hair, I recognized her as the eldest daughter of the local butcher. I had seen her in earlier days working in the back room of her father's shop, a small girl with a large cleaver, expertly separating a pig from its ribs. Her ears were small and dainty. They stuck straight out from the side of her head, as though always wide open to hear the death squeals of the pigs, cows, sheep, dogs, or chickens that her father spent eight hours a day slaughtering. He was a red, friendly man with a big belly and a loud cheerful laugh. He was well liked by all the neighbours, and as far as I knew didn't have a single enemy. Although he made his daughter work hard from a very young age, I knew he loved her, loved her better even than the two sisters or the cute little brother who spent their days playing in front of the shop without a care in the world.

No one guessed how she became pregnant. There was a rumour that it was not a man at all, but the big rutting pig that stayed in the shed one night in August. They say that in the morning, her father slit its throat and bled it until it died. She was so secretive and anxious that the rumour reached mythic proportions, and a neighbour said that the girl herself had confided in her this awful truth. No one suspected that it might be the newly appointed Official of Taxation, who had already sworn her to secrecy by threatening her father's shop. And then again, it might have been the barbarian king coming down from the north disguised as a beggar to learn the layout of the city. What if it had been? What if it had been a dragon instead of pig? A man instead of a monster? Would it have made a difference? Her father was desperate. His business dwindled and his favourite daughter was ruined. He tried to marry her to a poor, fatherless scholar in hopes of saving at least some face, but after hearing the story of the pig, the young man would not even look at her.

She came to me with a big belly, no hair, and her beautiful ears sticking sharply off the side of her head. Her child was born healthy and the three of us lived lived blissfully for year. One day a young woman appeared at the temple gates with a message from her father, asking her to go back. Without looking at me she began to gather her things. I grabbed her by the shoulders, took her to my room, and sat her down on the bed.

"Do you know what this is?" I asked, producing a clear crystal bottle with a thin black liquid inside. I swirled it so that it paled to a smoky purple against the side of the bottle.

"No," she said.

"It's poison," I told her. "One mouthful will kill a person almost instantly." Then, "I want you to stay with me. Say you'll stay."

I took a swig from the bottle and held it in my mouth. Her eyes widened.

"I'll stay!" she cried. I spat the arsenic out onto the floor and kissed her deeply. It was her first taste of death.

She spent the night with me and slipped out while I was sleeping.

 I'M NOT the meddlesome type. I know you don't believe me, especially as my reputation has been so much tarnished over the years. But I do have my principles; I never interfere with the lives of mortals based on personal interests. I see myself as a teacher with certain principles to uphold. But the line between morals and personal interest has gotten a little murky of late. A newly loosed spirit I met one night on a windy beach said it was a sad characteristic of the age that people can't tell the difference between what is right and what is self-serving, but I'm not sure. I think the world has always been like that. It's just that I am noticing it now—a characteristic of *my* age, perhaps? I don't know. That is one of the problems of living in exile—you don't have the experience of your elders to go by.

As I said, I don't like to meddle. But I had to get rid of Claude. She was disrupting Artemis' sleep, making my own nightly visitations more difficult and feeding a low-level but deeply resonant distress that results from too many years of unspoken history. I had to think of something. An old trick came to mind.

I stole an old dress from Claude's mother. She hasn't missed it to this day. I found it up in the attic of the house where the Chow family has lived for the last twenty years, in an old Kraft macaroni-and-cheese carton with the flaps crossed over one another to make it harder to open. It was the dress she'd worn the day the whole family had sworn allegiance to the Queen and received their citizenship papers. It was pale orange with splashes of red hibiscus. In the dead of night, I broke into the Value Village and slipped the dress between an awful gold lamé number and a gossamer-thin white cotton dress that swept the floor.

In the morning I followed Artemis through her day, making sure that she stumbled across it in the early afternoon.

Claude gave Artemis a strange look when she appeared on her doorstep in the dress later that evening. Of course, it had been fifteen years since she had last seen it, so she couldn't figure out why it seemed so familiar. Nevertheless, it made her uneasy and she squirmed all the way through *Thelma and Louise*.

My girl likes to shop, but it isn't often that she goes to the Value Village twice in the same week. I had to put the coveralls in the window to get her attention. They still reeked of mothballs. I don't know why Old Man Chow wanted to keep them. They were worn and stained with grease and now several sizes too small. It was the first pair he had ever bought in Canada, for his first day on the job at Hideo's Auto Repair in 1969. It was a bit of a risk—his first name, "Edwin," was emblazoned in large letters across the back. Almost half of the "W" and part of the "N" were worn off, but nonetheless, it was still perfectly legible.

Claude was disturbed by the coveralls. They brought to mind an incident at age seven, when she had come home from grade two to the sound of her father yelling at her mother in the kitchen. Something about laziness, she remembered. It was her first clear memory of her father yelling. She walked right past the kitchen on the way to her room, glancing briefly at her old man in the blue coveralls with his toolbelt still strapped around his waist, having quite lost control of his temper.

Again, Claude could not place what it was about her companion that made her uneasy, she knew only that she was having trouble getting her noodles down. She found herself getting snappy on the way to the video store.

I left the dandyish turquoise scarf that once belonged to Claude's brother on a seat in the bus. I couldn't possibly entice Artemis into the Value Village again that same month. It offset her short dark hair elegantly. But Claude's stomach did a double flip when Artemis appeared in her doorway with the scarf doubled around her neck. They argued through the night about something drearily political. I have a hard time with twentieth-century theory. It makes me cross-eyed and dries out my nose.

By morning their relationship was a throbbing mess and I knew my birthday preparations would soon be back on track.

Ø

"Who was that woman in your car?"
"Her name is Rachel Evans. She's
a photographer."
"Another fucking photographer!
I can never get away from them."
"She likes me."
"Of course she does. Why shouldn't she?"
"When I'm with her the nightmares go away."
"What nightmares?"
"The ones where I'm trapped in my parents'
basement and there are no windows—"
"You've never mentioned them before."
"Haven't I? I have them all the time."
"You never said. I would remember."
"Would you?"
"Of course."
"You don't always remember things I tell you."
"Like what?"
"Like the birthday gift you were supposed
to pick up for my mother last week."
"I'm sorry. I had a lot on my mind."
"You always have a lot on your mind. You always
forget things or break things. You're not reliable."

"Well, maybe Rachel Evans would be more reliable."
"What is that supposed to mean?"
"Nothing. I'm sorry."
"Are you trying to get rid of me?"
"No. I'm not. I'm just tired."
"You're reminding me more and more of my mother."

☎

"SHE PROBABLY shops at Leone's! She probably does sex tours of Thailand! It's disgusting, how can you let her touch you!" Artemis yelled out the back door of her apartment at Claude's small figure growing smaller as she vanished up the other side of the alley.

The nosy neighbour across the alley and one house down stuck her too-Romanesque nose out the back door. Artemis didn't care.

"I hope you get the yeasties! I hope you get crabs! I hope you vomit blood and shrivel up and die!"

Claude had long since disappeared. Down the street, an engine started and a car screeched away. Artemis thought she smelled exhaust and burning oil. The screen door rattled against her hand as she closed it and then she realized it was she who was rattling.

In the quiet golden light of this late October afternoon, she sat down at the kitchen table and abandoned herself to an old habit, imagining the lived detail of her own insults. She'd done this ever since she was a child, wondered where insults came from, and what it was that might have made the insult true in some way. It had started as a way of allowing herself some subjectivity when she felt she had none, of having a presence that didn't disappear.

"Chinky chonky chinaman sitting on a fence/Making a dollar out of fifteen cents." And she would imagine the father she had never met sitting on the clapboard fence that surrounded his house, dignified in his simple, tasteful suit, trying to sell cheap tin whistles or rubber balls for more than they were worth. The image, of course, was ridiculous, and so she would laugh to herself. She didn't consider herself any more frugal than anyone else she knew, but maybe she was, only they knew it and she didn't.

Today she was left with insults of her own imagining. She imagined Claude's new girlfriend, Rachel, stepping through the wide glass double doors at Leone's and feeling perfectly at home in a way that neither she nor Claude ever would. She imagined her shopping for crisp white shirts and linen pants and leather in expensive but tacky colours like rose-petal pink or muted cherry red. She wondered if the red curls were dyed, thinking red hair with red clothes looks tawdry, even if they are as costly as she is sure Rachel's clothes and hair are. She imagined Rachel conversing with snub-nosed women in their fifties wearing twinsets and Chanel No. 5 or browsing through silk scarves printed with geometric flowers or trying on lace-up boots lined with calfskin.

She thought of Rachel touching Claude, and felt her own belly buck to the remembered touch of Claude's lazy hand on a liquid afternoon before there was any such thing as Rachel. She remembered that hand, warm and heavy as the sun that pressed through the bedroom windows, drenching them in light. It was a hand that could find sex in every crevice of her body, the crooks of her knees, the dip of her collarbone, the base of her spine just before her bum turned out and curved in again to the quiet, pulsing place where she waited for that hand. Afterwards Claude would talk.

"Alexa wasn't soft like you. She had goosebumps all over her legs."

Alexa was Claude's most recent ex. Artemis giggled. "Goosebumps. Ugh."

"I'm so mean." Claude stroked the backs of Artemis' thighs. "It's hard not to be, you know. Especially since she ran off with a guy the same week we broke up. I swear she did it just to get to me. I told her she needed to see someone else so she could forget about me, but she started sleeping with this man. I should have known because she used to really get off on het porn. It was the one thing that would drive her crazy! All those big, juicy penises . . ."

"Claude! God! That is so ungracious!" Artemis sputtered, choking on laughter in spite of herself. "What if she knew you were telling me this?"

"Men and white women," said Claude. "Two things not to be forgiven."

Now she wondered what Claude would tell Rachel about her. There is nothing worse than knowing that your enemy knows the most intimate things about you.

The light coming in through the window diminished and the sound of that engine revving in the back alley had its final echo in her mind. Artemis got up from the table and dragged herself to the sink overflowing with dishes from their last meal together. Lunch, not dinner. Less of a chance of sentimentality. She pulled on the too-tight pink rubber gloves as though to shield her dry hands from the emotional outpourings of that last meal, the accusations and recriminations veiled in coconut milk and lemongrass, soy sauce and garlic. The stretched rubber tugged uncomfortably at the wide base of her palm as though it wanted a share of the blood that fed her fingers. As she ran water over the dishes, all the complicated scents and flavours of that meal rushed into her head, mixed with the smell of rubber, chlorine, and fake lemon scent from the detergent. They had had all afternoon to pull on that creeping smell of staleness and decay. Squirting more dish soap onto a rough green pad, she began to scrub. *Her hand touched this bowl like this. And this fork and this spoon have touched her lips. And her face was reflected in this plate, widened and distorted through the middle, but nevertheless recognizable and familiar in a way it will never be again, even in a perfectly smooth and truthful mirror.* Artemis was afraid she was going to cry, but the image of Rachel came back, glaring at her from the curved bottom of a bowl the way only a witch's can.

She scrubbed and scrubbed at the face in the bottom of the bowl, squeezed in more dish soap, perhaps a shake or two of some cheap abrasive cleaner, but the face wouldn't come out. Instead it began to laugh at her, or giggle, rather, insipidly, the way schoolgirls giggle at things they don't understand, the laugh of a self-assuredness about one's place in the world without the need to articulate it. The more Artemis scrubbed, the more the smooth fresh skin positively glistened. It was the sexy innocent face of the Noxema girl. The kind of face that inspired men in aftershave ads to lust, or at least to awkward phone calls that led to candle-lit pasta dinners and patriotic movies.

The bowl was not a fancy bowl. It was made of simple eggshell-white china with a blue band around the rim. It was one of a set of eight soup bowls that her mother had sent her when she moved into this apartment. Rachel was staring at her from the bottom of only one bowl. The others came clean when washed and dried evenly on the rack after a good hot-water rinse. She tried turning the bowl upside down, but the face still shone through the bowl's upturned bottom, gazing at her in perfect symmetry.

It wasn't because she thought she might be going crazy that she stopped. She stopped because she couldn't stand that face looking at her. So she pulled off the gloves and stepped away from the sink. As she did so, a whole scene gathered in front of her eyes, offering a small revelation. The cluttered counter, the sink still overflowing with dishes. A few clean ones steaming on the rack. Claude went home to such a kitchen except that in hers Rachel was already waiting. Dogs slept under the table. On the fridge, perhaps a shopping list: tea, rice, milk, soap . . . No need to do anything but keep it going.

She sat down at the table again and rested her head in her arms. Without quite falling asleep, she had a dream. It started with wings flapping, thousands of them, so many of them that they created a massive wind that blew leaves around the yard and in through her window, followed by an army of birds the size of cats with wingspans wide as human arms outstretched. Through her eyes she could hear claws scraping, closer and closer, and from her sockets came a piercing scream as the eyes were plucked from them and the world went black as the flapping of wings and then she was crying. She was crying with new eyes made of brown glass, beautiful and smooth as polished wood, so perfect that she almost believed she had her own eyes back. Then she could see again, and far in the distance a cloud of birds was rising over the mountains. And with those eyes she saw Claude moving towards her without ever coming closer. It was Claude and it was not Claude. The woman so identically reflected her own image she was no longer sure whether she was walking towards a woman sitting in her kitchen, or sitting in her kitchen watching a woman walk towards her. The woman recognized her too and was also puzzled and confused. They were both drawn to each other and terrified of each other at the same time. The forward motion continued but they never got any closer.

When she lifted her head again, the sky was dark and quiet as an empty bed. She got up and went to the sink, where the hot suds had become a cold scum sitting on top of cold dirty water, and the eighth bowl was just a bowl, and she was alone with it in her own familiar kitchen and there were no birds outside the window.

———

The scholar's study at the Dr. Sun Yat-Sen gardens in China-town was much too quiet. Artemis had chosen it on purpose, a subtle political statement, a many-layered dig at Rachel. But now she was sorry, because the quietness seemed to emphasize the strain between them, and there was nowhere to hide.

"It was not my intention to hurt you," Claude said.

"Big difference that makes. I don't place much stake in people's stated intentions."

"Is there anything specific you want to say to me?"

"No."

"I brought some things you left at my place." Claude reached into her knapsack and drew the items out one by one, placing them in a line on the long wood bench—a pair of jeans, carefully washed and folded, three pairs of clean underwear, a bottle of orange-scented bath oil, two paperback mystery novels, and a powder-blue cookie tin decorated with Roman statuettes surrounded by white wreaths.

"The tin isn't mine."

"It's not? I wondered. I found it in a strange place, in behind the laundry soap. I thought it was yours because of the style. You always liked all that Greek crap."

"It isn't mine. I don't want it."

"Well, it's not mine either. Let's look inside." She pried off the lid without waiting for a response. On top were two photographs of a young man, or rather a teenage boy. In one he stood beside a shiny green MG parked in front of a Vancouver Special, grinning his face off. In the other, he must have been sitting in front of the TV or something because an odd blue light flickered across his face. He seemed oblivious to whoever was taking the picture, lost in concentration. Underneath the photographs was a little stack of envelopes with the address typed neatly and no return address. At the bottom, on yellowed index cards with battered corners, were drawings of space-age killing machines with turrets and guns pointing off at every angle. On the flip side of each was a short typed message.

"Very interesting," said Claude.

"That's someone's private stuff. You should leave it alone."

"Don't be such a prude." She shuffled through the pile and took one card out at random. In a low voice she read:

Dear Diane,

I'm scared. Two men followed me home from the bar last night. I heard them behind me but didn't realize they were following me until I turned down my own street. I hurried home as quickly as possible without looking at them.

Hope you haven't told Mom and Dad about the other letters, but whatever you do, don't tell them this news. It will make them worry.

She pulled out another one.

Dear Diane,

I really don't think I'm being paranoid. I was followed again. One of the guys has dark hair, the other, red. I don't know if they're the same ones as before or not. Do you think I should call the cops? Or would that just make things worse?

"We shouldn't be looking at this," said Claude.

"So put it back."

"It doesn't make much difference, now that we've seen it."

"She didn't tell me this part of the story. Did she tell you?"

"I got some kind of story about her brother. But the way she told me, her brother's letters just stopped coming after a while, and then she found out he'd been killed."

"Do you think she had something to do with it?"

"No, I don't. But I think she must feel terribly guilty. Responsible even. For not acting. Why else would she make such a big secret of it?"

"You'd think she would have come after you for the tin."

"She might have. After I gave back what I thought was all her stuff, I refused to take her calls."

"But you've seen her since."

"You're not going to let me forget, are you?"

"No."

"Maybe she forgot I had it. Maybe she meant to ask, but didn't know how to without bringing up the past. I insisted that she not bring up the past."

"What are you going to do with it?"

"I don't know. I don't plan on talking to her anytime soon. Do you want it?"

"Why would I?"

"I guess I'll just hang on to it then."

They had almost forgotten to be bitter and distant with each other. But now there was a long moment of silence. Artemis swept up her stuff and shoved it into her shoulder bag.

 MY THOUSANDTH birthday is coming sooner than I thought. A week tomorrow, to be precise. I had not forgotten, it's just that I was having trouble calculating the exact date. I know I've become much too westernized. I've relied on the solar calendar for the last three hundred solar years. I have entirely lost track of the moon. My cousins would laugh at me if they could see. My grandmother would flick her left ear and turn away in annoyance if she were still alive, but she never made it past the first stages of immortality, bless her sleeping soul. It was not for lack of potential, but rather the iron fist of her own mother-in-law, who kept her night and day on all four paws tending to the sickly fox she married. I suppose we must take our fates as they are meted out by those silly sages in their palaces of the distant and as yet undiscovered Western Heaven. Who needs them anyway, with their stupid trailing beards?

The math was tough, I can tell you that. I'm no reader of almanacs. All those columns, teeny numbers, and strange symbols, half of which are circles with something or other sticking off them. I can never keep them straight. Especially not, as I've said, after having become accustomed to the easy glossy Roman calendars you can buy for $15.99 at the Book Warehouse. This year I got one with glossy colour photographs of foxes in their various habitats all over North America. My gentle cousins caught in the act of their daily ablutions, here scratching a flea bite, there licking clean that unmentionable place beneath the tail. Or scavenging bear leavings. Or rolling over each other in play or aggression. They're a mite intimate, these photographs.

If it were me, I'd find it intrusive—some long-lensed photography hack hiding in the grass ready to catch me stretching out of a good nap. But on the other hand, they're glamorous, and as we all know, glamour can go a long way in glossing over things we would otherwise find quite repulsive. I like the calendar. It keeps loneliness at bay.

So I worked out the exact date. The columns gave it up after an afternoon of wrangling. I got started just in time. If I'd decided to take a fishing trip up the coast as I'd vaguely been planning, it would have been over before I got back. Which would have been all right, I suppose, although I would really rather cele-brate at home. One's thousandth birthday is no small matter.

I'm not entirely sure what to expect, not having had anyone to instruct or support me since shortly after my arrival in Canada. But this is it, the stage beyond which there are no other stages. I imagine it will be something less vulgar, less visceral than the bodily transformation I experienced on my fiftieth and hundredth. Something more elevated, more sublime. Not that there is anything not-sublime about transformations of the body, mind you. I didn't mean to suggest that.

There's a tree in Stanley Park I would like to visit. Hollow inside and full of ancient, untouched spirits. The perfect place for a first lesson in twentieth-century haunting. It is history I'm interested in. History, and, I suppose, the future. If I'm to receive a birthday gift, I think that's what I'd like. The ability to read from the air who has breathed it in the past, and who will in the future. The accumulated emotions of any point in space.

 THE EARMUFFS that Ming handed Artemis had a hard plastic casing on the outside. They squeezed her head uncomfortably but blocked all sound except the sound of gunshots, which cracked as though from a long distance off. She pulled them down around her neck like a collar.

"I can't believe you've brought me here."

Ming nudged her gently into the booth and pressed the pistol into her hand, instructively folding the reluctant fingers into the correct position. The grip was cold. As soon as Ming let go, Artemis opened her hand and stared at the smooth dead metal.

"Don't point it at yourself, whatever you do. Or anyone else," Ming warned.

It was a dull gray colour, except for the six-inch barrel of shiny steel. Its angles were smooth and efficient, without any unnecessary curves or ornamentation. Is this what death has become, she wondered, so efficient and technological? She had seen photographs in one of the many coffee-table books Eden owned, of the .38 Colt through history, with triumphant soldiers or ancient, muscular warriors engraved into the ivory or mahogany stock or the base of the sleek steel barrel. Guns for known and respected enemies, not this bleak if elegant thing with its lean impersonal lines. And then, she thought, closing her fingers around the grip again, a gun is a gun.

Her face must have betrayed fear or anxiety, because Ming said, "I thought you might find this exciting, get your mind off Claude, and give you a taste of some twentieth-century action. I thought you might have some aggression to burn off. If it's gonna make you miserable, you don't have to do it."

"I wish you had warned me."

"If I hadn't told you it was a surprise, you wouldn't have come."

This she could not deny. "All right, what do I do?"

The figure at the end of the range, her target, had a human shape, a white outline tracing that ancient form, the shape of terror and vulnerability. From the chest area, a series of concentric circles rippled out, separated by single digits. A dartboard. A target. Closed and uncompromising. Ming showed her how to stand at forty-five degrees to the target, how to aim, lining the sights up with the bull's-eye without cranking her neck in an awkward position. She explained to Artemis how to hold her breath at the moment of impact so that her restless lungs wouldn't throw her aim off. Then there was nothing in the room but Artemis and that taunting figure. She squeezed the trigger slowly and blew a hole through the heart.

"Not bad at all for someone who acts so chickenshit," pronounced Ming cheerfully, pulling the little stub of steel from Artemis' hand. The gun's recoil had left her numb.

They fired a few rounds each. Ming had been practising. She

must have been, since she never missed, except when she experimented with the moving target. Artemis' results were more erratic, sometimes spot on, sometimes missing the figure altogether.

At one point, coiling all her concentration into her eye, she did not notice how badly her hand was shaking.

"Rest for a minute," said Ming. "You're not going to hit a thing if you're that nervous. Don't want you to shoot yourself."

"This is such a strange sport. These things have been designed for the express purpose of killing, and then we handle them so carefully to make sure we don't."

"You never know when you might need to. Then you'll be glad you know how."

"It must be a Catholic thing, to follow one's temptations right to the edge and then feel guilty for acting upon them."

"It's a self-defence thing," Ming snapped.

The intensity of this routine practice absorbed them so entirely they did not hear the rumbling laughter in the next booth. Not, that is, until a man on the other side of the thin wall growled, "Here's one for you, Charlie," and blew the head of the paper figure right off.

"I think we should leave," said Artemis.

"It's just some lame soldier who's still sore about Vietnam," said Ming.

"I don't care. We don't belong here. Let's go."

Ming levelled her eyes at her. "No. I'm not going to leave because some brainless gimp doesn't understand that I have every much a right to be here as he does."

A ruddy boyish face peered around the corner. "What did you call me, Chinaman?"

Another head peered around the corner. "Jeez, Phil, it's a girl."

"Fuck off, honky trash."

"Hey hey hey, what's going on here?" A burly security man appeared from nowhere and placed a heavy hand on Ming's shoulder. "We don't permit racist name-calling around here, young lady."

"But—"

He shook a finger at her as one would at a naughty child, and gently nudged the two young men back into their booth.

"Come on, I'm serious, let's go," Artemis urged.

"No." Ming lined up a round of bullets in the magazine, jammed it into the stock, and dropped into a firing stance. She released the whole round with scarcely a second between shots. Not one went even close to bull's-eye.

Artemis was relieved when Ming finally consented to leave and the glass doors swung shut behind them. It began to rain as they crossed the asphalt parking lot.

"I don't know what hurts more," said Ming, "bullshit like that from the outside or the games that women play with one another's heads."

"I can definitely relate, but what's happened to you lately?"

"Oh, nothing. I was just talking generally. Actually, I was thinking about you. Still bitter about Claude?"

"She gave back all my stuff yesterday."

"That's pretty final. Don't look so miserable. You'll get over it in time."

It was unbearable that Ming should patronize her. "Guess what was in the bundle?" she offered, too juicily.

"Tell me."

"A bunch of letters to Diane from her brother. She knew he was going to be killed."

"What?!"

"Shit. I guess that's a secret. Don't spill it, okay?"

Artemis woke up earlier than usual the next morning to the steady sound of hammering. Contractors had been working on the house next door for the past few months, but this was the first time they had started so early. Winter was coming on, and no doubt they wished to complete as much as possible before the heavy rain began. Artemis heard a stirring upstairs, heavy feet on the thin wood floor. She pulled a pillow over her head and the covers over that and drifted off for a few minutes more. But then she couldn't ignore the commotion that had started up outside. She leaned out the window.

The foreman was complaining in rising tones to two policemen, neither of whom would look him in the eye. One gazed vaguely at the workers who were watching from where moments ago they had been hammering or sawing. The policeman was shaking his head. The other policeman concentrated on his pad of tickets. Joanne had poked her head out the window right above her.

"Fine 'em lots!" she yelled. Behind her another woman was laughing and soon the two of them were in stitches. "Serve those foreigners right for not obeying the laws."

Artemis gritted her teeth and moved into the kitchen to make coffee. She had reading to do for a class that afternoon anyway, on Classical History. A lecture on military strategy during the Trojan War. Vaguely she wondered what it might have been like to be cooped up all night in the belly of a horse and then obliged to fight in the morning.

At ten o'clock Joanne banged on her door. "Those pigs sold the house today. To that yuppie 'artist' couple that were here at the beginning. Squeezed 'em good for a bunch more money by the looks of it. We're being evicted."

"Great."

"Yeah, but the bylaw requires them to give us three months' notice. I'm gonna stay and just delay paying my rent until I'm ready to leave."

"I couldn't do that."

"Sure you could. I'm here. I'll back you up."

"It wouldn't be right."

"If you're gonna let that stop you—"

The phone rang in the kitchen.

"It's Marlina. Better get it. Give the old cow some trouble for me, will you?"

 YESTERDAY someone I recognized crossed the courtyard. Her hair was loose and wild and her dress whirled around her like a storm. Was it her graceful dancer's step that made it seem as though she were flying? She fled through the courtyard and into the bamboo grove. At the place she entered, the slim green leaves shook for a moment and then returned to their flirtation with the wind.

What is a ghost? People say they inhabit tablets or trees or flowers or stones. I have never been so sure. There are ghosts that live inside me, wandering my arteries and veins, travelling into my heart and out of it again. Round the spirits go through my bloodstream in their own vessels, some close to the regular clunk of my heart, pounding like the sun, its red spot pulsing. Others orbit at a greater distance. It takes them a longer time to come back around. Lu Ch'iao was close for a long time, although lately her arc has grown wider. She sails through on her own wings like a wild swan or an angel. The gray feathers fall into my rushing blood, swirl down, and sink, get carried into my left atrium and lodge there, slowly amassing into a clot. Still her wings beat. I imagine the dense mass of muscle beneath the feathers, muscle that has been pounding for all these years like breath, never stopping. One day she will get tired or too many fallen feathers will accumulate. Perhaps I will die of a heart attack.

I imagine my father travelling in a sedan chair. He would like that, having gone on foot pretty much all his life. Four handsome bearers would carry him around inside his curtained box. Inside, he would have a storehouse of all those medicines that were familiar to me as a child, and many that were not—things that he had collected on his travels, far into the land of the West, pills that work their magic, healing instantly, only to reveal the ingredient for slow painful death years down the line. He will soon need a ship. He will meet many merchants on my oceans and rivers. Perhaps one will give him the black liquid smoke that the Chinese will suck into their lungs as they give away all the treasures of the Middle Kingdom to the white corporate dragon.

I imagine my mother as a crazy, irregular comet in beautiful colours, gold and lightning blue. She burns with an intense light from a great distance off, zigzagging through her orbit and glowing like a sunset on the ocean. I have stopped imagining her as a fairy godmother with gifts of finery and a magic vehicle that will take me away from myself forever. She is a star in the distant sky, endlessly falling.

And the butcher princess? Does she travel on the back of a horny boar, his sharp, coarse hairs spiking into her tender thighs? His hooves gallop against my heart like the most noble of horses. Will she betray me in the end, send me on my own travels in the other world, beneath the skin of someone who remembers me? Or will she turn my blood to arsenic that will coax my heart into stopping?

ARTEMIS descended from the bus and began her short trek through the wooded area behind the house. It was growing dark and the crows hung over her, cawing their usual cryptic warnings, which she ignored. She was just going around a bend in the path when Ming jumped out at her.

"What the hell!"

Ming grinned. "Today, Arty-Miss, I'm inviting you to my humble abode. I've got something to show you."

"You do?" Ming's theatricality set her suspicion alarms ringing.

"Don't look at me so funny. Come on, I've got my father's car while he's away."

"I thought you hated your father."

"I never said that." She paused. "You won't think any less of me because of the car, will you? It's a Volvo. A station wagon, though. It's a very practical car. Fits lots of stuff and should last forever."

"Where is your dad?"

"In China."

"What for?"

"Just business. I don't know what he does."

"Aren't you curious?"

"Not really."

"I thought you said he was doing something that upset you."

Ming squirmed and Artemis immediately wished she hadn't said anything. "Never mind. Why do you want to take me to your house?"

"I've got something to show you. A surprise."

The house faced directly onto the rushing traffic of Boundary Road, although there was a thick, raggedy hedge around it, blocking out the view, if not the noise. The place itself was a sprawling box, the lower half done in orangey brick, the upper half in white stucco that showed three large cracks and plenty of mildew. Ming opened the door to the smells of mothballs and stale cooking, not overpowering but still noticeable. It was carpeted in the dreadful browns, greens, and oranges of the seventies. The walls were dark wood panelling.

"Come meet my mother," said Ming, leading her up the green carpeted stairs over which a thick plastic runner had been riveted.

Upstairs, the walls were done in eggshell stucco with bits of sparkle in it that came off on your hands if you leaned too hard against it. The living room was huge and spotlessly clean. There was a cross over the mantelpiece, and a number of religious magazines neatly stacked on the glass coffee table. There were a few of the usual knickknacks—a sea anemone trapped under red-and-blue coloured glass, a ship in a bottle, photographs of the children at various ages against backgrounds that were gradated from hazy white to hazy blue and slipped into cardboard frames in fake wood colours—but on the whole, the place was unusually uncluttered.

"My parents are very wary of idolatry," Ming explained. The thick shag purred beneath Artemis' sock feet.

They found Ming's mother out on the deck, assembling what appeared to be a TV stand from a department store kit. It was the same brown panel colour as the walls downstairs. She knelt over it, laboriously twisting the screws into place.

"Pleased to meet you," she said to Artemis politely when Ming introduced them. "Get your friend a drink now, before you drag her all over the house. Maybe she'll talk you into coming back to church this Sunday."

"I'm fine," said Artemis as Ming rummaged through the fridge and emerged with a half-full bottle of Pepsi. You could tell it was flat by the way it poured. "Really. I don't need a drink."

"Just take it," said Ming, "or my mom will give me hell for being rude. I can't wait to move out."

The phone rang. Ming picked it up. "Yup . . . yup . . . uh huh . . . okay . . ."

"Is everything okay?" Artemis asked afterwards.

"Everything's fine."

They shuffled back downstairs. Ming threw open the door to her room. In contrast to the neatness upstairs there were clothes, books, newspapers, records, and photographs scattered all over the floor. The brown panelling had been painted over white on three walls and a dark eggplant purple on the long north-facing wall. If there had been carpet, it had been stripped back to the bare concrete.

"Ignore the mess," said Ming. At the back of the room was another door. Ming pushed it open. Artemis followed her into the dark. Somewhere in the centre of the room Ming fumbled for the cord that would turn on the bare yellow bulb.

Artemis blinked. Surrounding her on every wall were giant paintings of bodies tumbling through space, faces screaming, bolts of fabric uncoiling into nowhere, snakes, dragons, and birds with scales of gold screaming into a night of blinking stars. Drapes of real fabric, smooth silk or cotton with patterns of flowers and animals had been incorporated into one. Another was studded with bits of broken mirror, sharp and dangerous, reflecting back her own eye in a thousand biting pieces. In one, a gigantic woman with a mouth like a cave and teeth like stalactites was swallowing animals in a long line, pigs, sheep, goats, cows, bears, tigers, elephants, and a mangy dog. In the corner of another, a small figure crouched, stark naked, with her hands over her face.

"I started doing these after my father started going away all the time."

"Ming, they're incredible. You should try to get them shown."

"I don't know if I want to. Right now, I just want my friends to see them."

"These are nothing like what you had at the border that time."

"Well, it takes time. And the scale is important."

She was right. The things towered. They took you in, swallowing your whole field of vision.

It was dark and the wind was up when Ming dropped Artemis home.

"You want to come in?"

"I better get going."

"Come in for second. You've never seen my place and soon it'll be too late. We're being evicted."

A strange look crossed Ming's face. "Okay."

They stomped up the porch steps. Artemis flicked open the mailbox, took out the mail, and then, after some fumbling with the keys, found the appropriate one and stuck it into the lock. "Hey, it's unlocked. That's weird. I never forget—"

The door swung open. Even in the dark, she could make out the mess. She flicked on the switch. Furniture had been overturned, books pulled down from the shelves, sheets and blankets from the bed had been dragged into the hall and were covered with milk, spaghetti sauce, and broken eggs. The living room mirror had been broken and there were little shards of glass everywhere, like the ones in the paintings.

"Who would do this?"

"Jesus," Ming muttered under her breath. "I didn't think it would be this bad."

"What?"

"Nothing."

"I can't believe this has happened." Artemis stared blankly at the mess. Ming had a pained expression on her face. Artemis ran out onto the porch and banged on Joanne's door. Joanne clattered down the stairs, came out in a bathrobe, wet hair sticking to her head.

"A woman was here earlier," she said. "A Chinese woman. I assumed she was a friend of yours. She seemed to know where to find the spare key." She looked inside. "Shit. You know, I thought I heard some commotion, I don't know why, I just figured it was okay, you know, because I'd seen her and she looked like a normal person."

"Who could it have been? Diane? But why would she do this? I mean, we're not the best of friends but—"

"She was looking for the letters," said Ming.

"You knew? You knew! You were in on it with her. Goddamn it, Ming!"

"I had no idea she would wreck the place."

"How did she know about the letters in the first place?"

Ming's vaguely pained look was now more a look of panic.

"You told her. You bitch. I can't believe it. I don't even have the fucking letters."

"Think about how she must feel that you know about her brother, you know, that she knew what would happen to him—"

"Get out of my house."

"Art—"

"Get out."

Ming slunk down the front stairs. As the lights of the Volvo station wagon went on and the engine started, Joanne wrapped her arms around Artemis.

"Never mind," said Joanne, rocking her back and forth. "We have to move out anyway."

"I wonder if I should call Claude, to warn her."

As if on cue the phone rang, and it was indeed Claude.

"Diane was here," Artemis began.

"I know, you idiot. She was here too. Why did you tell Ming? How could you be so stupid?"

"Don't yell at me."

"Why the hell not? You're the one that fucked up."

"Did she trash your house?"

"No, she hurled plenty of abuse my way, though."

"She didn't trash your house?"

"No, but—"

"Well, good-bye then."

"Don't you dare hang up on me."

 YOU ARE FAMILIAR, no doubt, with stories of forbidden love, where the soul of the lover, quite unbeknownst to her, leaves her body to be with the beloved. But perhaps you have never heard of such a thing happening for more complicated reasons.

There was once a student who did not keep to her books as much as she should have. Indeed, she was rather vain. She spent much of her time casting her eye about looking for reflections of herself, in mirrors, in lakes, in flowing rivers and other moving creatures. If she liked what she saw, she would gaze endlessly at the reflection until it melted away or transformed into something unbearably hideous. If she did not, she turned her eyes politely to the side and pretended not to notice.

One day in a garden (for as you know, meetings in stories of this sort always take place in gardens) when the air was redolent with the scent of roses, she met a painter. It was not the painter's beauty that struck her, although the painter was very beautiful. Rather, it was her awkwardness, which was at once endearing and annoying, but terribly magnetic all the same because she saw herself in it.

"Who is that painter?" the student asked her friends. But none of them could tell her. She watched the painter investigating the roses, studying the range of tones from the base of a petal to its lip, wondering how to translate scent into colour.

Eventually the painter meandered down the path. The student found herself following her. She trailed her past roses, past marigolds and maple trees all the way to her home. She followed her straight through the front door of the house. Nobody tried to stop her. Indeed, nobody even noticed that she was there.

The walls of the house were covered in stupendous paintings, so realistic that as you walked down the hall, you believed yourself in a forest, surrounded by strange beasts with glittering eyes. When you strolled into the main reception room, you could easily believe yourself beneath the water, pushing aside wavering alien plants, seaweed, and shimmering fish that flashed by like angels or sudden memory. Sitting in the painter's room you might think you had fallen into a sky of tumbling stars; the dark was so realistic it enveloped the student like breath.

The painter lit a candle, illuminating the student's face. Without a word she took out a chess board. They began to play chess. They played and drank right through the evening and the following day, enjoying themselves immensely. But on the third day things got competitive. Perhaps they had tired of one another's company. The painter shifted the pieces on the board slightly when the student was not looking. The student replaced her own defeated queen in the middle of a game when she thought the painter was too drunk to notice. And so it went until the accusations began to fly.

Suddenly, they both drew pistols from the depth of their coats, but the student was a faster draw. She shot the painter in the head. The body fell to the ground with a clunk and blood sprayed over the playing board. Shocked at what she had done, the student hurried to the front door, dissolved right through it, and fell unconscious. When she woke, she was lying at home in her own bed. Her friends were gathered around her with nervous, exhausted expressions on their faces. They told her she had fainted in the park and remained passed out cold for three days.

 THERE WAS a place where time was not yet a measurable thing, where it didn't stretch like a long jet of water shooting into the night but meandered and twisted, curling and eddying without haste or care. It was a place where the dead moved among the living more easily than they do now. In that place grew a tree. Not the kind that spreads haphazardly, allowing anything to blow through its branches. This was a closed tree, shaggy with leaves. The leaves were small. Precise points and sharp angles. If you stood under the tree, a curious thing revealed itself. The tree was entirely hollow inside, a planet composed of space and dark branches. The leaves all pressed outwards, competing for sun and air. Inside, it was dark. Not the sweet, warm dark of sleep and enfolding arms, but a troubled dark, broken by chips and splinters of light that fell through before the greedy leaves could spear them. Enough light to make shadows and feed the spirits that lived in the elbows of the branches. Here and there, a small pale leaf hung without the strength to push to the surface.

The trunk was ten times as thick as the torso of a strong man and robed in gray-brown bark dense and wrinkled as the skin of a sorceror. Its roots trammelled the ground above and below, rearing up like horses now and again, displacing earth. Who knew how far below the ground they reached? They could have marked trails to cities inside the planet.

Buried in the loamy soil beneath a heap of leaves and bracken was the body of a young woman.

PART 4

When Fox
Is a
Thousand

"I HAVE HEARD every rumour in the book. I don't think I can stand it anymore."

Artemis rolled over on her futon, absently brushing the dirt that probably came from the soles of Diane's shoes off the bed, without actually waking. She pulled the spare sleeping bag that had survived the rampage unharmed up around her chin.

"They've checked out every Asian man who owns a leather jacket, they're so sure it's gang-related. Couldn't pin it on anyone local, so now they're saying it's a New York-based Triad. They say three members flew in, did the deed, and flew out, even have plane ticket stubs to prove it. Drug related, of course."

"I heard the body was clean."

"Yeah, so? Drug-related family retribution. Orientals are into that kind of thing."

The voices came from beneath the window. She was tired. She pulled the covers over her head to shut them out. But the voices grew louder as the men beneath the window became more engaged in their conversation.

"You know that closet-case faggot I told you about? What's his name? Jimmy? He thinks it was queer-bashers who mistook the girl for a man. But he's too afraid to say anything about it for fear they'll ask questions about him. Williams, the one with all the Oriental girlfriends, he thinks it was racist skinheads and we should be watching Pender Island a whole lot more closely. Chen says there's no way it could be skinheads. He believes the gang theory, or at least that's what he says. I wonder if he's worried about losing his job."

She got up and went to the window. She opened it and leaned out. Cool, damp morning air rushed into her nostrils. There was no one there. She returned to her bed, bones packed with the lethargy that comes from not wanting to acknowledge something that has happened, no matter how close it may be.

She closed her eyes against the slow light that filled the room, watched the lids pulse red. The red faded not to black, but to white, the whiteness of clean white sheets on a white bed. Curled like a question mark in the hollow of her own weight lay a woman. A perfect, sleeping face, flickering eyelids, slack jaw, red lips. Diane. She leaned close. It was not Diane but Ming sleeping on the cloud-white sheets. Artemis' heart was suddenly pumping with uncontrollable rage. In the bright light that poured over the bed she reached for the woman's neck. Flesh oozed between her fingers. She wrung and wrung with a fury that saw nothing but bright light and white sheets. A trickle of blood ran past perfect lips. She woke screaming just as the phone began to ring.

"I'm looking for Artemis Wong."

"Speaking."

"I hope you don't mind me contacting you like this. I talked to the woman who adopted you."

"My mother. Jeanne."

"Yes. She gave me permission to call. I'm your biological mother."

She gave an address in Richmond. They agreed to meet that evening, but after she hung up the phone, Artemis decided not to go. At midday, she changed her mind. At three she changed it again. Who was this woman, barging into her life as though she had any right?

The forest lay in a deep twilight. It was a short walk through the woods to the bus stop, but at the moment it felt as though trees covered the whole planet, as, she reflected, they must have once. There was nothing but greens and browns and shadows and small fragments of light like broken glass scattered across the path. The smell of oxygen combined with the purple smell of decay. The ground was tender as flesh. She stepped into the dark as though entering her own house through the back door, and began to work her way up the path.

The first time she was not even sure she saw a fox cross in front of her. The second time the creature moved more slowly and she was more certain about the flash of red.

Around a bend in the path stood a woman. She wore a pair of

snug-fitting Levi's, fraying at the hems, with a hole in the left knee, and a white T-shirt with the sleeves cut off. The leather of her steel-toed army boots looked as if it was ready to give and was brown and nubby in places. Beneath a revolutionary workers' cap, the stranger's long hair flowed freely in the wind, and Artemis noticed that the back was shaved off, right to the occipital bone. In the grown-out ends, there were traces of a blonde bleach-job. All the air in the forest was relatively still, but there was a breeze that kept the stranger's hair constantly in motion, crossing her face and coming free and crossing again, and the face seemed different every time it emerged. Artemis had a vague feeling she had been in this woman's presence before, but she didn't know when or where and in the stillness of the forest the planet seemed to spin around so fast she could not be sure of anything but the trees.

"Where are you going?" asked the stranger.

"I'm going to catch a bus to see my birth mother in her apartment in Richmond," said Artemis.

"And how do you know you will get there safely?"

"Of course I will. It's only a short walk to the bus stop and then the bus will take me right to her door, almost."

"Did you hear they found a woman's body in Stanley Park last night?"

"No, I didn't," said Artemis, wondering for a moment if she ought to be frightened.

"Never mind," said the stranger. "We're a long way from there."

This kind of talk made Artemis nervous. She began walking up the path towards the stranger, who stood directly in her way. For a moment Artemis was worried that the other woman might not take the hint and step aside. She hoped she wouldn't have to say something rude. But the stranger turned and walked beside her in long, even strides.

"What are you bringing your mother?"

"Maybe roast duck if I have time to pick one up from Hon's."

"And what route do you plan to take?"

"Whatever bus comes first that will go over the Oak Street Bridge."

"Hmmm," said the stranger, "I see."

Artemis didn't see how, but the moment her back was turned,

the stranger vanished into the sunlight winking on the ground beside patches of shadow.

Her legs were aching by the time she got to the gravel shoulder where the bus stopped. She wasn't sure why. She'd just been lying in bed all day and the walk up the path was quite short.

The bus wound through the streets and got to the Oak Street Bridge just in time for her to see the whole city glowing orangey-gold in the sunset and the small blue streetlights coming on. Wind rushed through the open window.

There was a bit of a jam on the bridge because of roadwork. A woman in a hard-hat with an orange flag waved them by.

Still, by the time she got to Hon's there was only the slightest hint of natural light left in the sky, like the dampness of a just-wiped countertop. She was just pressing her weight into the cool glass door when the stranger from the woods nudged the door open on the other side, arms loaded with boxes of sweet cakes and roasted meats. She winked at Artemis. Too astonished to do anything else, Artemis winked back.

The butcher grinned at her. He abruptly ended his cheerful Cantonese conversation with the previous customer and asked her in English what she would like. She answered in Cantonese, her accent stilted.

"Half a roast duck, okay!" he said. "You Japanese, or what?"

She shook her head and smiled an embarrassed smile. He took a glossy duck down from its steel hook in the window, poured the juices through the neck hole into a waiting bucket and expertly cleaved it in two.

The same woman Artemis had seen in the woods behind her house, and again in the butcher shop answered the door.

"You're late," she said.

"You're not my mother, are you?"

The woman shook her head gravely.

"Who are you, then?"

"Better come in. This will take some time."

Artemis hesitated for a long moment before stepping over the threshold.

Then she remembered a stormy night on an island somewhere

far away, the rain passing back and forth across the hills like cattle.

"What big eyes you have," said the strange woman.

"I don't get it," said Artemis.

There were plates of meat on every surface, the desk, the side tables, the coffee table, the window sills. Tall red candles and long sticks of incense made the place glow and flicker like the interior of a temple. She laughed at the absurdity of it.

"What's all this for?"

"To feed the ancestors. They're hungry tonight. And to celebrate my birthday."

"How old are you?"

"I'd rather not say."

"I think this is weird. And it really wasn't very nice, the trick you used to get me here."

"I wanted to make sure you would come."

"Well, I'm leaving now."

A look of dismay crossed the woman's face. "No, please don't leave. I went through so much trouble . . ."

"I don't know you. And I find this all much too strange for me. I have enough problems as it is, without some weirdo trying to suck me into her life."

"Look, I'm very sorry. I didn't mean to trick you. I'm not used to the conventions of this . . . country." She was going to say "century" but caught herself.

"Good-bye. Please don't call." Artemis turned to the door.

"No! Come back. I'll tell you everything."

"I don't think so."

But the woman began in a voice that was mesmerizing and other-worldly. "There are creatures who live below the earth and creatures who live in the air above it. And there are those who can travel between both. Foxes, we are called." She crouched low to the ground and then sprang up towards the high loft bed that dominated the room. The Levi's, T-shirt, cap, and boots fell away and landed on the floor with a soft fabric thud, except for the steel-toed boots, which landed with a loud crash. A diaphanous green robe that might have been made of moths' wings fluttered down, swirling and billowing as it covered the Fox, bestowing the power of flight. Her hair sailed up like a black cloud and swirled around her. All the candles in the room blazed and the incense smoked madly like a barely contained house fire.

"Come here," said the Fox.

Artemis approached the bed with some trepidation.

"Come on."

She began to climb the ladder up the side. It seemed to go on forever. She crawled onto the bed and sat at a respectful distance from the imposing figure of the Fox.

"It's all right. Come closer," said the Fox.

Artemis edged a little closer.

"Really." The billowing and fluttering calmed down considerably. Artemis moved closer. The spirit gestured towards her lap and Artemis shyly placed her head there.

"Now," said the Fox, I'm going to tell you a story.

THE NUN

A Buddhist nun was walking to the temple in her flowing orange robes, with a bowl of tsai to share with her sisters.

"I thought you said it was red," said Artemis.

"But in my mother tongue, red and orange are the same thing."

On the way through the woods, a fox crossed her path, waving a bushy tail.

"Where are you going, and what have you got in that bowl?" she asked.

"Buddha's Delight and mock duck made of wheat gluten," said the nun, "and I am going to the nunnery to share it with my sisters."

"Oh," said the fox, and took off into the woods.

As soon as she was out of the nun's sight, she turned into a spirit and flew to the nunnery, where she hid herself in an urn and howled like a human ghost until all the nuns fled in terror. Then she came out of the urn in the form of a beautiful young woman with long flowing hair and a gauzy green dress. She found an orange robe in a small storage room and covered herself with it. She waited for the nun with the tsai to arrive.

As the nun approached the temple a gentle breeze shook the trees. No hair got in her eyes because her head was shaved. As she came through the door, she called to her sisters, but no one answered. When she walked into the main hall, the young woman appeared as if out of nowhere.

"All the sisters have gone on a pilgrimmage, but left me behind to greet you," said the young woman. "I am the new novice."

"What long hair you have," said the nun. "You should shave it, if you want to stay here."

"The better to charm you with," said the fox.

"And what delicate skin you have," said the nun.

"The better to please you," said the fox.

"What tender lips you have," said the nun, and kissed the fox spirit before she could speak again. And so they fell in love and lived happily ever after in the temple, even after the gwei lo came from overseas and tried to convert them to Christianity.

As the story progressed, Artemis found her eyelids becoming heavier and heavier. The moment it ended, she dropped into a deep sleep from which nothing could have roused her. She woke in the morning to find herself surrounded by the familiar walls of her own bedroom.

———

"Your phone number was in her pocket. She wasn't carrying any ID, so you're our only lead. I'm sorry to inconvenience you like this, but you do understand."

"Yes, of course. I'll be there as soon as I can." Artemis felt the words come too easily out of her mouth, like precious coins she wasn't sure she wanted to spend. A woman's body lay in the morgue, and it was someone she knew. Someone who was carrying her phone number when she died.

"Inconvenience," he had said, as though her phone or water pipes might be momentarily disconnected, or the street she lived on blocked off for construction for a day or two. "Inconvenience . . . understand . . ." she mumbled to herself, trying to fend off the nervous breath that rose from her diaphragm. She felt like bone jelly inside a hard casing.

She knew there was no point dilly-dallying, but she somehow didn't feel ready to go. Not yet. It's not right. There had to be a ritual. To begin with, she must be clean. No point going to her first experience of death dirty and unprepared. She walked slowly to the bathroom, slippers flapping against the worn wood floor. She ran scalding water into the tub and added bath salts — why not, this was a special occasion of sorts. The smell of lavender and eucalyptus was soothingly familiar, for a moment, but then she noticed for the first time a rough, soapy chemical odour underneath. The pleasure seemed tainted and the horror of what she was about to see returned, filling her stomach with that soapy chemical smell, and a memory from childhood which she had thought was lost for good. It was the memory of going into fever, late at night, when dreams swell to a disproportionate size, engulfing the child who has conjured them.

She was perhaps ten years old and in bed sick with the flu. Her mother and father were asleep in the next room. Eyes wide open, she dreamt of a huge cloud of steel machine parts: coils, hinges, gears, and blades whirring through the sky like mutated clockwork. It was headed straight for her parents' room, so she climbed out of the high bed that her father had made her, and went into their room in time to see one cloud settle on each parent like a giant vulture and begin to feed. She screamed and screamed, but nothing came from her throat but a bone-dry rasp.

For the next year, it was like that every time one of them left the house. She was so afraid the dream meant one of them would die in a car accident or fall from a tenth-floor window or be knifed in a shopping mall parking lot. But they always came back, day after day, perhaps with a little less blood in their faces each time, though she didn't notice that until years later. In the meantime, the nightmare eventually faded away.

But the metal bird was back now, and the rusty hinges and gears scraped and creaked through the convolutions of her brain, dripping gluey black oil as her body soaked up all the chemical stench of the bath salts only thinly masked now by the stale perfume of flowers and trees. More than ever she felt an urgent need to be clean. With a generous amount of soap and an old washcloth she scrubbed and scrubbed herself until her skin felt raw. She climbed quickly out of the tub, dried off, and dressed.

Her hair was still wet when she arrived at the police morgue.

"You mustn't be alarmed," said the tall policewoman who

greeted her, "by the cuts around her face and down the centre of her body. We had the autopsy done this morning. We had wanted you to identify her first, but it has taken us a couple of days to get hold of you."

Artemis nodded. "The phone was off. Do you have any idea who it is?"

"There are tattoos, but they don't help unless somebody can identify them."

They arrived at a pair of gray swinging doors.

"She's just in there."

Artemis stood at the doors for a long moment, until the police-woman gently pushed her from behind. She in turn pushed the doors and they swung wide. The body was right there, an all-too-simple human shape flat on its back on a steel table. She didn't know what she had expected, whether it was clothing, or gore, or a familiar if unhealthy face to look her in the eye and smile feebly, as though death were nothing but an extremity of sickness. The body lay there. The flesh was gray except for a few bruises on the forehead, left cheek, arm, and ribs. There was a long cut down the centre of the torso, which bifurcated just above the belly. It had been coyly sewn shut, as though to tastefully conceal something lewd or embarrassing, as though death and naked-ness were not enough. It was not frightening to be here in the way she had expected. There was a familiarity to this feeling. A familiarity to this woman. It was not the familiarity one has with a living acquaintance, of knowing someone because you've worked with them before or maybe gotten stoned together once.

Trying to see the body as someone she might have known was a different task again. The tattoos, of course, were familiar, but death had made this woman a stranger. Artemis approached more closely, searching the dead eyes for a sign, trying not to stare at the wiped-clean bullet wound in the side of the head. She gazed at the face and let the features settle on her mind. She looked down the length of the bruised and sliced and examined body as though gazing at broken wheels of cheese in a deli. The body was small, but it filled the room with its gray deadness in much the same way a horse or any large beast fills one's con-sciousness with its presence.

And then she was tumbling into a memory so vivid she almost lost her balance and fell across the corpse. In the pink dressing room of the bathhouse she saw Ming, nonchalantly shedding her clothes, revealing the bright new tattoos, the rounded belly.

The body on the steel table was the same body. When the realization struck her, she screamed but nothing came out except a bone-dry rasp. The policewoman took her gently by the shoulders and guided her back out into the hallway where the lights and the walls were comfortably, generically institutional.

"Are you okay?"

Artemis nodded her head a bit feebly. Someone handed her a glass of water and she drank it. As it went down her throat she thought of rats in a sewer. She looked up at the policewoman.

"Can you make a positive ID for us?"

"Yes, she's Mercy Lee." Her voice came out flat and expressionless, like she was acting in a suspense thriller but didn't really know what to do. "She has family in Burnaby, I think."

"When was the last time you saw her?"

"I'm not sure. I've been sick. A week ago, maybe two. Was she murdered?"

"We think so," said the policewoman. "Any idea why someone might want to kill her? Was she involved in a gang or anything like that?"

"I don't think so. She was an artist and a student and sometimes a writer, working for feminist media and stuff like that, but nothing that heavy-duty."

"Why do you suppose your number was in her pocket?"

"I really don't know."

The moment she got home, Artemis went straight to the bathroom and ran herself another bath.

 I STILL REMEMBER the first time I ever saw a dead fox. I was young. It was still years before I'd even heard of such things as rope and poison, of brown bottles and pig's bladder. By the bank of a river, fishing for trout, a fox had taken a hunter's arrow in her side. She was young, perhaps my own age. Blood gushed out of the wound, matting her fur. Her eyes were closed and already flies were buzzing greedily about. Between her paws lay a half-eaten fish, its dead eyes staring.

I felt a deep sorrow. I lay down beside her and pushed my

moist snout against her dry one. I thought I heard her sigh. My mother came rushing out of the hedge just in time.

"Don't!" she cried. "Don't you know that's the most dangerous thing you can do? Foxes can help each other in life, but you must never try to animate a dead fox. She will drag you down into the Ninth Fox Hell with her and you won't stand a chance of reincarnation for another thousand years."

The thought of that close call still makes me shudder, even in the wake of my new-found immortality.

 ARTEMIS STOOD at the magazine rack, flipping through the latest issue of *Vogue*. Out of the corner of her eye, she saw the Fox in the same human form as last time. She was dressed in torn jeans and a T-shirt. Artemis didn't quite want to believe it was her. But the Fox rummaged aggressively in the poultry department, poking and squeezing at the cellophane-wrapped packages of chicken parts. She spotted Artemis and ambled over carrying a red plastic shopping basket containing two large chickens. The packaging was coming apart and pink juice trickled onto the floor.

Artemis was flipping through a section on new lingerie for spring, which featured a short-haired Eurasian model. She heard the sound of boots approaching but didn't look up.

"Sleep well?" Under the bright fluorescent supermarket lights the Fox looked remarkably human. The Levi's and T-shirt, both of which were desperately in need of washing, were the same ones she had had on in the woods. Her skin looked tired. There were bags under her eyes and a few pimples forming to the side of her nose.

"Yeah, I slept fine," said Artemis.

The Fox smiled and put her arm around Artemis like a long-lost friend. "You don't look so well. Did you eat today? Maybe your blood sugar level is low. You need some protein."

"All of this is very stressful, you know. I think I'm going crazy."

"I feel bad about the little trick I played on you the other night. I thought I would make it up to you."

"How do you plan to do that?"

"Any information you want about the past or the future, I'll find the answer for you."

"You can do that?"

"I think so."

"Who killed my friend Ming?"

"That will take some time. How would you like to come to my place for dinner?"

The Fox picked up the *Vogue* magazine and tossed it into the basket with the chickens. She took Artemis by the arm and walked out the door. Nobody seemed to notice that she hadn't paid for her groceries.

Out in the parking lot the sun glowed softly behind the clouds. The smell of rain lingered in the air. Artemis slumped back into the cool black leather seat of the Fox's BMW.

They circled around the industrial-turned-yuppie district of Yaletown for a good fifteen minutes looking for parking. Finding a spot, the Fox pulled up close to the car in front. She didn't notice until it was too late that her right-hand mirror was too close. There was a loud crunch and the left-hand mirror cracked off the other car.

"Ooops!" she cried, laughing, and pulled away. "I guess we'll have to park somewhere else. "Boy, some stuffed suit is gonna be mad!"

Artemis chuckled nervously. "I thought you lived in Richmond."

"No, no. Rented that. I thought it added to the plausibility."

The Fox found another parking spot and they walked three blocks to her front door.

"Maybe it's time to move out of Yaletown," said the Fox. "It's being taken over by too many expensive furniture types."

They went up to the third floor in an enormous freight elevator.

For a warehouse space it was not particularly big. It had been divided into several sections with white rice paper screens. Against the far wall was a long row of windows beyond which the city glowed. There were thick wool Chinese carpets scattered randomly about, and soft couches, low to the ground and generously loaded with brightly coloured cushions. Halogen lights dangled from the ceiling, glowing dimly. Artemis found herself wondering how the Fox had managed to steal all this stuff.

The Fox indicated a couch facing into the kitchen. "Sit down."

Outside the sky had begun to darken. Artemis slumped into the cushions. The Fox handed her a snifter of brandy and the *Vogue* magazine, from which she had carefully wiped the chicken juice. Artemis thanked her shyly. She sat back and watched as the Fox unwrapped the chickens, put them in the sink, and rinsed them. She took a board from the cupboard and a cleaver from beside the stove and expertly chopped the chickens into small accurate pieces, clicking the blade against the board after each passage through flesh and bone. Her hands were quick and strong. She cut in such a practiced manner that Artemis wondered whether she was older than she looked.

There was the sweet odour of onions and soy sauce and chestnuts and rice. The comfortable smell made Artemis drowsy and she dozed for a moment among the soft cushions. The sky was black when the Fox woke her with a stubby hand on her shoulder. The table was set with tall silver candlesticks, heavy silver chopsticks, and cloth napkins. But there was only one dish, which struck Artemis as odd for a Chinese meal—chesnut chicken and rice. The Fox produced a bottle of good red wine from the cupboard above the stove and generously filled two glasses. Whatever the meal might be lacking in variety, it did not lack in quantity. The Fox filled Artemis' bowl, and when it was empty, she filled it again. They didn't speak. The Fox ate quickly and noisily, her nose twitching every now and then. Artemis ate slowly and sipped steadily at the wine.

The wine made her head heavy, so heavy that she could not finish eating, but had to rest her head on the table. She woke once to find the Fox had gone. She could barely stagger to the sofa before she sank into sleep again.

Sometime in the night, there was a hand on her shoulder. It was the Fox. "While you were sleeping I went to the Court of the Underworld to check up on your friend. This is what I saw."

THE JUDGE OF THE UNDERWORLD

In the High Court of the Underworld five young women are lined up on their knees in front of the judge. He adjusts the wings on his cap and strokes his long, sparse gray beard like a smooth trail of smoke. The young women wear white linen shifts with clean lines. Varying lengths of smooth black hair hang down their backs, each tied with a single white ribbon, except for the one whose hair is cut close like a boy's. Their faces are identical, right down to the mole beneath the right eye. Between the young women and the judge hangs an immense veil of gauze, so that he appears as a ghost to them, and vice versa. Incense and torches burn all around them, generating great clouds of smoke. From a distance, way above their heads on the surface of the earth, comes the eerie sound of professional mourners wailing, an impersonal kind of wail, which makes it all the more perturbing.

"How is it that you all come to be here on this day?" the judge asks.

The young women remain silent.

"Do you know one another? Are you sisters?"

"No," says the girl with hair like a boy. "I've never seen any of these women before." The other four girls nod their heads to indicate that they are experiencing similar confusion.

"All right," says the judge. "Then we shall have to begin with each individual's story. Family history and circumstances of death. You first." He points to the girl at the right.

"I am the daughter of a forklift driver," she says. "He worked mostly in shipyards, so I never saw him. He used to be a doctor in Vietnam, but nobody cares about that in Canada. I was a student in Engineering. I wanted to be a boss at the kind of places where my dad had to work. How did I die? I love the ocean, you see, so I often went for walks on Kits Beach or English Bay. On this particular night the moon was full and orange. I was walking in Stanley Park. There were lots of Asian families fishing for smelt in the tide that had swelled so high it could have lapped right over onto the path. I felt safe walking there, knowing these families were all around. So I walked, and maybe I didn't know how far I had walked. I was surrounded by four young white men with shaven heads and baseball bats. They said something about Orientals taking over the city and putting white people out of work and then all I remember is a long dark tunnel." She falls silent.

The judge strokes his beard with one hand arched in the shape of a "v" and nods his head gravely.

The second girl, the one with hair like a boy, begins. "My mother was a successful businesswoman, but she's dead now.

She died of cancer. My father is a Chemistry professor. I was walking with him around the seawall. He was telling me about his childhood, and how the Japanese had invaded Guangzhou during the war. His family hoarded rice because they were afraid there would be a shortage. We walked a long way, and then my father went to use the public washroom. I waited just outside the door. Two men with jeans and crewcuts approached me. 'Faggot,' they said. 'Bum-fucker.' I began to explain to them that I wasn't, and that I was waiting for my father, but they said they knew by the way I walked. They were carrying little cudgels like the kind English policemen have. They used them to beat against my skull until it cracked. I passed out. I woke up just once before I died to feel dirt being shovelled into my face and then that was it. I don't know what happened to my father."

The third girl speaks with a firm British accent. "I was being sponsored into Canada by my aunt, who is very rich and owns a flat in Richmond. My mother and father are both garment workers in Hong Kong. He is an overseer, she is a seamstress. I was studying for a business degree at the University of B.C. I was lucky. My aunt was very kind to me. When she was not in town, I looked after her flat, and sometimes drove her car. It was new and red and driving it felt like flying. Some young men found out where I lived and started asking me to get money from her to prevent them from beating me. I got a couple of hundred dollars from her by saying I needed it to buy books, but when they wanted thousands, I couldn't ask. They broke into my basement suite late one night and made me drive them to Stanley Park in the red car. I was beaten to death with a crowbar."

The fourth girl says, "My father is a conductor and my mother was an opera singer in Taiwan, but she doesn't sing anymore. She could sing both European- and Chinese-style opera. She clicked her castanets and sang *Carmen* so well my father was afraid that bullfighting might be imported to Taiwan. She made a lot of money, but when they were married, my father didn't want her to perform anymore. I think it was because as the conductor of a second-rate orchestra he made far less than she did. They're divorced now, but she still doesn't sing. She willed me her fortune and all her fabulous dresses. When I was little I learned to play the violin, Suzuki method, you know. When my husband married me, it was my music he loved, not me at all. The minor keys made him weep. The major keys made him dance. But when he discovered that I cried when I was sad and my breath stank in the morning, he started sneaking out with a trombone player. Maybe he thought those deep substantial tones were something he could catch in his hands. I suppose it was my money they came after me for. As a person, I had long since become invisible within the walls of his house. I began to walk regularly in the park at night, wishing for violence because my heart was broken. When it came, it was like sleep being granted to a woman without eyelids."

The fifth woman winds her hair around her finger as she speaks. "My father works in a café as a short-order cook and my mother works there as a waitress sometimes, but she spent a lot of time with me and my brothers while we were growing up. I married an Asian Studies student when I was eighteen and studying at the community college to be a nurse. I quit my own studies to pay for his, working as a waitress in a girlie bar. My family, had I told them, would have been very upset, so to them I pretended nothing had changed. Until I found myself drawn to one of the dancers. After hours in a Mickey Mouse sweatshirt and blue jeans she was the loveliest thing I had ever seen. It was not my husband who came after me, but my brother. He thought it had something to do with his honour. One night he came after me with his hockey stick. If I was found in the park, he must have somehow buried me there."

"Well," says the judge, stroking his beard more gravely than ever, "only one young woman was found dead this morning, so only one shall find rest within this jurisdiction of the under-world. We shall determine who it is, and the rest shall become wandering ghosts, unless you can find another county to take you." The incense smoulders madly and the flames of the torches burn higher. A faint breeze nudges the gauze in a gentle wave, so that the judge's body seems to undulate for a moment, and then is still again.

"That doesn't help," said Artemis. "All the killers are elusive."
"I know," said the Fox. "Guess I couldn't be of much help on that one. Tell you what. I'll help you find your birth mother."
"I don't know. I'm not sure I want to find her. I'm very tired.

Can we talk about it some other time?" She rolled over and was fast asleep and snoring again before the Fox could express her urgent desire to try her new-found powers.

Artemis' eyes were closed so she didn't see the way Fox vanished and the green light rushed like a gas through the vents and under the windows. A thin green smoke followed, but she didn't notice anything until there was the sound of breaking glass and a cold blast of air from the direction of the broken window. Amongst the shards on the concrete floor stood a small, wiry young woman with long black tresses that billowed about her like an ad for moisturizing shampoo. Forget those golden-haired, trumpet-sucking angels in their chaste robes with their sickly chicken-white feathers! Their pimply pink complexions have nothing on this creature. She smelled faintly of quality cosmetics; her make-up was subtle, barely noticeable although it made her skin look unnaturally moist and blemish-free. She wore a well-fitted dress of crushed silk the colour of old ivory and two marvellous diaphanous scarves that swirled and shimmered in the breeze that blew through the broken glass so that she looked as though she had just stepped down from a cloud. Two heavy, shiny black wings with the power of sweating horses were spread wide behind her.

Artemis opened her eyes wide. "Who are you?"

"My name is Nenuphar." There was something of the Fox about her, but Artemis just smiled to herself and said nothing.

Nenuphar grinned, and Artemis noticed that one of her front teeth was missing. The rest were yellow and crooked. She had sweetened her breath with mouthwash, but underneath was the quiet but persistent odour of rotting meat.

"Put your shoes on, let's go."

Artemis couldn't remember having removed her shoes. There they were placed neatly side by side at the end of the couch. She put them on, careful not to pull too hard on the frayed left lace, which threatened to snap any moment. Nenuphar watched.

As soon as she was done, Nenuphar stepped towards the door with a slim-hipped gait, leaving the broken glass behind. Down the elevator they went and into the cool night.

The sky was spitting gently and the whole night seemed to be bathed in a barely perceptible version of that same chemical green glow. Artemis trudged behind Nenuphar, who walked in strides too long for her own legs, giving her an affected kind of toughness. The great black wings remained closed against her back although a slight up-and-down motion betrayed the working of her lungs. Although Nenuphar was not quite Artemis' height, Artemis found herself struggling to keep up with her rapid pace.

"Where are we going?"

"East."

"How far?"

"Far. Better hurry or we won't make it on time."

"On time for what? Can't you slow down a bit?"

"You'd be faster if you hadn't drunk so much."

"I won't make it at all, at this rate."

The angel continued her pace and turned right on Georgia. The rain came a little harder as they began their trek across the viaduct. The city was a cozy, hazy orange to their right and the warehouses beneath them were dark. Cars flew by, spraying their faces with water. Artemis found the wine fog beginning to clear and her breath even out. She wiped the spray from her face.

"Come on, hurry up." Nenuphar twitched her wings in frustration, spraying more water backwards. Artemis' nostrils filled with a smell not unlike that of a wet dog. As they came off the bridge onto Prior Street, she stopped.

"Okay, enough now. My legs hurt and I'm drenched to the bone, and you won't even tell me where we are going."

Nenuphar ruffled her feathers. Her eyes went dark in her small, sharp-featured face. Artemis noticed thin lines beneath them and wondered how old she really was.

"I've been on this planet for nine hundred and eighty-one years more than you. Don't you think I know what I'm doing?"

"I don't appreciate your patronizing attitude. It's unfair."

"Well, sometimes life is unfair."

"Isn't there a better way than walking? We could take the bus."

"Can't have people looking at me."

"What about a taxi? You could sit in the back and I'll chat to the taxi driver so he doesn't notice."

"No."

"Well, steal a car then. I can't walk anymore," said Artemis, only half joking. She sat down on the curb, her feet in the gutter.

"Stay here." Nenuphar walked off and disappeared behind a tree, the metal taps on the heels of her cowboy boots clicking loudly against the pavement. Artemis stared after her, gritting her teeth as a trickle of cold rain rushed down her back.

As she sat, she imagined dragons in the cracks in the sidewalk. The coolness of the night had washed away the alcoholic blur. She waited. The familiarity of that act allowed a heightened sense of reality to sift slowly into her mind, and for the first time all evening, it struck her as vaguely absurd that she was following a Chinese angel through the streets of her city as though it were the most normal thing in the world.

Nenuphar pulled up beside the curb in an iridescent champagne-pink Mazda hatchback. She leaned over and unlocked the door. The dashboard glowed a soothing hi-tech blue. Nenuphar stepped down hard on the accelerator before Artemis even had a chance to close the door. The night twisted away behind them faster than the speed of light. With her foot on the accelerator, Nenuphar told a story.

THE CAT MOTHER

There are gaps in the flow of reality that can't be filled. They can grow even between close places, between the shore and the sea, between the fields and the house. I used to forage for chickens in a village of women. All the men were away in the city, earning money to send home. One night after a meal of fresh chicken, I met a ghost by the village well. This is the story she told me:

"My sister and I worked in the family fields. We didn't want to, we would have preferred to go to Guangzhou, to work in a factory and own lots of shoes. We complained about it often to our mother, who just sighed and said that women had to resign themselves to their fate. This was something we didn't want to accept and we often chided her for being old-fashioned.

"One afternoon our old mother came to the fields. We thought she was bringing lunch, but she had come to scold us. She carried on through the worst heat of the day, cursing us and pelting us with stones. This carried on for many days, until one evening, after supper, I asked her the reason. My mother was shocked. She said she had not left the house in months except to go to the well for water or to her sister's house, where the grain was stored.

" 'It must be some evil spirit plaguing us,' she said. 'You should kill it the next time it comes.'

"In the hottest part of the day during the second planting of rice, our old mother worried about her daughters. She put fresh barley water in a jug in order that we might have a cool drink, and set out for the fields. We saw her coming. We mistook her for the evil spirit, and forced her head under the leechy muddy water of the paddies until she drowned. We buried the body in the dyke along the eastern edge of the property and hurried home to celebrate. Our mother was there with a feast already prepared. We did not think to ask how she knew in advance of our telling her, but sat down to enjoy the meal. The spirit cooked well. There was fresh fish at every meal for the next year. The family worked hard and lived relatively contentedly until a wandering nun paid us a visit the following summer. She took me aside and said, 'Your mother has a strange smell about her.' I laughed at the nun and asked her what cause she had to say such a rude thing when she was a guest in our house, but the nun had already begun chanting. She walked into the kitchen where our mother leaned over the stove, her voice sliding up to a higher pitch. Our mother dropped to the ground in the form of a cat and rushed out under the gap below the back door. Realizing we had killed our real mother the year before, my younger sister jumped into the well and drowned herself. I turned the situation over in my mind one last time, and then I leapt after her."

"What are you trying to tell me?" Artemis asked.

"I'm not trying to tell you anything. The story is whatever you make of it."

"You're saying there's never any going back."

"I'm not saying any such thing."

"I think we should turn around now."

"But we're so close."

"I don't want to meet her. I don't want to know what she's like. She's probably some miserable garment worker who will shed all these tears and make me feel guilty. Or an evil real estate agent that I'll have to be embarrassed about for the rest of my life."

"Surely you want to know where you came from."

"Do you know where *you* came from?"

"Only loosely. I mean, I know about the foxes. I know a little about the Poetess, although there is one matter I've never been able to clear up."

"What is that?"

"Whether she did or did not murder her companion."

"Why haven't you tried to find out?"

"As a matter of fact, I did try. I went to the Library of the Western Heavens while you were sleeping."

 SHE CAN BE pretty nosy when she wants to, that much is certain. I was very pleased with my new powers of transformation. Now no longer reliant on corpses, I could change at will into any shape I could imagine. The angel Nenuphar was amusing, although next time I will have to remember to do something about her teeth. And the black wings? Perhaps brown would be more subtle.

I wanted to see if I could travel any faster than I used to. I wasn't much faster than a twentieth-century airplane before my thousandth birthday. Not that it mattered. I hate travelling. But I wanted to know.

On the morning of my thousandth birthday, I changed into an eagle with a human head. I don't think I imagined the head carefully enough. It looked suspiciously like that of the poor woman I inhabited on my fiftieth birthday. But I was impatient to get going. I hurried as fast as I could over oceans and undiscovered continents to the Islands of the Blest, farther to the West than any human can imagine. (For, if you know how to travel it, the world is not round at all, but a spiral that keeps circling outwards. Every three hundred and sixty degrees things may look the same as on the previous round, but that is an illusion.) I wanted to check the scrolls on the Poetess's life to find out what had really happened on those last mad days of her life, whether, as they said, she had strangled the young friend she employed as a maidservant, or whether she was entirely innocent of the deed.

The library was a great sprawling complex with rolls and rolls of paper tucked into many shelves. Between the reading rooms were courtyards with living fountains and singing birds and butterflies that would tranform into handsome young women to guide or entertain anyone who stayed there any length of time. I saw one among the stacks, explaining an older style of calligraphy to the newly appointed Heavenly Marine Official of the South China Sea. In another wing a librarian stepped from her chrysalis for the first time, reciting T'ang Dynasty poetry to the flowers. That was how I knew I was in the right section.

A powdery wing brushed against my cheek. I turned in time to see a rainbow-hued creature with a wingspan twice the width of my palm vanish down an aisle. A moment later, a librarian stepped from the same aisle and looked me dead in the eye. "Can I help you with something?" She was not at all the willowy creature I had expected, but I suppose aesthetics change with the times in the Western Heavens as they do in the secular world. She was a muscular, large-boned woman with a heavy squarish jaw and thick glasses with a heavy black rim. She wore a Western-style men's suit in light herringbone tweed with a tasteful and well-ironed white shirt and a showy silk turquoise tie that made my eyes hurt.

"I'm looking for biographical material on the T'ang poetess and Taoist priestess Yu Hsuan-Chi," I explained, carefully.

"Hmmmph," she said. "Just got your credentials, did you? What are you? A good-hearted geisha saved by some simpering lower official?"

"I beg your pardon!" I cried. "There's no need to be rude. For your information, I'm proud to say I am a Fox who has just reached her thousandth birthday."

She looked down at her shiny black patent-leather shoes, so I could not gauge her reaction, but I hope she wasn't smirking. "You will find, if you are a true scholar, or spend any length of time here, that in those days very few records were kept on women, if any at all. We may have a few items collected from the mortal world. Let me take a look." She took me to a computer terminal at the end of the aisle. "Aha. Here. Two anthologies, one with two of her poems in it, one with four. One of them is also available in English translation."

I could see this was going to be difficult. "I want to know

whether or not there was any real justification for her execution," I said.

"Oh yes, you did say biographical, didn't you?" Her efficient fingers moved rapidly over the keyboard. She shook her head. "Nobody's really taken an interest in that kind of thing for thousands of years. Oh, okay, wait. There is a young man who was recently appointed to a newly created post, Heavenly Official of Immigration." She put a thick palm up to the side of her mouth. "I think he might have foreign blood." And then, in a normal voice, "I believe he made a donation of some T'ang Dynasty research materials recently. But none of it has been catalogued yet. Have a seat, will you. I'll go down into the stacks and see what I can find."

I strolled into the courtyard and lay down on an elegantly carved stone bench with dragons' legs beneath, a lion's head on one end, and a dragon's tail on the other. It had been placed beside a little fountain that tossed water up into the air and brought it down again in brilliant colours. The sound of water against stone was soothing. I dozed.

I awoke to a rough hand on my shoulder. "You shouldn't fall asleep. The guards will think you're a bum and have you kicked out."

"Sorry," I said.

"They're all in English, I'm afraid," said she. "The new official was an American when he was living. And they're bound books, not scrolls at all."

"I don't suppose I can take them with me."

"Absolutely not."

I spent a few hours flipping through them, and then copied out key sections. This is what I copied.

> "When the patron came and knocked at the door, I told him through the door that you were not in. Without a word, he rode away. As for romantic sentiments, it has been years since I had such feelings. I pray that you will not suspect me." Hsüan-chi became even more incensed. She stripped Lü-ch'iao naked and gave her a hundred lashes, but the latter still denied everything. Finally, on the point of collapse, Lü-ch'iao asked if she could have a cup of water. Pouring it on the

ground in libation she said, "You seek the way of the Taoist triad and of immortality, yet cannot forget the pleasures of the flesh. Instead you become suspicious and falsely accuse the chaste and righteous. I shall certainly die by your evil hands. If there is no Heaven, then I have no recourse. If there is, who can suppress my fervent soul? I vow never to sink dully into the darkness and allow your lascivious ways to go on." Having spoken her mind, she expired on the floor. Frightened, Hsüan-chi dug a pit in the backyard and buried her, assuring herself that no one would know of it.

—SAN-SHUI HSIAO-TU
translated by Jeanne Kelly

Of her many lovers, Yu Xuanji became particularly attracted to a handsome young poet named Li Jinren. The two had frequent meetings but one day Li Jinren arrived only to find that his paramour was not at home. While waiting for her to return, he was entertained by the maid Luqiao. When Yu Xuanji arrived at the convent, she saw her lover with Luqiao and fell into a jealous rage. In her fury, she grabbed the hapless maid and flogged her to death.

—100 CELEBRATED CHINESE WOMEN
illustrated by Lu Yanguang,
translated by Kate Foster

She was accused of murdering her maid, and although her poet friends tried to save her, she was executed about 870.

—WOMEN POETS OF CHINA
translated by Kenneth Rexroth and Ling Chung

Yu Hsuan-chi resumed the wild life at the Hsien-i-kuan, where she held open house for all elegant young scholars and officials, and had numerous amorous attachments. But as she grew older her popularity waned, and one after the other she lost her influential patrons. She got into financial difficulties and became involved in trouble with lower police-officials. Finally she was—probably wrongly—accused of having beaten a maid-servant to death, and was convicted and executed.

—SEXUAL LIFE IN ANCIENT CHINA
by R. H. Van Gulik

The Governor, flooded with letters from high-placed persons all over the Empire in favour of the poetess, was about to give a verdict of not guilty, when a young water-carrier from the Lake District came forward. He had been absent for several weeks, accompanying an uncle on a journey to the family graves. He had been the maid's boy friend, and stated that she had often told him that her mistress importuned her, and beat her when she refused. The Governor's doubts were strengthened by the fact that the maid had been found to be a virgin. He reasoned that if robbers had murdered the maid, they would certainly have raped her first.

—POETS AND MURDER (fiction)
by Robert Van Gulik

 THEY SAY my temple is haunted, but they say that about many things in this village. I heard a tune last evening as I leaned out a south-facing window. A wooden flute or an old man's falsetto. No, a flute, definitely. A strange, sad little tune, all wind and minor cadences. They say the Black Fox Shrine just on the other side of the bamboo grove has a new priestess. A young thing with pale skin and black hair. She has a corpse for a lover and sleeps with the foxes at night. Every other day she goes to the execution grounds and brings her lover a new skull for a head.

A sound comes across the courtyard again. Or is it a motion? Something smooth and cool, like water.

The police came again last night, calling for me, but I hid from them in the closet where the sutras are stored.

No, I am sure of it, a sound. A melody, frail and liquid, in a key you could call romantic or you could call eerie, depending on how you were listening. Outside the sun has melted and the courtyard is almost dark, but there is someone dancing out there, I'm sure of it. Is that a shadow I see moving? Only the quiver in the wind lets me know for sure.

In the village, a poor woman farted in the presence of a strange visitor. The next morning a bucket of dirty water she had left by her bed turned into a bucket of gold. In the village, a rich woman forced a fart in the presence of that same visitor. The bucket of water she left by her bed at night turned into a bucket of snakes which stung her to death. They say that foxes are taking over the village.

The sound takes me by the hand and we run into the courtyard, through the grove of bamboo. I imagine something furry against my legs. Little flashes of red fur running on either side of me. Through the grove and up a stony incline. In the dark, I cut my arms and legs on the sharp edges. There at last, just over the top of the hill, sits the black shape of a shrine, growing clearer as we approach. The foxes run in the front gates and I follow them. The lover is waiting for me with her toothy smile. A small skull today—a child's, perhaps. At the back of the back room, Lu Ch'iao is sitting leaned against the back wall, cuddling her foxes. She looks the same, only dirtier. There are faint circles under her eyes and her hair is loose and matted in places. Is that the same dress I saw her in before she disappeared? It is tattered and colourless. She smiles when she sees me, and I know she is alive.

"I was beginning to think you would never come," she says. The shadows of the bamboo leaves outside come through a crumbling window and play across her face.

"You remember me, then," I say, "so you're not mad."

"What is madness anyway?" she asks. For a moment, her eyes are all dull and unfocussed. Then they become suddenly clear and sharp. "I hear they say the same about you."

"Really?" I ask. "All this time, I just thought they thought I was evil."

"Isn't it the same thing?" she counters.

"Perhaps," I say.

Her hands are bathwater, warm and almost liquid.

The memory of sex is never the same as when it is actually happening. Sometimes between the act and the memory there is a longing that builds up, quietly feeding on the soul, a longing almost like the longing for home, or the longing for death. The longing has its own tense beauty, all salmon and mauve and indigo, like the sunset, riding on the belly like the need to urinate, or at the base of the skull like a dream of falling. We return to the memory through different doors each time. We return to it in fragments, a flash of desire flooding through the chest, or moist breath travelling a jawbone. Here and there a moment of pain, sometimes intended, sometimes not—hipbone in the spine, a pinch, a bite, a scratch . . .

I never knew humans could get rabies. The infection went straight to my heart, and my heart loosened from its anchor and fell into my body.

———

We used to be reluctant to admit we enjoyed the company of men. It was a living. But lately it has been more a question of spite, though I don't know why they take to her, thin and dark as she is. Maybe they find a certain charm in decay. A casual observer would say we care for each other, although we amuse ourselves with men and quarrelling.

After our last fight we promised each other we would not let any male creature come between us again, but she knew the young scholar Jinren was mine, so I don't know what she was thinking. She says she did not even open the door to him, but then I'd like to know about the muddy footprints twice the size of her feet leading away from the back of the temple. They are fresh. It doesn't take a dog's nose to figure that out.

So that is why she wouldn't come to the princess's funeral with me. It must have been something important to miss an event like that. The emperor's favourite daughter, Princess Tongchang, had just died. He spared no expense to express the depth of his mourning. The funeral was magnificent. There was a procession fifteen kilometres long, with forty camels just to carry food and drink for the coffin-bearers. They didn't burn paper houses, boats, and clothes, but ones made of real silk studded with gold and precious stones. Many people risked immolation to cart away the hot ashes riddled with treasures.

Perhaps that is why she didn't come to the execution of the princess's thirty lazy doctors either. Lazy or evil, for poisoning her. That's the rumour. Although I'm not sure why so many clever men would devise such a feeble plot. They should have known it would only bring them to a sorry end. So the emperor weeps blood one week and hot jewels the next. How wonderful, to be able to express such grief!

The emperor has his problems and I have mine. I try to talk to her and she admits to letting Jinren in but she says she didn't talk to him. Only gave him a cup of tea and asked him to wait. I don't believe her. Her eyes are as innocent as the sky, but I know better. I told her so and she started to sing. She hates singing so I know it was just to annoy me. She sang in that opera voice I taught her when we were young. She knows she can sing better than me and she likes to keep me on the edge about it, meting her voice out like it is something to be conserved and measured.

Where is she? Gone to play with her foxes again? That headless doll of hers gives me the creeps. Jinren says he saw her at the execution ground yesterday collecting skulls. What does she need so many skulls for?

Was it wrong of me to beat her? I didn't mean to or maybe I did but I didn't think I was beating her very hard. Then all of a sudden there was all this blood and she fell down. I thought she was just being dramatic, so I left her there and went back to the funeral ground to see if there were any ashes left. When I came back she was still there, in the same position I had left her.

 "DO YOU THINK Ming will come see me today?" Artemis stared at her reflection in the mirror. It is dull, faded like a photograph that has been lying out in the sun for too long.

"I don't think so," the Fox whispered tenderly into her ear, have stolen unnoticed into the bathroom.

She took a last glance. Her hair was a mess. She couldn't remember the last time she had brushed it. Her skin had a yellowish tint, that could almost but not quite be a suntan, she thought.

"Ming is dead," said the Fox, her face growing serious. She guided Artemis by the waist back into the bedroom, where they had been sitting or lying for weeks, writing poems and playing chess. She sat down among the tangled sweaty sheets at the foot of the bed. The Fox sat at the head, by the night table.

"Ming is dead?"

"Yes."

"Does that mean she won't come see me?"

"Not necessarily."

With a firm swipe of the hand, the Fox pushed half a dozen empty bottles of Johnny Walker Red onto the floor, and, smiling, produced a fresh one from the depths of her skirts.

"Where did you get that?"

"Bought it."

"With what money?"

"From the envelope in the kitchen drawer."

"That was rent money." Artemis didn't say this angrily but with the sort of resignation that comes from Taoist philosophy at its worst. Resist nothing. Let happen what will. Time was running out on her apartment. The new owners would take possession in less than a month.

The Fox poured scotch into freshly rinsed glasses. Freshly but not thoroughly rinsed, so that the dried yellowish scum of last week's drinks lingered at the bottom and floated up through the drink in brown flakes.

Artemis took a sip and crinkled her nose. "It stinks in here."

"More poems," said the Fox. "I'll clean up tomorrow."

 THEY COULD BLAME it on the kidneys, the starting point for the well of memory. She has a lot to remember, how it began, who she placed trust in and for what reasons. Memory is a sneaky thing, so easily coloured by emotions, by illusions of beauty and power.

I come to her daily now, in fact, I never leave. She likes me here. She needs me to keep her company, to bring her whiskey and write her poems and play chess.

We write poems to the Poetess, trying to dream through what nobody's records could tell us. Poems that turn into tales that fall back on themselves the way night falls into day.

She can't take care of herself. She moans in her sleep. The name was not enough to hold her. They didn't fill her quiver with arrows before setting her loose and hungry into the world. The name was not nearly enough. It was just a thin covering, a disguise to get her through a few doors. It didn't weigh enough. No more than a small bag of coins, not even enough for a ghost to buy her way down the river. A name must carry you into the past and the future. It needs roots to tap the water deep below the surface of the earth, to prevent the soul from being swept away by any old tide that happens to wash in.

At least I am here. She clings to me in the night, she aches for my hands to soothe her, my poems to whisper her under the dark. That is what I can do, so that is what I do. I wait with her. I try to comb her hair, but she complains loudly that it hurts her scalp, and so I just stroke her head and wait. Her breath is hot. If I were to return to my original form, she would singe my coat off with it, so I don't. I stay in the Poetess's body. But we are both getting dirty. The place smells like a den. I don't mind it so much, having been born into such a place, but it bothers her and yet she refuses to wash. The place grows grayer. She subsists on a diet of scotch and cigarettes. I haven't seen food pass her lips in weeks. She is growing yellower and yet somehow she continues to hang on, tenaciously. Perhaps there is more to that name than I thought.

 MY CELL IS COLD and at night I have to fight with the rats for enough space on the stone floor to sleep. I would have starved to death by now if not for one of my students, the daughter of an Arabic salt trader with a gift for poems on the topic of loneliness. She brings me steamed bread, roast meat, and pomegranates which are in season now. There is her and there is a woman I've never met before, extremely ugly, with a mischievous light behind her eyes. She brings me chicken and the most up-to-date news she can garner concerning the status of my case. My trial is to be postponed again because of the possibility of another witness who heard Lu Ch'iao and I fighting the night before she died. She says a number of scholars from all over the kingdom have pleaded with the judge in my favour, but that he is determined to find me guilty and is just waiting to find the right evidence. Which he almost certainly will, she says mournfully, whether it is true or not. They always find their evidence when they need it.

I am past caring. Outside my tiny window I can see stars at night. Six of them that move through the tiny rectangle over the course of the dark hours and vanish by morning. I ask the salt trader's daughter to bring me a candle, paper, ink, and a brush so that I can write while I am here. This she does faithfully every week and takes my finished poems with her, in order that I may have a trace of life in the outside world. She says she hears people discussing them in the teahouses, and that is a comfort to me, although I am quite aware of the possibility that she tells me this precisely for that reason and not because it is true.

The ugly woman wants to know from my own mouth whether or not I am guilty, but I don't trust her. She says if I tell her, she will bribe the guards and help me escape, but I turn her down. She continues to bring me chicken and sometimes clean clothes or a bottle of wine.

It is raining the day she comes to see me for the last time. She tells me the judge has found his witnesses, the eldest daughter of a local butcher and the Official of Interior Taxation, formerly in charge of expunging foreign religions from the land. The butcher's daughter claimed to have heard Lu Ch'iao and I fighting as she cut around the outer walls of the temple the night before Lu Ch'iao died. The official said he had seen me burying a body beneath a cherry tree in the garden in the wee hours of the following morning. My trial has date has been set, and I have no doubt about the outcome.

 I AM SCARED. I am scared we will be discovered. The place reeks now. No longer of dirt, but of death, lingering patiently in the air, waiting for the perfect moment to swoop down, or perhaps simply settle like ashes after a fire.

I am scared because these are classic symptoms of a fox's haunting. The victim pale and thin with eyes that blaze and hair too lush and thick to be human. It was never my intention to haunt like this. I came for the warmth, for the breath. I came as a friend, to comfort. I never expected her to place all her hopes and desires in me, to rail at me as she sometimes does in her sleep, lashing out with nails and teeth as sharp as the claws and fangs of something feral.

I am scared for her. I am scared for myself. I am scared of the men with the charms and poisoned liquor.

 THE NEWSPAPERS INSISTED on drugs. It was the only way they could explain the tattoos. They devised an extensive map of meaning that led to high-flying Triad members based in New York. A local television station ran a two-hour special on Asian gangs in large North American cities. For them, Ming's change of name and appearance was a wilful attempt at deceit, to hide illicit activity. Her friends are not so sure. The drugs they found in her bloodstream were prescription, but that explained nothing. Although the dull silver Smith & Wesson 3913 Ladysmith was found in her stiffly clutched fingers, many police and friends speculated that someone else had placed it there. She may well have been capable of killing herself, but surely she could not have buried herself too.

The ceremony was Claude's idea. None of them knew what they were supposed to do, what their ancestors might have done on a similar occasion.

She bought a lot of white candles, joss sticks, some oranges, and a steamed chicken. She called everyone, even Diane, and talked them into coming. The only one Claude couldn't reach was Artemis, who did not answer her phone. She drove by on the day of the ceremony and rattled the door until a thin, straggly-haired woman opened it. The place was a mess, as though a hurricane had hit it, or, as was more likely the case, as though Artemis had not cleaned up since Diane's little rampage. She stood in the doorway and stared at Claude.

"What happened to you?" Claude asked.

"I'm sick. Leave me alone."

The house reeked of stale tobacco and spilled liquor.

"Come on. Everyone went a little crazy after the murder, but things don't need to get this bad." She pushed her way into the apartment. "We're going to do a little ceremony at Ming's death site. I think you should come. I'll wait for you to take a bath. Do you have any clean clothes?"

"You want me to get into a car with Diane *and* Rachel *and* yourself? Fucking no way."

"I rented a van so no one has to sit too close to anyone they don't want to. Go on. People are waiting." She pushed her with a gentle, encouraging hand.

In the van, with all of them there, you could almost feel Ming among them, some new scheme on her lips, the tattoo-dragon on her arm winking.

Rachel sat on the floor beside Claude, in the gap between the two front seats. Her hand lay on Claude's thigh, burning. Diane slouched at the back, her discomfort nearly audible. She pulled a little cast-iron monkey out of her pocket, one that she had recently taken to carrying wherever she went. She turned it round and round in her hands. It grew warm with their heat. The little metal eyes twinkled with sympathy. Artemis sat somewhere in the middle, wrapped in her own arms, rocking herself, not really thinking about who was in the van with her at all. Eden, whom Claude had tracked down through an address on the back of one of Ming's photos, sat beside her, feeling large and clumsy and out of place. Claude kept her eye on the road and said nothing.

The park came up ahead and the dark trees swallowed them. The night folded around them, as they rolled towards the vision of themselves walking single file through the wooded park, each bearing a tiny yellow flame.

 THERE WAS a chicken at the foot of the hollow tree. I found it halfway through my morning stroll. I'm not trying to imply that morning strolls are a regular thing with me. As you know, I'm much more a creature of the dim hours. But this morning I decided I would take a walk, and in my original form at that. I hadn't gone out in my vulpine shape for ages, having long since lapsed into the habit of falling asleep in the Poetess's body, or whatever form I had invented for the moment, before I got around to changing back. But I am an immortal now. Why shouldn't I do as I please?

I ate the chicken. It was a plump one, steamed to tender perfection, although a bit smudged with ashes and dirt. All traces of the body they had found there nearly two months ago had vanished, but there were clusters of burnt-out joss sticks poking out of the soil like little red antennae, and here and there a solidified pool of white wax.

I remember coming across the body while it was still warm on one of my evening forays less than a week before my thousandth birthday. I am disturbed, but also proud, to admit it did not interest me in the way it would have in the past. The urge to investigate did not burn through me, although it was certainly still present. I did go take a look. Once I was there, what could be wrong with a little animation? I nudged the mouth open with my snout and blew my soul inside. Up and down the seawall we walked, six inches above the earth, scaring night fishers, amorous young men, and old derelicts alike. I rode a cloud into the city and paid a visit to my new friend while she was sleeping, curled like a child in her blankets. I was careful not to wake her. I never meant to go close, but some perverse instinct drove me through the window, right up to the edge of her bed. Her face was soft and relaxed, all the tension of guilt and worry washed from it by sleep. I crouched beside her, certain that she would be terrified should she wake to see me there—the animated body of her friend, with my soul peering out of it. I reached out to stroke her cheek, not realizing how cold my hands were. Her eyes opened. I was caught. I expected her to scream, but she didn't, only gazed evenly at me as though she had already dreamt of Ming's death and felt reassured by the appearance of this strange shadow. It was my eyes that froze in hers. After a long moment, she released me by merely closing them again. I rushed back to the park. Scratching diligently at the earth, I dug a grave of respectable depth beneath the same tree, and put the body to rest.

But on my return to the spot this morning I thought to myself that my time has come. The constellations have shifted from their original positions in the black bowl of the sky. Surely congress between the divine and the mortal should not take place with such sordid regularity. I must be heedful of my new situation. My selfishness in this most recent haunt has been childish beyond my years. It is time for me to move on. I will tell her so this evening.

She will not be sad. Her soul, like mine, is an old one. They have been intertwined since an herbalist and an oil seller made a promise to one another more than a thousand years ago in another country, when they were still neighbours. Since a chance meeting on a hill beneath a temple in the rain. I know we will meet again.

Source Notes

I AM FOREVER INDEBTED to the sixteenth-century writer Pu Songling and the unnamed storytellers whose stories he collected. Many of Fox's monologues in this book are adapted from tales contained in Pu's popular collection of tales, variously (though incompletely) translated as *Strange Tales from a Chinese Studio* (Herbert A. Giles (trans.), Hong Kong: Kelly and Walsh, Limited, 1968); *Strange Tales from Make-Do Studio* (Denis C. and Victor H. Mair (trans.), Beijing: Foreign Languages Press, 1989); *Strange Tales of Liaozhai* (Lu Yunzhong, Chen Tifang, Yang Liyi, Yang Zhihong (trans.), Hong Kong: The Commercial Press, Ltd., 1988); and *Selected Tales of Liaozhai* (Yang Xianyi and Gladys Yang (trans.), Beijing: Panda Books, 1981). Ten newly translated selections are available in *Renditions: A Chinese-English Translation Magazine* (Hong Kong: The Chinese University of Hong Kong, No. 13, Spring 1980).

For the Poetess's story, I relied on R. H. Van Gulik's *Sexual Life in Ancient China: A Preliminary Survey of Chinese Sex and Society from ca. 1500 B.C. till 1644 A.D.* (Leiden: E. J. Brill, 1974). Other sources included *Traditional Chinese Stories: Themes and Variations* (Y. W. Ma and Joseph S. M. Lau, eds., New York: Columbia University Press, 1978); *Poets and Murder: A Chinese Detective Story* (R. H. Van Gulik, London: Heineman, 1968); *Women Poets of China* (translated and edited by Kenneth Rexroth and Ling Chung, New York: New Directions Publishing Corporation, 1972); *100 Celebrated Chinese Women* (Cai Zhuozhi (Kate Foster, trans.), Singapore: Asiapac Books, 1994); *Tales of Empresses and Imperial Consorts in China* (compiled by Shang Xizhi, translated and edited by Liang Liangxing, Hong Kong: Hang Feng Publishing Co., 1994); and *Tales About Chinese Emperors — Their Wild and Wise Ways* (compiled by Luan Baoqun, translated and edited by Tang Bowen, Hong Kong: Hang Feng Publishing Co., 1994).

The epigraph, translated by Jan Walls, comes from *Sunflower Splendor: three thousand years of Chinese poetry* (co-edited by Wu-chi Liu and Irving Yucheng Lo, Garden City: Anchor Books, 1975). The quote from the

I Ching comes from Brian Browne Walker's translation, *The I Ching or Book of Changes: A Guide to Life's Turning Points* (New York: St. Martin's Press, 1992). The translation from *Hsuan-chung-chi*, on page 88, is by R. H. Van Gulik, in *Sexual Life in Ancient China*, cited above. The quotation from *San-shui hsiao-tu*, on pages 225–6, comes from *Traditional Chinese Stories*, also cited above. "The Cat Mother" is adapted from a version appearing in *The Man Who Sold a Ghost: Chinese Tales of the 3rd-6th Centuries* (Yang Hsien-Yi and Gladys Yang (trans.), Beijing: Foreign Languages Press, 1958). The image of snakes and doves originates in Betty Bao Lord's *Spring Moon: A Novel of China* (New York: Harper and Row, 1981).

About the Author

BRENDA MILLER

LARISSA LAI was born in La Jolla, California. She currently lives in Vancouver, British Columbia, where she works as a community activist, writer, editor, and critic. Her poetry and fiction have appeared in such publications as *Bamboo Ridge, West Coast Line, The Asian-American Journal, CV2, Matrix, Room of One's Own,* and *Estuaire,* and in the anthologies *Many-Mouthed Birds* and *Pearls of Passion*. She is a regular contributor to *Kinesis* and has had articles and essays published in *Fuse, Video Guide, Harbour, Rungh, Yellow Peril: Reconsidered,* and *Matriart*. In 1995 she was the recipient of an Astraea Foundation Emerging Writers Award.

Press Gang Publishers has been producing vital and
provocative books by women since 1975.

A free catalogue is available from
Press Gang Publishers,
101–225 East 17th Avenue, Vancouver, B.C.
V5V 1A6 Canada